LIGHT FANTASTIC

Recent Titles by Graham Ison from Severn House

DIVISION
WORKING GIRL

LIGHT FANTASTIC

Graham Ison

This first world edition published in Great Britain 2003 by
SEVERN HOUSE PUBLISHERS LTD of
9–15 High Street, Sutton, Surrey SM1 1DF.
This first world edition published in the USA 2003 by
SEVERN HOUSE PUBLISHERS INC of
595 Madison Avenue, New York, N.Y. 10022.

British Library Cataloguing in Publication Data

Ison, Graham
    Light fantastic
    1.   Police - England - London - Fiction
    2.   Murder - Investigation - England - London - Fiction
    3.   Detective and mystery stories
    I.   Title
    823.9'14 [F]

    ISBN 0-7278-6011-9

Except where actual historical events and characters are being
described for the storyline of this novel, all situations in this
publication are fictitious and any resemblance to living persons
is purely coincidental.

Typeset by Palimpsest Book Production Ltd.,
Polmont, Stirlingshire, Scotland.
Printed and bound in Great Britain by
MPG Books Ltd., Bodmin, Cornwall.

'Hello Bravo Six, Bravo Six, from MP. Outside number twenty-seven – two seven – Durbridge Gardens. Sec Mr Jim Wise, a milkman, re believed collapse behind locked doors. Ends origin Information Room zero-nine-one-one. To Bravo Six, over . . .'

One

The house was probably Georgian, but I'm not much good at identifying architectural periods. What I did know was that it was in that part of Notting Hill where an asking price of a million pounds wouldn't even raise an eyebrow.

A blonde policewoman, preening herself and trying desperately hard to appear photogenic, stood at the foot of the short flight of steps leading to what remained of the front door. The television cameras hadn't arrived yet, but I suppose she was living in hope. 'Can I help you?' she asked brightly, moving herself sufficiently to stand in front of me, at the same time casting a suspicious glance at my black detective sergeant, Dave Poole, known in the trade as my 'bag-carrier'.

'Detective Chief Inspector Brock, SCG West,' I said, waving my warrant card as I informed her in policeman's shorthand that I was from Serious Crime Group (West) at New Scotland Yard, even though my office was at Curtis Green in Whitehall. 'And DS Poole.' I cocked a thumb at Dave just in case she thought his name was SCG West.

The policewoman appeared disappointed and stepped aside. After all, she was doing an important job and perhaps didn't know, and would probably have cared even less if she had known, that my colleagues and I were responsible for all the serious crimes from Westminster to Hillingdon.

However, don't be misled into believing that because my area of operations covers much of the better class district of London there is an absence of crime. Believe me, the rich and famous are often up to some sort of villainy. Even if they're peers of the realm they're not disqualified from pumping themselves full of cocaine.

The detective inspector from the local nick – he introduced himself as Ted Fellowes – was standing under the portico in front of the shattered front door. He seemed a bit young for a DI and I suspected that he was a graduate of that forcing process known as the Special Course at Bramshill Police College, a wondrous scheme that frequently elevates callow young constables to levels way above their competence. Even so, he'll probably be a commander before I make superintendent.

'So what have we got, Ted?' It was the standard copper's question: a way of finding out what the situation was. I knew that I was dealing with two suspicious deaths – the phone call to my office had told me that – but it's always nice to know how the Old Bill had got to hear of it. I just hoped he wouldn't tell me in the strangulated prose known as Bramshillese.

'A milkman called police—' Fellowes began.

'Funny name for a milkman,' muttered Dave, having also sussed out that the DI was probably a Special Course man.

Fellowes gave Dave a withering glance and started again. 'A milkman called police at about ten past nine' – he pointed down the steps: a man in a striped apron was smoking a cigarette and leaning against a milk float – 'after he found that yesterday's milk hadn't been taken in. He knocked but got no answer. The rapid-response car turned up but couldn't effect an entry. Bloody good timber they used when they built these places,' he said, kicking a jagged piece of wood down the steps. 'The crew called the fire brigade and they banjoed the door.'

Good, he spoke English. 'Do we know who the victims are?'

'They've not been positively identified, sir, but we believe them to be a couple called Light: Andrew and Kim. At least, they're the names on the electoral roll.' Fellowes led us into the house and pushed open the sitting-room door. 'The man's body is in here and the woman's is in the

4

master bedroom on the first floor. They both appear to have been shot. The scenes-of-crime lot are outside in their van. They've laid the platforms, but they can't do anything else until the pathologist turns up.'

We picked our way across the small platforms that were designed to prevent the importation of material from outside, material that might confuse the white-suited scenes-of-crime experts.

The sitting room was sumptuously furnished and richly carpeted. I let out a silent sigh of envy: the whole of my pad in Wimbledon that I'm forced to share with my estranged wife Helga – lack of finances prevent us from going our separate ways – would probably have fitted into this room and still left space.

A pair of sofas upholstered in velvet faced each other at right angles to the fireplace. A low coffee table between them held a silver rose bowl, an edition of *Country Life* magazine and a copy of *The Sunday Times*. Over the fireplace hung a painting that would undoubtedly have paid off my mortgage with money to spare.

'Nice bit of crenellation, guv,' said Dave, gazing up at the ornate ceiling.

'How the hell d'you come to know a word like that, Dave?'

'Read it in a book, guv.'

'What sort of book?'

'A dictionary, guv.'

'And when did you have time to study a dictionary, Dave?'

'When I was reading English at university,' said Dave smugly, with a smirk that said he'd got one over on the governor.

Isn't it amazing? Dave had been working with me for over a year now, but you learn something about your colleagues every day. My fault really: I should have looked up his personal records, but the say-so from a DI on division that Dave was a good detective was enough for me to take him on.

The dead man's body, clothed in a short, gold-coloured dressing gown – silk by the look of it – lay face down on the floor near the windows, across which the heavy, damask curtains were still drawn. There was a round mark at his temple and a pool of blood beneath the head: as Fellowes had suggested, it was probably a bullet wound, but in this game you learn never to make assumptions. The pathologist would tell me. Much later, of course.

'Been shot,' said Dave.

I cast an acid glance at my sergeant. 'You're coming on a treat, Dave,' I said. 'But as you've got nothing better to do, nip out and have a word with the milkman. Then he can go on his way. I'd hate to have complaints from the locals that they'd been deprived of their milk by the police. These days they'd probably sue for damages.'

I examined the body more closely. A full head of brown hair, expensively cut, and a signet ring on the little finger of the right hand. And a lingering aroma of aftershave adulterated by the unique odour of blood.

The main bedroom was immediately above the sitting room and was white: rich white carpet, white fitted wardrobes and dressing tables, and a huge bateau bed, also white.

On the bed – on a white fur coverlet – lay the body of the second victim. She too appeared to have been shot in the head. I guessed that she was in her early thirties, a good-looking girl with long black hair. I was left in no doubt that she had a gorgeous figure: she was naked. Her breasts were so firm and shapely that I thought she must have had implants, but Dave would undoubtedly tell me later: a bit of a boobs man is Dave.

The girl's right hand clutched a pink, silk peignoir – most of it beneath her – her left arm flung carelessly across the pillow. Legs slightly apart, the left one hanging over the edge of the bed, bent at the knee.

One of Fellowes's detectives appeared in the doorway. 'Pathologist's here, sir,' he said.

Downstairs, Dr Henry Mortlock stood just inside the

fractured front door. 'Morning, Harry. Business looking up, is it?'

Mortlock was a Home Office pathologist with whom I'd worked on several cases. If there had been an Oscar for black humour, he would have had a row of statuettes on his mantelpiece. We shook hands and I explained what was known so far.

'I'll start down here and work my way up,' said Mortlock, without the glimmer of a smile. Putting on his rimless glasses, he took off his jacket and handed it to a DC whom he'd clearly mistaken for a manservant of some kind.

I stood in the doorway of the sitting room and watched Mortlock at work. He hummed a few bars from *Tosca* as he knelt down beside the body, opened his bag and set out his instruments. 'Are you there, Harry?' he asked, speaking to the body.

'One knock for yes, two knocks for no,' I said.

'Rigor mortis seems to have passed off,' said Mortlock, pointedly ignoring my flippancy.

'I have the feeling that you're going to tell me something significant, Henry.'

'Rigor usually disappears thirty-six hours after death,' continued Mortlock, selecting one of about three thermometers from his collection of goodies. 'It could be, therefore, that death occurred at least that long ago.' But then he ruined it. 'It's a very unreliable indicator though,' he added. 'I'll be more certain after the post-mortem.' He stood up. 'Where's the other one?'

'Upstairs in the front bedroom. OK to let the SOCOs in, Henry?'

'Yes, let them do their worst,' said Mortlock.

I sent a runner to roust the scenes-of-crime officers from their van and Henry and I went upstairs. He examined the body of the dead woman, took a few temperatures and said the same thing again about rigor mortis.

'That ties in with what the milkman said, guv.' Dave Poole appeared at my elbow.

'And what *did* your very good friend the milkman say, Dave?'

'He says he left milk here at about nine yesterday morning. This morning it was still on the step. That would square with their being murdered the night before last.'

I shook my head. Oh, if only it were that easy. 'There are a number of flaws in your reasoning, Dave,' I said. 'Firstly, we don't know they've been murdered. It could have been a suicide pact. One kills the other and then shoots himself. Or herself.' I shot an arch glance at Dave, testing him.

Dave picked at his teeth with a pin. 'So where's the weapon?' He was always very good at getting to the point.

All right, it was a wind-up. I had to admit that what I was dealing with here was a double murder. 'Secondly,' I continued, 'the deceased may have been the sort of idle sods who couldn't always be bothered to bring in their milk. Or maybe it was the maid's job and she didn't turn up yesterday, and the deceased aforementioned wouldn't demean themselves to bring it in.'

'Maybe the butler did it,' said Dave churlishly.

Henry Mortlock declared himself reasonably satisfied with his on-site examination – he never committed himself further than that – and departed.

The next couple of hours were taken up with the scenes-of-crime team taking photographs, searching for fingerprints and generally sweeping the place with their E-vac machines in the hope that some speck of dust or shred of fibre might solve this double murder for me.

'There's been a break-in, Mr Brock,' said a young lady in a fetching white boiler suit and latex gloves. She told me her name was Linda Mitchell, and that she was the senior SOCO.

'Happens all the time,' I said, 'but right now I'm dealing with two dead bodies.'

Linda smiled – someone had obviously told her about my sense of humour – and led me down to the kitchen at the rear of the house. 'It looks as though entry was made that way,' she said, pointing to a window over the sink.

The original windows at the back of the house had been replaced with a type of sealed, UPVC double-glazed units. The window that had interested Linda had had its glass removed, apparently from the outside, presumably by the simple expedient of stripping away the rubber mounts that held it in place. It would have been an almost silent operation.

'It's beginning to look like a professional hit,' I mused. And if I was right, it was guaranteed to make my job ten times more difficult than it promised to be already.

'The glass is standing against the wall outside,' said Linda.

'Anything else of interest outside?' I asked.

'It's being examined now. There is a driveway at the back that gives access to the garages for this row of houses.'

'Good. Let me know what you find, if you find anything.' On the face of it, it appeared that someone had broken in at the rear of the house and murdered the occupants. But why? Why murder, I mean. A burglary gone wrong? It seemed a bit heavy, even these days, for a burglar to carry a firearm, but it has happened before.

Or was that what the murderer would have me believe?

Right now I was not happy about any of it. The single shot to the head in each case looked more like an execution than a spontaneous shooting and I wondered if there was more to Mr and Mrs Light than was immediately apparent.

'Has the front door been examined yet?' I asked.

'Yes,' said Linda. 'It was fitted with a mortise deadlock and a deadlock night-latch. And both were locked.' She paused and smiled shyly. 'Before the fire brigade got at them, that is. The back door was also locked, again with a mortise deadlock.'

'Bolts?' I asked.

'No bolts on any of the exterior doors,' she said.

I returned to the main floor. A carpenter had arrived and was waiting for the go-ahead before setting about repairing the damage that had been done to the front door. But he'd have to wait. He was probably getting paid by the hour anyway.

'There's a message on the answering machine, guv,' said Dave.

'Splendid,' I said. 'Grab the tape and we'll analyse it at our leisure.'

Dave gave me a sorrowful look. 'It doesn't have a tape, guv. It's one of those digital wire electronic gismos.'

'Yes, I suppose it would be,' I said. I hadn't got a clue what he was talking about, in fact I thought he was making it up, but I was in no position to argue. I'm a pencil and paper man. Not much can go wrong with that. 'I'd better have a listen, then.'

The message was terse. A man's voice simply announced that he would be there as arranged. The caller did not identify himself, presumably because he knew that the recipient would know his voice, but the small window on the answering machine showed '1537 hrs 11 June'.

Dave dialled 1471 but the caller's number had been withheld. So what? The last caller may not have been the one who left the message anyway.

'Well, that doesn't tell us much,' I said. 'Could be confirmation of some sort of prearranged business meeting, I suppose.' I turned to Fellowes, who was sitting on one of the plush sofas. 'Any idea what this guy Light did for a living, Ted?'

'Not yet, sir,' said Fellowes, 'but I reckon it paid well, whatever it was.'

'Morning, Harry.' DI Frank Mead stood in the doorway and nodded approvingly as he took in the luxury of the Lights' sitting room. 'Looks like a tricky one. I see they've just taken out two bodies. Is that it or have you got a few more stacked up somewhere?'

Frank – a former Flying Squad officer – was responsible for supervising a team of twelve or so detectives who would carry out all the follow-up enquiries. A thorough investigator, he could be trusted to get on with the job without any interference from me. And what I didn't think of, he would.

'No, just the two, Frank.'

'So, what have you got for me?'

I counted off the immediate 'actions' on my fingers. 'Positive ID. The local DI thinks they're called Andrew and Kim Light. I want to know what he did for a living and whether he was involved in anything dodgy that might have given some nutcase a reason for walking in here and topping him and his wife. Oh, and see if there were any staff: cleaning woman, housekeeper, cook, that sort of thing. By the look of the female victim's hands she wasn't in the habit of doing much in the way of housework.'

Frank was busily making notes on his clipboard as I spoke. 'House-to-house enquiries?' he asked, glancing up.

'Yes, ask the usual questions.'

'And we'll get the usual answers probably,' said Frank drily. '"Well, we heard something, officer, but we thought it was a car backfiring." Or, "We didn't want to bother the police."'

'Particularly if it was likely to interrupt their cannabis parties,' I added, attempting to match Frank's cynicism.

There was a commotion outside the room and I stepped into the hall. The blonde policewoman was arguing with a man near the front door. 'I'm sorry, sir,' she said to me, 'but this man says he lives here and that his name's Andrew Light.'

Two

'So you're Mr Andrew Light,' I said, steering the man into the sitting room. He was well dressed – if slightly crumpled – his suit, shirt, tie and shoes clearly of good quality.

'Of course I am.' The response was terse, hostile almost. 'What the hell's going on?' he demanded, glancing at the patch of blood on the carpet where the male victim had been found. 'What are all you police doing here? What's happened?'

'I think it would be as well if you sat down, Mr Light,' I said, affording him the courtesy of the name he claimed was his, even though I was by no means sure that he was the rightful occupant of the house. Publicity-seekers have been known to talk their way into crime scenes before, have even been known to confess to crimes they hadn't committed. Don't ask me why, but it happens. 'I'm afraid I have some bad news.' Well, I thought I had. If this man proved to be Andrew Light, was I right in assuming that the woman we'd found upstairs was, in fact, his wife? 'Do you have any form of identification?'

The man fumbled in an inside pocket and produced a passport. It was in the name of Andrew Light, aged thirty-five, the photograph undoubtedly that of the man sitting opposite me. He also gave me a visiting card bearing the address of the house in which we were now sitting: 27 Durbridge Gardens, Notting Hill.

His identity confirmed, I told Light as briefly as I could how the police came to be in his house and what we had found.

Light stared at me white-faced. 'But . . . I mean . . .

12

why ... what ... ?' he stuttered, before lapsing into confused silence.

'I'm still trying to establish what happened,' I said.

'But are you sure? That it's my wife, I mean.'

'No,' I said. 'At first we assumed that the victims were you and your wife, and that means that there's a rather painful task that I'll need you to perform.'

Light nodded slowly; he'd obviously guessed what was coming next. 'You want me to identify her?'

'Yes, I'm afraid so.'

Suddenly, the shock and emotion of the moment overtook Light and he buried his face in his hands, his whole body shaking as he began to sob. It was a reaction I'd seen many times before.

'Can I get you something?' I asked.

Light raised his head for long enough to point to a satinwood side table that stood against the wall opposite the windows. There were a number of bottles and glasses arranged on it. 'There's some brandy over there.'

'I'll get it, sir,' said Dave. He was always formal in the presence of members of the public.

Light took a gulp of the Courvoisier that Dave handed him, and then asked, 'But what happened?'

'We don't know as yet, other than to say that both victims appear to have been shot at close range. From our initial enquiries it would seem that an intruder gained entry through a kitchen window at the back of the house.'

'But that's double-glazed,' mumbled Light, slowly regaining his composure.

'Our enquiries are at a very early stage,' I said, deciding that now was not the time to tell him that double-glazing was nowhere as secure as a lot of people thought. Or as secure as some double-glazing companies led them to believe it was. 'We're assuming that the murders took place some thirty-six hours or more ago, although I'm waiting for the pathologist to confirm that.'

'Oh God!' Light sank his head in his hands again. 'If only I'd . . .'

'If only you'd what?' I asked.

'Not had to go away,' Light said, looking up. 'I've been abroad on business, you see.'

'Where?'

'Sweden.'

'And what is your business exactly, Mr Light?'

'I'm a barrister.'

I knew all about barristers, oh yes, and how. Knew that their travel pattern was usually triangular: chambers, law courts and wine bars. And, more frequently than I could afford, expensive restaurants and exotic far-flung places for holidays financed by their exorbitant fees. 'What sort of business would take a barrister abroad?' I asked.

'I don't practise at the bar. I'm a commercial lawyer.'

'I see. And when did you go?'

'Monday night.'

'That would have been the tenth of June, then.'

Light thought about that. 'What's the date today?'

'The thirteenth,' I said.

'Yes, the tenth would have been right. It was certainly Monday. I flew SAS from Heathrow to Stockholm.'

'And when did you get back?'

'This morning. I've come straight from the airport.'

'In that case, would you rather have a break before going to the mortuary, Mr Light?' I hoped that he would say no: I didn't need that sort of delay.

Light looked at me with a pathetic tear-stained face. 'No, I'll go now. Get it over and done with.'

I took Dave to one side. 'Get on the blower to Henry Mortlock and tell him not to start carving until we've been to view the bodies,' I whispered, and returned to my seat opposite Light. 'What is concerning me at the moment is the identity of the dead man,' I told him.

Light withdrew a handkerchief and wiped his face with it, but remained silent.

I knew that my next question was going to be misinter-preted – as I intended it should be – but I tried to frame it as tactfully as I could. 'Did you and your wife have any male friends who might have called here during your absence?'

Light frowned: he knew what I meant. 'If you're insinuating that my wife was having an affair,' he said angrily, 'then the answer is definitely no.'

But I knew from my own bitter experience that the husband was often the last to know of such a liaison. It had been a long time before I found out that my German wife Helga had been having it off with a doctor from the hospital where she worked as a senior physiotherapist. Not that it mattered: the death of our only son in a drowning accident some years ago – for which I had quite justifiably blamed her – had put a gulf between us long before that.

Andrew Light needed only one quick glance at our female victim to identify her as his wife Kim. He volunteered the information that she was thirty-three years old.

'You're under no obligation, naturally, but it may help us if you'd be prepared to look at the male victim, Mr Light,' I said.

I suppose that, as a lawyer, he had some understanding of the problems facing police in a murder enquiry, and he reluctantly agreed. Casting a cursory glance at the second body, he shook his head. 'I've no idea who he is,' he said.

'You've never seen him before?' I wanted to be absolutely certain about this.

'No, never.' Light shook his head, either in denial or bewilderment. 'I wonder what the hell he was doing in my house. Perhaps he'd come about the insurance.'

'The insurance?'

'Yes. I had a car accident about three weeks ago on Albert Bridge. Only a touch, but even so there was quite a lot of damage. But I thought it was all settled. Maybe they sent someone round to inspect the repair work.'

'Yes, maybe,' I said. 'If you'll give my sergeant details of the insurance company concerned, he'll check it out.' I didn't think it was an opportune moment to tell Light that when we found the victims, Kim Light was naked in the bedroom and that the man was wearing nothing but a shortie dressing gown. You don't have to be a detective to put words and music to that little scenario.

Dave took a brief, formal statement from Light and I told him that he was free to go, but not to Durbridge Gardens, at least not until the SOCOs had finished their work.

'I wasn't intending to,' he said. 'I'll put up in a hotel until the house is sold.'

'The house is on the market, then, is it?'

Light gave me a look that managed to combine pity with hostility. 'It will be, very soon,' he said tersely. 'I couldn't possibly bear to live there after what's happened. There'd be too many reminders of Kim.'

I felt sorry for the guy. Not only had he returned home to find his wife murdered, but must by now have suspected that she had been having an affair. Even though he had vehemently denied that possibility. 'Perhaps you'd let my office know where you're staying,' I said, handing him one of my cards. 'We're almost certain to need to talk to you again.'

Light took the card and handed me one of his own in exchange. 'That's where I work,' he said, 'should you need to contact me.' The address was that of a prestigious city banking house. 'And I'll let you know which hotel I finish up in.'

'Thank you. Apart from anything else, we'll need to take your fingerprints at some stage. For elimination purposes.'

After the macabre little scene at the mortuary had been played out, Dave and I returned to the house at Durbridge Gardens. The scientific team had still not completed their work and Linda, the senior SOCO, was waiting to speak to me.

'There are finger marks all over the place, Mr Brock,' she said. 'We've lifted those that we think are capable of comparison, but I'm afraid it's going to be a long job. When it comes to it, we'll doubtless find those of Andrew and Kim Light' – I'd told her that we'd positively identified the woman, and knew that the murdered man wasn't Andrew

16

– 'and all sorts of visitors. But,' she went on, 'in all probability, none of them will have a record anyway.'

That was always the problem. In the United States fingerprints have to be provided for just about everything, but in Britain, where we're obsessed with civil rights, the only fingerprints on record are those of convicted criminals. 'You're so optimistic,' I said.

Linda smiled. 'We found quite a few glove marks in the kitchen,' she said. 'Most likely made by a domestic rubber glove. The sort you'd use for washing up, Mr Brock.'

'Me wash up?' I murmured. 'Don't you kid yourself.'

Linda smiled again: I imagine she was getting used to me. 'You'll have to wait to see if they're all the same, but we found them on the glass removed from the kitchen window, on the draining board and on the doors to the kitchen, the sitting room and the master bedroom.'

'What about the garden?'

'Nothing that an initial examination turned up, but you may consider a fingertip search useful.'

I turned to Dave. 'Get Mr Mead to organize that,' I said. I glanced at my watch. 'Time we got back to the office.'

'By way of somewhere to eat, I hope,' said Dave with a mournful sniff. 'My stomach thinks my throat's cut.'

We grabbed a bite to eat at my favourite Italian restaurant and returned to Curtis Green.

Not many people know where Curtis Green is. An eight-storey building, it used to be called New Scotland Yard North in the days when it was a part of the Scotland Yard that lay between Whitehall and Victoria Embankment, but that was back in the sixties. The Metropolitan Police are great movers and shakers. They'd moved further up Whitehall from the original Scotland Yard in 1890 because the building was overcrowded. And they'd moved again, in 1967, because the building was overcrowded, this time to Victoria Street. Which is now overcrowded. I reckon we must be due for another move about now.

Detective Sergeant Colin Wilberforce, the incident-room

17

manager, had already got the basic administrative essentials of the enquiry up and running. Computer screens were flickering, books were laid out, binders had been prepared for the hundreds of statements – most of them probably useless – that we all knew would be taken before the murders were solved, and a board upon which photographs of the victims would shortly be exhibited, along with those of anyone else who interested us. It was all as neat and tidy as Colin himself, who was always well groomed and sat behind a desk as immaculate as he was. Even the pens were lined up, not daring to lie there any other way.

'Bit of a juicy one, sir,' said Colin. 'Still, it's a nice neighbourhood.'

I gave him a sour look. 'Yeah, thanks,' I said, and signalled Dave to follow me into my office.

'So where do we go from here, guv?' asked Dave, flopping down, uninvited, into my only armchair.

'We wait, Dave,' I said. 'Wait until we get the results of the post-mortem and the scientific examination and the house-to-house. But the most important thing is to identify the male victim.'

'Bit of a problem that,' said Dave, giving the impression of being completely uninterested in the task facing us. But it was an illusion: he was thinking hard.

Dave was a dedicated detective prepared to give as much time as needed to a complex investigation. It was, I suppose, fortunate that his wife Madeleine was a ballet dancer and worked most evenings. Some time ago, he had taken me and my girlfriend, Sarah Dawson, to see her perform. Madeleine was petite and gorgeous, but at five-feet-two I could not visualize her giving the six-feet-tall Dave a duffing-up, which is what current scuttlebutt at the Yard would have you believe. Mind you, marriages are funny things, and I should know.

I lit a Marlboro and tossed the packet across the room to Dave.

'Thanks, guv,' he said. 'You've given up giving up, then?'

18

I ignored his criticism of my weakness. I'd been trying to give up smoking for years now. In fact, ever since a master caught me at it behind the school bike sheds. He'd cuffed me round the ear and told me that his brother had died of lung cancer. 'Did you organize the taking of fingerprints from the victims, Dave?'

'All done and dusted, guv. On their way to Fingerprint Branch as I speak.' He lit his cigarette and threw back the packet. 'By the way, I got the Woodentops to take the numbers of all the cars parked in the vicinity,' he added, using his usual derogatory term for the Uniform Branch.

'Really? You into collecting car numbers, then?' I said, but I was glad he'd thought of something I hadn't.

'If we can match up all the index marks to living persons except one, then the missing one could be our male victim.' Dave spelled it out as if he were talking to a two-year-old.

'We'll make a detective of you yet, Dave,' I said.

But that particular strand of the investigation was overtaken when, ten minutes later, I received a telephone call from Linda, still at Durbridge Gardens.

'I think we've identified your victim, Mr Brock,' she said. 'There was a black sweater and a pair of chinos in the wardrobe in the master bedroom. In the back pocket of the chinos was a wallet containing several credit cards in the name of Duncan Ford.'

'Where are those credit cards now, Linda?'

'Still here. D'you want me to send them round?'

'Is DI Mead still there?'

'Yes, he is,' said Linda.

'Good. Perhaps you'd hand them over to him and ask him to get full details of this man Ford as soon as possible.'

'Got a result, guv?' asked Dave, when I'd finished talking to Linda.

'Perhaps,' I said cautiously and explained what had been found. But I'd been disappointed too often in the past to get excited. 'You'd better give the name to Fingerprint Branch, Dave. It might help them to shortcut their search, but knowing our luck I don't suppose he's got a record. You never know, though.'

Colin Wilberforce appeared in the doorway with a computer printout several miles long. 'First batch of results from Notting Hill nick, sir.'

'Results of what?'

'Collecting car numbers.' Colin nodded at Dave Poole. 'It was his idea,' he said defensively.

'Anyone called Duncan Ford on that list, Colin?'

Wilberforce shuffled the long printout rapidly through his fingers. 'Yes, sir. There's a Range Rover here that goes out to a Duncan Ford of Flat two, thirteen Sawbridge Street, SW1. That's Pimlico, sir.'

'Excellent, Colin. We shall sally forth, Dave and me, and see what's what.'

Three

Taking the set of keys that Linda had found in the pair of chinos at Durbridge Gardens, Dave and I made our way to the address of the Duncan Ford that the Uniform Branch had turned up.

Sawbridge Street was a turning off Pimlico Road. Flat two, on the ground floor of number thirteen, was one of six flats in the converted, three-storey terraced house. And, miracle of miracles, one of the keys on the ring fitted the door. Perhaps it was an omen.

I opened the door and, not knowing whether Ford lived alone or perhaps had a wife, called out to see if anyone was there. There was no answer, but the flat was so clean and tidy that I imagined there must be a female somewhere in Ford's life. My current girlfriend, Dr Sarah Dawson, a forensic scientist at the Metropolitan Laboratory, would doubtless have had a few critical words to say about that assumption. She'd told me on more than one occasion that my concept of a woman's place being in the home was not only outdated but blatant male chauvinism. Perhaps I was influenced by my estranged wife's determination – the cause of many rows – to continue her career even after our son was born.

The flat was tiny: a small sitting room separated from a kitchenette by a counter, and a bedroom with the smallest en suite shower room I've ever seen. It didn't take very long to search the entire flat but it yielded nothing in the way of evidence that would point to Duncan Ford's killer.

A loosely bound typescript lay open on the floor between a television set and an armchair. On closer examination it proved to be the script of a play: *The Importance of Being*

Earnest. I skimmed through it and saw that the part of John Worthing had been underlined throughout in red.

'Oscar Wilde wrote that,' said Dave, looking over my shoulder. 'I studied him at Goldsmiths.'

'Thank you, Dave,' I said. 'I'm not entirely without some literary education.' I paused. 'What is Goldsmiths?'

Dave sighed. 'It's part of London University, sir.'

'I see.' I knew I'd irritated him: he'd called me 'sir' instead of the usual 'guv'.

'D'you reckon this guy's an actor, then, guv?'

'It looks like it,' I said, putting the script of the play back on the floor and pointing to a framed photograph of the dead man – obviously a publicity print – that was in a prominent position on the wall. 'But I suppose he was resting.'

'Sure as hell he is now,' said Dave, without the trace of a smile.

'Have a look round and see if you can find any corres.'

'Corres' is policeman's shorthand for correspondence and covers anything that is written on, or is capable of being written on, including letters, receipts, credit-card accounts, bank statements and anything else that may shed some light on the lifestyle of the subject of police enquiries. Nowadays though, a lot of people rely on computers rather than paper, which is unfortunate. Certainly as far as I'm concerned. I can just about use one, but I don't really understand the damned things, don't want to and don't trust them anyway. Luckily Dave Poole is what is described as computer literate. That, however, is in my view an oxymoron.

'Want me to have a go at his laptop, guv?' asked Dave.

'Do what?' I asked testily.

'His laptop, guv.' Dave held up a small grey plastic box. 'It's a computer.'

'OK. See if you can make it work.'

Dave gave me a wounded glance, sat down in the armchair with the computer on his knees and opened it. For a few minutes he fiddled with various keys and muttered strange imprecations like a magician casting a spell. For all I knew, he might have been doing just that.

'Nothing,' he said eventually.

'What d'you mean, nothing?' I asked.

'There's a few bits and pieces on the hard disk, but nothing that tells us anything,' said Dave. 'And there isn't a thing in his email folders. Either he's dead cunning or no one sends him anything.' He looked around the room, a helpless expression on his face. 'I s'pose he's got some floppies here somewhere.'

'You're beginning to sound like a nerd, Dave,' I said. 'If you come across anything useful let me know.' I pretended ignorance because I was easily irritated by computer wizards, all of whom seemed to have an overwhelming desire to tell everyone how their damned machines worked. After all, people don't go about telling you how the telephone works, do they?

'Yes, sir,' said Dave and then muttered to himself. He was calling me 'sir' again. Obviously deciding against telling me what he was doing next, he crossed to a small writing table and opened the drawer. 'Aha!' he said, and took out a cable.

'What are you doing now?' I asked, against my better judgement.

'I'm going to try getting into his server, if I can get the modem to work.' Plugging one end of the cable into the telephone socket and the other end into the computer, Dave tapped a few keys. 'Bugger it!' he said. 'It needs a password.'

'What's that mean?'

'It means that we can't get into it to see if he's got any emails waiting. Best thing is to get one of the computer guys at the lab to hack into it.'

'What a good idea,' I said, having not the faintest idea what he was going on about.

Dave put the laptop on the floor and wandered off, obviously in search of Ford's floppies. It didn't take him long. 'Bastard hasn't got any,' he said as he ambled in from the bedroom reading a piece of paper. 'Doesn't make sense.' He looked up. 'There weren't any at Durbridge Gardens and there aren't any here, so where the hell are they? No good having a computer if you haven't got floppies.' He clearly regarded such gross inefficiency as a personal affront.

'For Krissakes stop rabbiting on about it, Dave. And what's that you've got?'

'A letter dated the seventh of January from some bird called Eve.' Dave handed me the document, now shrouded in a plastic envelope.

It was a scribbled note – there was no address – to 'Dear Duncan', thanking him for 'a wonderful dinner and an even more enjoyable night'. The last word was followed by four exclamation marks. 'I wonder who this woman Eve is,' I mused.

'Some scrubber he's screwing, I should think,' said Dave with all the subtlety of a sledgehammer.

'I'd more or less worked that out,' I said, and handed the letter back.

'I know, guv,' said Dave in resigned tones, 'find her.'

'Is that the only corres you found?' I asked.

'Yeah, there's nothing else.'

'How very odd.' Most people have got an address book, a list of phone numbers or a Filofax, that sort of thing. 'Is there an answering machine anywhere?'

'There's one in the bedroom, but there's nothing on it.' Dave sat down in the armchair again, clearly frustrated at the late Duncan Ford's lack of co-operation. 'Has anyone searched the Range Rover that goes out to this Ford finger, guv?' he asked. 'Might be something in there.'

'I hope so,' I said, suddenly realizing that I hadn't issued any specific instructions for it to be done. 'Get on to Mr Mead and ask him to get it shifted to the lab at Lambeth – on a flatbed truck – and get the boffins to examine it. Oh, and ask him to organize a fingerprint team to give this place a going over.'

'Right.' Dave took out his mobile and made a call. 'All in hand,' he said, moments later. 'And Mr Mead said that there's no trace of Duncan Ford in CRO.'

What Dave meant was that Duncan Ford had no criminal

record. But like me, he still used the term CRO – Criminal Records Office – even though I think it's been changed to National Identification Bureau. At least, it had the last time I looked. I think. God knows why the *wunderkinder* at the Yard keep changing the names of things. Last thing I heard was that they've ordained that accidents aren't accidents any more, they're collisions. Makes them look clever, I suppose, but I just can't keep up.

'What now?' Dave glanced pointedly at his watch.

'A pie and a pint, I think,' I said. 'Then we'll go back to the office and find out what's happening.'

Dave looked disappointed and I wondered if Madeleine had got a rare night off. 'Shall we take that?' he asked, pointing at the publicity still of Duncan Ford. 'Might come in handy for showing to witnesses.'

'Good idea,' I said, although I couldn't immediately think of any likely witnesses. Like I said to Linda, it was beginning to look like a professional hit.

Dave crossed the room and took the photograph from the wall. 'I'll pop into the mortuary and leave a receipt,' he said drily.

After a quick snack and a couple of pints of best bitter in the Red Lion, Dave and I made our way back to Curtis Green.

The commander, an indecisive Uniform Branch buffoon who had been administratively translated into a detective and thought he was one, was poking about in the incident room. Much to the restrained annoyance of Colin Wilberforce, who disliked anyone interfering with his paperwork. And that included me.

'Ah, Mr Brock,' said the commander, peering at me over his glasses and giving his moustache a quick tug. 'How's it going?'

It was one of his favourite expressions and I was never quite sure whether he was enquiring after my health, bank balance, place in the seniority list or just wanted a summary of the investigation so far. I opted for the latter and gave him a thumbnail sketch of what had happened to date, which, apart from identifying the bodies, wasn't much.

'Good, good,' said the commander. 'I'll see you in the morning, then.'

Surprise, surprise. It was nearly half past six in the evening of what had been a very busy day, and the commander was usually out of the office on the stroke of six o'clock, disappearing like a rat up a drainpipe. I think Mrs Commander nagged him. Although that, in my view, was as good a reason as any for staying out to all hours.

'Any idea why the commander was still here, Colin?'

'Not really, sir,' said Colin, 'but he did say something about there being a lot of influential people living in the Notting Hill area.'

That reckoned. The commander was a bit of a social climber and if he was out to dinner somewhere posh this evening he would like to pretend that he was in charge of this latest tasty murder enquiry. Well, I suppose he was really, but I knew – and he knew – who would be doing all the bloody work.

I adjourned to my office, to be followed minutes later by Dave with three cups of coffee.

'Who's the third one for, Dave?'

'Mr Mead's just arrived, guv,' he said. 'Got the results of the house-to-house.' He opened a packet of Silk Cut and tossed one on to my desk.

'Have you heard that they've made the Yard a smoke-free zone, Dave?' I asked, lighting my cigarette.

'Thought it always had been, guv. Never seen anyone burst into flame over there.'

Frank Mead was carrying a sheaf of papers when he came into the office. He stared menacingly at Dave. Dave surrendered and moved to an upright chair. 'Have a comfortable seat, guv,' he said.

'I haven't had time to put this together yet, Harry, but I thought I'd give you the gist,' said Frank, sitting down and starting to shuffle through the forms that the Uniform Branch had used to gather information from the Lights' neighbours.

'Anything riveting?' I asked.

'The Coopers, who live next door, told police that the Lights moved in about two years ago, in July to be exact. Mrs Cooper said that the Lights argued quite a lot. She and her husband heard raised voices occasionally and once there was a public row between Andrew and Kim on the pavement outside their house.'

'What about?' I asked.

Frank shrugged. 'Your guess is as good as mine, Harry. What do married couples usually argue about?'

I could have told him, and how. 'This and that,' I said.

'Last Christmas morning they invited the Lights in for drinks,' continued Frank, 'and Kim Light turned up in a very revealing black dress – low cut, no back and split up the side to her thigh – and proceeded to chat up all the men. There were about thirty people there altogether: husbands and wives . . . or girlfriends. It didn't go down too well apparently, not with the womenfolk anyway. Mrs Cooper described her as a flighty piece.'

'How delightfully old-fashioned.'

'Some other neighbours, the Dyers, were also at this drinks party. Kim Light told Charles Dyer that she used to be a dancer and—'

'Where?' I asked.

'Don't know,' said Frank. 'She didn't say, or if she did Dyer doesn't remember. But wherever it was, it was where she met her husband.'

'How long have the Lights been married, do we know?'

'No, not yet.'

'I'll get it done, guv,' said Dave, who by now had a notebook open on his knees. He scribbled a few lines and would doubtless lumber some unsuspecting DC with a search at the General Register Office. 'And I suppose you want me to find out where she was a dancer.'

'Well spotted, Dave,' I said, and turned back to Frank. 'Anything else?'

Frank shuffled through a few more questionnaires. 'The couple opposite the Lights – the Wilsons – seem to know

27

all that's going on. At least *Mrs* Wilson does. She claims that she saw Andrew Light getting into a taxi one morning – this was about three or four months ago – laden with a grip and a suit-carrier. She assumed he was off on a business trip. In fact, she was sure because she *happened* to see him come back again about three days later.' He looked up and grinned. 'However, she reckons that within an hour of Andrew Light's departure, a guy turned up in a Range Rover and was admitted to the house by Kim. This guy stayed for about four hours, she said.'

'She didn't get the number of this Range Rover, by any chance, did she?' I asked hopefully.

'No,' said Frank.

I glanced at Dave. 'Get someone to show Mrs Wilson that publicity still, see if she can identify him. No, on second thoughts, I think I'll go and see her, when I can fit it in.'

'Unfortunately,' said Frank, 'the people on the other side of the Lights from the Coopers – they're the Stows – are away on holiday. I think it'll definitely be worth having a word when they get back.'

'When's that likely to be, Frank?'

'The Dyers at thirty-one said the Stows will be back on Saturday. They've gone to the Algarve apparently. Flew out about three weeks ago, according to Charles Dyer.'

'Why d'you think the Stows in particular will be worth seeing?'

'According to Charles Dyer, the Lights and the Stows are close friends,' said Frank. 'Even went on holiday together last year.'

'Did they indeed? Yes, I'll definitely have a word with them. Saturday, you say?'

'Yes, but I don't know what time.'

'That's OK. They'll keep till Monday.' Even in a compli-cated murder enquiry – and I was quite sure that this was going to be one – I tried to avoid working on a Sunday. It's not that I'm religious or anything, I just think that even CID officers are entitled to some time off. There are times when I wish I was a television detective: to be able to solve a murder in two hours, including commercial breaks, would be marvellous. But I'm afraid the stress of being an actor would be too much for me. Early-morning shoots in the freezing cold. No, not for me.

'By the way,' Frank said, 'I went with the Range Rover to Lambeth.'

'Anything?'

'No. I had a good look round inside it, but there was nothing beyond the usual: owner's handbook, a couple of unpaid parking tickets, a pair of driving gloves and a membership card for the AA. I'm getting the lab people to give it a good going over, but I'm not expecting miracles.'

It was no more than I'd expected, but it did beg the question where did Duncan Ford keep his personal corres and the computer floppies that Dave was so worried about. 'Let me know if they find anything interesting.'

'The SOCOs found a mobile phone belonging to Ford at Durbridge Gardens. They're going through the directory to see what phone numbers he had stored. Might turn up something useful.'

And that was really all we could do. I glanced at my watch: it was nearly eight o'clock. 'Time to go home, I think,' I said.

Dave stood up immediately with an about-bloody-time expression on his face.

Four

C opies of Henry Mortlock's post-mortem report and the SOCO's, preliminary findings had already been sent through on the secure fax by the time I arrived at the office the next morning. I selected the post-mortem report first.

'There's a bit of a surprise in that one, sir,' said Colin Wilberforce, who made a habit of reading everything that passed across his desk.

I was skimming through the report when my eyes stopped at a paragraph about Duncan Ford's sexual habits. *There is evidence,* Mortlock had written, *that Ford indulged in regular homosexual activity.* Well now, there's a thing! I read on. *But DNA tests indicate that Ford had also recently had sexual intercourse with Kim Light.*

I looked up: Colin was leaning back in his chair, arms folded, gazing at me with a smile on his face. 'Bit AC-DC our male victim, sir,' he said, summing up the situation in his usual succinct way.

The rest of Henry's report comprised no more than I had expected. There was all sorts of esoteric stuff about split entry wounds and how the bone of the crania had been carried away through the exit wounds, but it was the next part that was of interest to me: each victim had been shot with a single round at close range – Henry estimated about three feet – with, and he admitted to guessing here, a .38 handgun. Why, I wondered, had he guessed? Then I found out.

I looked next at the report which set out the findings of the scientific examination team. Unfortunately for my investigation, it recorded that the murderer had been careful enough to remove the rounds fired from the murder weapon, one from a wall in the sitting room, the other from a wardrobe door in the bedroom. Even if we found what we believed to be the weapon, we'd have one hell of a job proving that it fired the fatal rounds.

But it was the next paragraph that jolted me. Linda Mitchell, the senior SOCO, had examined the window through which it was originally thought the killer had gained entry.

One sentence leaped out at me: the glass had been removed from *inside* the house.

Although she didn't go so far as to state that it had been done to suggest that an intruder had committed the murders – it wasn't her job to say so – it was clear that I was meant to draw such an inference. And I did. She went on to explain, in technical jargon, just how the removal of the window pane had been achieved. And if Linda said it was so, then it was. I reached for my cigarettes.

'Problem, guv?' asked Dave.

'You could call it that.' I handed him the report and pointed out the telling paragraph.

'Inside job, then.' Dave was always very quick at getting to the nub.

'I reckon so, but who? The only aggrieved party in this set-up was Andrew Light, who might have suspected his wife of having an affair – even though he denied any such knowledge – but was in Sweden at the relevant time anyway.'

Dave reached across and took one of my cigarettes. Without asking. I shall have to tell him about discipline one day. 'Are we sure, guv?'

'Are we sure what?'

'That he *was* in Sweden at the time of the murders.'

'That's something we still have to check,' I said.

'Just talked myself into that one, haven't I?' said Dave, taking out his pocket book. 'He said he went to Stockholm from Heathrow on Monday the tenth, didn't he?'

'That's what he said.'

31

'And got back on Thursday the thirteenth in time to find us trashing his pad in Notting Hill.' Dave was scribbling away. 'Did he say where he went in Sweden?'

'No, other than Stockholm, but it shouldn't be too difficult to find out.'

'No?' Dave looked up with a quizzical look.

'No, we'll ask him,' I said, taking out the business card that Light had given me. 'And there's no time like the present.' I pointed at the phone. 'See if he's at work.'

'I'm surprised to find you here, Mr Light,' I said, when Dave and I were shown into the plush office that was assigned to the bank's legal adviser.

Light stood up, shook hands and asked his secretary to bring in some coffee. 'Why should I not be here?'

'I thought that with the death of your wife, you might have taken a few days off.'

'I think it's much better to immerse oneself in one's work,' said Light, somewhat piously. He was urbane now, fully in control of his emotions and exuding a self-confidence that, unsurprisingly, had not been present when I told him of the death of his wife only yesterday morning. It might, of course, have been a façade: some people are very good at hiding their grief.

Nevertheless, I felt myself disliking the man, but that was no reason to let it inhibit my approach to the investigation. 'You will appreciate that in a case of this sort, I have to check everything.'

'I should hope so,' said Light. 'I want to see the killer of my wife apprehended even more than you do.'

'Now, you say that you flew to Stockholm on Monday the tenth of June, and returned on the Thursday, the morning that we discovered the bodies of your wife and Duncan Ford.'

'That's correct.' Light's brow furrowed. 'But who the hell's Duncan Ford?'

'Ah! The man found dead in your sitting room was a Duncan Ford, thirty-six years of age, who lived in Pimlico. We believe him to have been an actor.'

'*An actor!*' exclaimed Light disdainfully.

I got the impression that Andrew Light was not much taken with thespians. 'So it would appear,' I said, 'but we're still checking that out.'

'But what on earth was an actor doing in my house?'

'I don't know,' I said. 'I was hoping you might be able to help us over that.' I had nearly said, 'shed some light on him', but fortunately realized at the last moment how inapposite such a comment would be. I'd no intention of telling him though – at least not yet – that the pathologist's post-mortem examination had revealed that Ford and Kim Light had engaged in sexual intercourse. Anyway, I was damned sure he'd guessed as much. If he hadn't he must have had a pathetic faith in his wife's fidelity.

'I've never heard of him,' said Light, the expression on his face clearly indicating that he was having difficulty taking all this in. 'Have you checked with the insurance people?'

'The insurance people?' Although I looked blank, I knew exactly what he was talking about, but it isn't always a good thing for policemen to appear too clever. A lot of people think that we're a bit thick and it can sometimes be useful not to dispel that misconception.

'Yesterday morning I suggested to you that the dead man might have been from the insurance company. You remember I mentioned the accident I had on Albert Bridge and that—'

'Oh yes, so you did,' I said smoothly. 'We have it in hand and it is being checked out by one of my team of officers.' But I knew bloody well that Duncan Ford was nothing to do with insurance – even though actors often have to do other jobs to make ends meet – but if Light was trying to convince himself that a passing insurance man just happened to be in the wrong place at the wrong time – wearing nothing but a dressing gown – rather than someone who had called with the intention of enjoying Mrs Light's favours, so be it. 'However, to get back to your trip to Sweden, would you tell us where exactly you went in Stockholm.'

'Certainly.' Light opened a drawer in his desk and took

out a business card. 'You can keep that,' he said. 'That's the man I went to see. I spent most of Tuesday and Wednesday with him and on Wednesday night had dinner with him and his wife at the hotel where I was staying.'

'And which hotel was that?' asked Dave.

'The Grand, in Castelgaten,' said Light, pausing briefly to acknowledge the arrival of the coffee with a word of thanks. 'Not a very imaginative name, is it?' he added with a smile. 'But, as a matter of interest, why d'you want to know all this?'

It was my turn to smile, a disarming smile, I hoped. I took a sip of the coffee that I suspected came from the vending machine in the entrance hall: it was awful. 'I'm sure you'll understand that my report to the Crown Prosecution Service has to cover every particular, Mr Light. You know and I know that what you did on your trip is irrelevant, but if I don't put in the details, someone will ask why they're not there.' It was absolutely true. I knew fine that where Light had gone in Sweden had nothing to do with the murder of his wife, but sure as hell some nit-picking pedant – from my commander right up to the Director of Public Prosecutions, and anyone in between – was likely to query its omission and rightly ask how I knew that Andrew Light hadn't murdered his wife and her lover. But I wasn't going to tell Light that. 'It's the bloody lawyers, you know,' I added, smiling.

Light had the good grace to laugh. 'There is, however, the question of the funeral, Chief Inspector,' he said, becoming serious once more. 'Are you able to say when my wife's body is likely to be released for burial?'

'Not at this stage, sir, no,' I said, 'but I will enquire of the coroner's officer and let you know.'

'I happen to know the local chief superintendent here rather well,' said Light. 'We're in the same livery and all that. D'you think it might help if I were to . . .' He inclined his head and adopted an apologetic expression.

'It won't help at all, sir,' I said. 'The City of London Police have nothing whatever to do with my enquiry.' And I could have added that they wouldn't know what the hell to do if they were faced with a double murder like mine on their patch. But I did know: they'd send for the Met. I stood up. 'Thank you for your time, Mr Light. I'll let you know of any developments, and I'll certainly see what I can do to have your wife's body released as quickly as possible.'

'What's the best way of tackling this, guv?' asked Dave when we were back at Curtis Green, and waved the business card that Light had given me.

'Try a phone call,' I said. 'The budget won't stand you gallivanting off to Sweden to make an enquiry that will rule out a suspect who isn't a suspect. Anyway, Madeleine would play merry hell with me for letting you go.'

I was certain that Dave's ballet-dancer wife would not be best pleased at the prospect of her husband roaming the fleshpots of Stockholm, doubtless suspecting that no copper could resist a pretty girl, particularly some shapely Swedish beauty. At least, that was the view held by my wife Helga, and she had said so in the days when we were speaking to each other. I don't know what it is about these Nordic girls, but the mere mention of a Swedish au pair is guaranteed to strike terror into the hearts of English wives.

'I don't speak Swedish, guv,' said Dave.

'Wouldn't be any good you going anyway, then, would it?' I said. 'But my understanding is that most Swedes speak English. However, to be on the safe side ring Special Branch. They're bound to have someone who speaks the lingo. If you tell him what to say, he can make the call for you.'

The upshot of that suggestion was that although Dave persuaded a Special Branch linguist to call Jan Johannsson – the man Light said he had seen in Stockholm – it proved to be unnecessary: Johannsson spoke perfect English. He confirmed that he had spent most of Tuesday the eleventh of June with Andrew Light discussing business. On Wednesday the twelfth, Johannsson took Light sightseeing, had dinner with him and ran him to Arlanda airport next morning in time to catch the early British Airways flight to Heathrow.

In the meantime – even though I knew it was a pointless

35

exercise – I told Dave to ring the insurance company that had underwritten the repairs to Light's car.

Ten minutes later he returned with the expected information that the company never sent anybody to check that damage had been satisfactorily repaired. And neither did the body-shop repair company that was contracted to the insurers.

'Well, that's that line of enquiry closed,' I said.

'It was never open in my view,' muttered Dave, turning a page in his 'action' book. 'The lab reports that Duncan Ford's laptop computer was empty,' he said, 'but there were a few telephone numbers in his cellphone directory.'

'Anything interesting?'

'The only one that we identified immediately was Andrew Light's. It doesn't mean that he knew Light, but he sure knew Light's wife Kim. The rest we're doing subscriber checks on. I'll let you know as soon as we have anything worthwhile.'

'This Ford guy is turning into a bit of a mystery man,' I said. 'No corres to talk of in his flat, or in his car, and nothing on his answering machine.' I wondered which way we should go next. 'You remember the script we found in his flat . . . ?'

'*The Importance of Being Earnest* by Oscar Wilde,' Dave said smugly.

'Exactly. See if you can find out where that play was going to be put on, will you? Might just give us a lead.'

That took the triumphant smile off Dave's face. 'How am I supposed to do that, guv'nor?' he wailed. 'There are hundreds of theatres in the country, and there was no indication that it was likely to be in London.'

'I'm sure you'll find a way,' I said. 'And don't forget that you were going to find out where Kim Light was working as a dancer . . . and when.'

'Can't we lumber Mr Mead's team with that?' Dave asked plaintively.

'Sure,' I said. 'It was just that, as your wife's a dancer, you might have known a few contacts.'

36

Dave gave me a withering glance. 'Madeleine is a classical ballet dancer, guv,' he said in a pained voice. 'From the look of Kim Light, I reckon you'd more than likely have found her in some sleazy nightclub.'

I laughed. 'Yes, you're probably right, Dave,' I said. 'Go for it.'

But that enquiry was to be rendered unnecessary by the appearance of Colin Wilberforce brandishing a sheet of paper.

'I've got the results of the fingerprint examination of the scene here, sir.'

'Don't tell me,' I said, 'it's a blow-out.'

'Not quite, sir. Firstly the glove marks. Those found on the pane of glass removed from the kitchen window were identical with those found on several of the internal doors. Those that were capable of comparison, that is. Secondly, the only identifiable fingerprints anywhere on the premises were those of Andrew Light, Kim Light and Duncan Ford. There were several other unidentified marks—'

'They probably belong to people who had legitimate access,' said Dave. 'And that could be a lot.'

'Brilliant,' I said, but I hadn't expected anything more. The sort of murderer who had entered Andrew Light's house and carried out the killings in the cold-blooded way that he had done – or for that matter, she – was unlikely to have left any evidence in the form of fingerprints. The rubber gloves were testimony to that. Neither was there any property missing, so it was doubtful if it had been a burglary that had gone horribly wrong. On the other hand, if that had been the case, no sensible burglar would have taken property that could eventually be traced to him from a murder scene, because it would also tie him to the murders.

'But there was one other identifiable mark, sir,' said Colin. 'One of the prints found in the master bedroom where Kim Light's body was found goes out to a Jonathon Wheeler. The print was on the door leading to the en suite shower room.'

'What sort of form's this Jonathon Wheeler got, Colin?'

I knew he had to have at least one conviction, otherwise we wouldn't be holding his prints on record.

'One previous for GBH, sir. Eighteen months ago he got six months suspended for striking a hunt saboteur with his whip, as a result of which the guy fell and broke his arm. The address for Wheeler shown in CRO is The Willows, Little Matcham in Hampshire. It's just outside Winchester.' Colin handed me the Criminal Records Office printout.

'So what the hell was he doing in Kim Light's bedroom, I wonder?' It was a jocular remark. It was bloody obvious what he'd been doing there.

But Dave, as always, came up with a cynical alternative. 'Having it off with Andrew Light perhaps?'

Colin produced another sheet of paper. 'We've also had a report about the letter found in Duncan Ford's flat, sir, the one signed Eve.'

'What does it say?'

'Fingerprint Branch found a few smudged finger marks on the paper,' said Colin, 'but there weren't enough points for any sort of ID. However, the lab reckoned there were traces of Poison on the paper.'

'What sort of poison?' I took a sudden interest even though the administration of a noxious substance appeared to be irrelevant to the Durbridge Gardens murders.

Dave had been reading the report over Colin's shoulder. 'Poison is an expensive perfume by Christian Dior, guv,' he said with a smug grin.

'Smart-arse,' I said. 'Right then, tomorrow morning you and I, Dave, will go to Little Matcham and interview Mr Wheeler –' that'll take the smile off your face, I thought – 'and see what excuse he comes up with for being in Kim Light's bedroom.'

'As if we didn't know,' said Dave.

Later that afternoon, I decided to return to twenty-seven Durbridge Gardens and have another look around.

We moved methodically from one room to another, but by the time we'd finished, I was no further forward than when we'd started. I examined the holes where the murderer had dug out the bullets that had killed Ford and Kim Light, but had to admit that if the SOCOs hadn't found anything useful, I was unlikely to do so now.

'This one's going to be a bugger, Dave,' I said.

'It might look better through the bottom of a beer glass, guv,' said Dave.

Jonathon Wheeler's house was a large, rambling country pile that dominated the village. Although it was called The Willows there was no sign of any. A dark-green Bentley lounged on the gravel drive.

A young girl – I guessed she was about nineteen and probably Wheeler's daughter – answered the door.

'Mr Jonathon Wheeler, please,' I said.

'May I say who it is?' asked the girl.

'Yes, we're police officers.'

Leaving us on the doorstep, the girl retreated into the house.

The man who appeared moments later was large in every respect. He wore a well-cut suit in Prince of Wales check – complete with waistcoat, despite it being high summer – and a Paisley handkerchief that overflowed from his top pocket. His florid cheeks gave the impression that he was no stranger to gin.

'The girl says you're coppers,' he said loudly. 'Always glad to see you chaps. Don't see enough of you round here, dammit. Come in, come in, and tell me what I can do for you.'

The sitting room was untidy. Copies of *The Field* littered a large table and the two Labradors which were spread across the centre of the carpet gave us a baleful stare as we entered, but then went back to sleep again. A shotgun stood in a corner by the leaded-light windows.

Wheeler noticed my glance. 'It's all right, it's not loaded. Normally keep it locked in a cabinet, don't you know. Fully conversant with all the rules, you see, but I've been cleaning it this morning.' He took a copy of the *Daily Telegraph* from a sofa and dropped it on the floor. 'Have a pew, gentlemen.' He sat down in an armchair. 'How's my old chum the chief constable?'

I'd met Wheeler's type many times before in the course of interviews. The opening gambit was always a blatant claim to have friends in high places, but I doubted that the Chief Constable of Hampshire even knew of his existence.

'I've no idea,' I said. 'We're from Scotland Yard. I'm Detective Chief Inspector Brock and this is my colleague, Detective Sergeant Poole.'

'Ah!' Wheeler brushed his moustache and frowned at my sergeant. Dave smiled back. 'So what brings you to God's own county, eh?'

'Jonno, I wonder if –' A tall, angular woman was framed in the doorway, but she stopped speaking abruptly the moment she saw us. 'Oh, I'm sorry, I didn't realize we'd got company.'

'A couple of coppers from Scotland Yard, m'dear,' said Wheeler. 'This is my wife Lydia,' he added, turning to us.

'Don't get up,' said Mrs Wheeler as we both began struggling to our feet. 'You've not been getting into trouble again, have you, Jonno?' She spoke haughtily and looked down her nose at her husband.

'Heavens no, m'dear,' said Wheeler, but nevertheless looked decidedly guilty.

Obviously disbelieving him, Lydia Wheeler said, 'Well, I'll leave you to talk your way out of whatever you've been up to. I just hope you don't get dragged through the courts again, that's all.' And with that, she left us, shutting the door firmly behind her.

'Women!' muttered Wheeler. 'Well now, what exactly are you here for?'

'Kim Light,' I said.

'Who?'

'Mrs Kim Light.'

'I'm sorry, old boy,' said Wheeler, managing a convincing air of bewilderment, 'but I haven't the faintest idea what you're talking about.'

It was possible, I suppose, that Wheeler's fingerprint had been left in the Lights' house before the Lights moved in. He may even have been a previous tenant.

'Are you familiar with the address twenty-seven Durbridge Gardens, Notting Hill?' I asked.

'Never heard of it,' said Wheeler, but looked noticeably uncomfortable.

'Mr Wheeler,' I said, 'we recently had occasion to examine that address. In the master bedroom we found your fingerprints.' *Now talk your way out of that.*

'How the hell . . . ? I mean what right do you chaps have . . .'

The blustering was about to start. I knew the signs, but I also knew the kind of man we were dealing with. It was time to prick his balloon.

'A week ago last Thursday, a Mrs Kim Light was found murdered at that address along with a man called Duncan Ford,' I said. 'I am investigating those murders.' I handed Wheeler a photograph of the dead woman.

'Good God Almighty!' said Wheeler. 'It's Gloria.' Dropping the photograph, he stood up and made for a heavily laden drinks table. 'I think I need a drink.' Pausing, he cast a glance over his shoulder. 'Can I get you something?' he asked.

'No thanks.'

With a shaking hand, Wheeler swirled a whisper of Angostura bitters around a glass and poured in a substantial measure of gin.

'So perhaps you'd tell me what you were doing in Kim Light's bedroom and when you were last there,' I said.

'Christ!' said Wheeler, almost collapsing into his armchair. 'How the hell did you know they were my fingerprints?'

'Easy,' said Dave, speaking for the first time. 'Eighteen months ago you were convicted of causing grievous bodily harm to a hunt saboteur, as a result of which you were given a suspended sentence of six months imprisonment. You were fingerprinted at the time and those prints have been kept on record.'

Wheeler cast a withering glance in Dave's direction. 'That case was a fucking scandal,' he bellowed. 'It was the bloody man's own fault. I flicked him with my crop and the damned fool fell over and broke his arm. He was on private land anyway, but I don't suppose you johnnies did anything about that, did you?'

'Hampshire's out of our jurisdiction,' said Dave mildly. 'Perhaps you should speak to your friend the chief constable.'

'To get back to the point, Mr Wheeler,' I continued, 'what were you doing in Kim Light's bedroom?'

Wheeler was perspiring quite freely now and glanced several times at the door, perhaps fearing that his wife was listening to our conversation.

'What the hell d'you think I was doing? I was shafting the girl, of course.' Wheeler gazed wistfully, but unseeing, into the empty fireplace. 'She was pretty bloody handy with a riding crop, too, I can tell you,' he added.

'You mean she rode to hounds with you?' I posed the question out of sheer devilment. As I've said many times before, it sometimes pays to let the public think that policemen are a bit on the dim side, and Wheeler obviously thought I was being serious.

'Oh, don't be so bloody naïve, old boy,' he said. 'She rode all right, and damned well too, but not to hounds.'

I could sense Dave suppressing a laugh. 'How did you meet her, Mr Wheeler?' I asked.

'Lap-dancing club,' muttered Wheeler gruffly.

'Where is this club?'

'Can't remember the name but it's in Lavenham Street, Soho.'

'And that's where you picked her up, was it?'

'Not exactly, although that was the usual form. If you fancied one of the girls, you just handed the owner a fifty-quid note and he made the intro, provided the girl was under starter's orders. They weren't all on the game, you see. Some of the poor little bitches were so innocent that they thought nude dancing was the first rung on the ladder to stardom. But by the time I decided that Gloria would make a good screw, she'd started working part-time and was only there occasionally. That's what the bouncer told me.'

'How did you make contact with her, then?'

'I used to pop into the club fairly regularly, usually after I'd been to London for a board meeting. That's what I told Lydia, anyway,' Wheeler added, lowering his voice. 'But after a month or two, I noticed that Gloria wasn't always there, so I dropped the bouncer a twenty and asked him where she'd gone.'

'And what did he tell you?'

'He said that she'd more or less retired from lap-dancing and had set herself up as what she called a "home entertainer". We both knew what that meant and had a laugh about it, but he gave me her mobile-phone number and told me to ring her between nine and ten in the morning to make an appointment.'

'When was this?'

'About six months ago, I suppose.' A sudden look of alarm crossed Wheeler's face. 'I say, old boy, there's no need for Lydia to know anything about this, is there?'

'I shan't tell her if you don't,' I said, but I'd already got the impression from Lydia Wheeler's brief conversation with her husband that she was a woman well aware of his infidelity and probably dismissed it, with a sigh, as the sort of thing that men do. 'And so you rang her, I presume.'

'Yes. I gave the girl a call one morning and she told me to go round to her place in Notting Hill at two o'clock that afternoon. I was there for a couple of hours and she charged me five hundred quid, but it was worth every penny.'

'How often did you visit her?' I asked.

Leaning back in his chair, Wheeler spread his hands across his expansive belly. 'Twice more, I think,' he said eventually.

'Why?'

'For more of the same, dammit. What did you think I went there for, afternoon tea?'

'No, I meant why only twice. Why not more often?'

'Oh, I see. To tell you the truth, I found another filly who was even better and she didn't cost a penny. I mean to say, Gloria was bloody good, but five hundred a screw was a bit much, don't you know.'

'Where were you on the eleventh of June, Mr Wheeler?'

'Was that when the poor little bitch got her come-uppance?'

'Yes.'

Wheeler took a diary from his pocket. 'Yes, of course,' he said. 'Epsom races, all that week. Stayed in a hotel near the racecourse. And if you need any confirmation ask my secretary. She was with me all day every day. And all night every night.' He chuckled as he put the diary away. 'But for Christ's sake don't tell Lydia.'

'I shan't,' I said, 'but I will have a word with your secretary. What's her name and where can I find her?'

Wheeler shot forward in his chair. 'I say, old boy, is that really necessary? I was only joking when I suggested asking her.'

'I'm investigating a murder, Mr Wheeler, and I would remind you that your fingerprints were found in the dead woman's bedroom.'

'Jesus Christ!' muttered Wheeler. 'What a bloody mess.' He scribbled a name and a telephone number on one of his visiting cards and handed it to me. 'But you will be discreet, won't you?'

'Of course,' I said. 'I shall confine my questions to asking her if she slept with you during the week beginning the tenth of June.'

Five

'Well, that's opened up a whole can of worms,' said Dave gloomily, when we'd stopped for lunch at a pub on the way back to London. 'It means that any one of a dozen punters could have topped her. A hundred even.'

What Dave had said was true. 'And right now there's no way of telling who they were, either,' I said with equal despondency. In a way, we were lucky that Jonathon Wheeler had a criminal record, otherwise we would probably never have known that Kim Light had been working as a call-girl at her home.

The sudden sheer enormity of such an enquiry was daunting and even though I hated computers, I thought that HOLMES, the Home Office Large Major Enquiry System, might for once come into its own.

'One thing's certain,' I continued. 'Andrew Light must have known about this. The lifestyle that those two enjoyed must have been contributed to in no small part by Kim's earnings. If she had one punter in the morning and one in the afternoon, Monday to Friday, she'd've been netting five grand a week, tax free. Plus a bit of lap-dancing in the evening. Busy girl.'

'You going to do Light for living on immoral earnings, guv?' asked Dave.

'I shan't worry too much about that, Dave,' I said, 'except perhaps as a lever to put the arm on him.'

'What about the guy who runs the lap-dancing club, and who cops a fifty every time he fixes a punter up with one of his girls? To say nothing of his bouncer.'

'Yes,' I said thoughtfully, 'it would be nice to knock

45

someone off for something. So far we're not having a lot of luck. Unfortunately we don't have the time, but I'm sure the Vice Squad at West End Central nick will thoroughly enjoy feeling the collars of those two. After we've given them a going over. And that we'll do this evening.'

Dave groaned.

The lap-dancing club in Soho's Lavenham Street, described by Jonathon Wheeler, was not difficult to find. A large man barred the entrance. He wore evening dress and had 'bouncer' written all over him. Metaphorically speaking, of course.

'Are you a member, sir?'

'That do?' I asked, producing my warrant card.

The bouncer took a pace back. 'Of course, sir. Always pleased to welcome members of the force.'

I'm sure you are, I thought*, and wouldn't Internal Investigations Command love to know.*

'I'm here on official business. Where can I find the guy who runs the place?'

'Bear with me for a moment, sir, and I'll get hold of him.' The bouncer turned to a telephone and made a call.

Within minutes another dinner-jacketed individual arrived. He was fat, bald-headed, sweating and breathless. 'Good evening, gentlemen,' he said. 'I'm John Rose, the proprietor. How can I help?' I could almost see the wheels whirring inside his skull as he raced through a catalogue of vicarious errors and omissions that might have interested the police.

I steered Rose out of the bouncer's hearing. 'I want to talk to you about one of your dancers,' I whispered. 'Preferably somewhere private.'

'I think you'd better come into the office, then,' said Rose and led us into the interior of the dimly lit club.

It was a glitzy sort of place now, at the start of the evening's business, but I wouldn't mind betting that first thing in the morning it was a tip that smelled of spilt beer and stale tobacco smoke.

The tables were set in a horseshoe around a small floodlit

stage. The clientèle, as yet few in number, were drooling at a solitary girl – attired in nothing more than a microscopic G-string – performing the most suggestive gymnastics around a slender chromium pole that rose from floor to ceiling.

'Training to be a bus conductor, is she?' asked Dave, as we made our way around the edge of the large room and up a short flight of stairs. The proprietor laughed, nervously.

'Can I tempt you gentlemen to a drink?' Rose asked, once we'd reached his office. There was a window on the wall at right angles to his desk that gave a perfect view of the contortionist.

'No, thank you,' I said. I was not averse to drinking on duty, even though it is frowned upon by those now in authority but who probably drank on duty themselves when they were down where I was in the pecking order. It's just that I don't like being beholden to anyone whom I may have occasion to nick sometime in the future. And John Rose looked as though he could well be in that category.

'Now, about this girl . . .' I said, and showed him a photograph of Kim Light that we had taken from Durbridge Gardens.

'Ah!' said Rose. 'That's Kim Scott, but she was known as Gloria here. Her professional name, you know.'

'So I gathered,' I murmured. I presumed that Scott was her maiden name.

'What's she been up to, then?'

'She got herself murdered, Mr Rose.'

'Good God! When did this happen?'

'Last Tuesday or Wednesday.'

'I didn't see anything about that in the papers.'

'She was murdered in her married name of Kim Light,' said Dave drily.

Rose obviously didn't know whether Dave was joking or not. Come to that, neither did I. 'What happened?' he asked.

'She was found shot to death at her home in Notting Hill,' I said, 'along with a man called Duncan Ford.'

'Good God!' said Rose again, and after digesting that

piece of information, asked, 'So how can I be of assistance?'

'For a start, you can tell us when she left your employment.'

'It must have been about a year ago.' Rose crossed the room and thumbed through a large ledger on top of a filing cabinet. 'Yes, it was June last year. That's when she stopped coming full-time.' He shut the book and sat down again. 'But she'd come in occasionally to do an evening if we were short.'

'When was the last time?'

'About two months ago, I suppose.' Rose imparted the information reluctantly, as though to do so brought him too close to the murder.

'I'm told she met her future husband here, a man called Andrew Light, a lawyer. A barrister, to be precise.'

'She may well have done.' Rose spread his hands. 'I'd be very surprised if some of the clientèle weren't attracted to our artistes. After all, the sight of a naked girl dancing on a table right in front of your nose tends to get the juices going, doesn't it?'

'I imagine so,' I said, being in no doubt about it.

'We try to discourage liaisons in the club, but to be honest there's very little we can do about it. If a girl accepts a client's offer to dinner somewhere else and gets herself bedded . . . well, I'm not my brother's keeper, so to speak.'

'Sister's,' said Dave.

'What?' Rose stared at Dave.

'It would be your sister's keeper, not your brother's.'

I suppose having a degree in English made Dave a bit of a linguistic purist. But, it seemed, only when it suited him.

'And *did* Kim get herself bedded?' I asked. 'Or was there anyone who took a particular interest in her?'

'Not that I know of,' Rose said defensively.

Lying bastard. But he probably had in mind the legislation about keeping brothels and living on immoral earnings, to

48

say nothing of that delightful, outdated law about disorderly or bawdy houses.

'Do you recognize this man?' I produced a photograph that one of Frank Mead's team had covertly taken of Andrew Light leaving his office yesterday evening.

Rose studied it closely and then shrugged. 'He could have been one of a hundred men who regularly come here,' he said. 'I certainly don't know him.'

'Try this one, then.' I handed him the photograph of Duncan Ford.

'No, sorry. I don't recall ever having seen him either.'

That didn't surprise me. Ford might only recently have been converted to the delights of straight sex by Kim Light. I made a mental note to have some enquiries made of known gay clubs and haunts.

'Was she a good dancer, Mr Rose?'

'The best,' said Rose enthusiastically. 'In fact, too good.'

'Meaning?'

'Too explicit, really sexy. More the sort of thing you'd see in blue films.'

'You would?'

'Well, you know what I mean. The punters used to go wild when she came on. But I had to warn her about it. Told her that if she kept it up, we'd have the law round here.' And then, remembering that he was talking to the police, Rose added, 'No offence, of course. You've got your job to do.' He 'washed' his hands and forced a smile.

'Was there anyone that you know of who bothered her?'

'What, like a stalker, you mean?'

'Yes.'

'Not specifically. All the girls get a bit of grief from time to time, but I don't remember that she was particularly singled out. What basically happens is they mention it to my chief security officer, Tony Lambert – he's the chap you met on the door – and he and his team usually have a few words with the individual concerned.'

'You mean they give him a duffing-up?' asked Dave conversationally.

'Good heavens no. I'd never condone that sort of thing,' said Rose with just a little too much indignation to be genuine. 'Er, perhaps you'd like to have a word with Tony.'

'Good idea.'

Rose picked up the phone and tapped out a two-digit number. 'I'll get him relieved and bring him up.'

Tony Lambert looked even more menacing in the confines of Rose's office than he had at the front door, and I imagined that he could be extremely intimidating when it came to 'advising' a client that he was no longer welcome at the club.

'You sent for me, Mr Rose?'

'These gentlemen want to ask you some questions, Tony,' said Rose.

'D'you remember Kim Scott, who was known here as Gloria?' I asked.

'Not half,' said Tony enthusiastically. 'A real scorcher, she was.'

'Was there anyone that you can recall who paid her particular attention?'

Tony sucked air through pursed lips and, placing one fist in the palm of his other hand, cracked his knuckles. 'No, guv'nor, definitely not. Not in the club anyway.'

'So there was no one you told to get lost for bothering her?' asked Dave.

'No.'

'If there had been such a person, you'd've roughed him up, I suppose.' I shot a quick glance at Rose, who appeared to be praying.

'Bless you, no, sir, nothing like that,' said Tony. 'This is a respectable establishment.'

I showed him the photographs of Andrew Light and Duncan Ford but, like Rose, he claimed never to have seen either of them. I was inclined to believe Tony rather than Rose. With people like Rose one always wondered if their evasive answers were covering something else. And as for Tony, I thought that he appeared too thick to be cunning, but in that I was wrong. When the ship looked as though it was foundering, Tony proved to be first in the lifeboat.

'Thank you, Mr Lambert,' I said.

Rose took the hint. 'That'll be all, Tony,' he said.

Once Tony had left us, I returned my attention to Rose. 'Did anyone enquire after her recently?'

Rose screwed his face into a thinking mode. 'No, I can't recall any such person,' he said eventually.

'You're sure about that, are you?'

'Absolutely,' said Rose, a touch too quickly.

'We have been speaking to a witness' – I used the word witness deliberately to make Rose think that we were on the verge of going to court – 'who tells me that he paid you fifty pounds to introduce him to one of the girls who works here. An introduction for the specific purpose of prostitution.' That wasn't quite what Wheeler had said – he'd claimed to have bribed the doorman – but I was sure that other clients had greased Rose's palm.

Rose had been perspiring when we'd arrived, but now the sweat began to run freely. He took out a large handkerchief and mopped at his face. 'I don't know where you got that from, Mr Brock,' he said. 'This is a very competitive business, you know, and there are always people who will tell lies to get you shut down. Some of them will stop at nothing.'

'The information was confirmed by several other people we interviewed,' I said, gilding the lily outrageously and thereby increasing the pressure on this odious creep.

'What can I say?'

'You can start by telling me the truth, Mr Rose, because obstructing police in a murder enquiry is a very serious matter.'

'I might have helped out a valued client once in a while,' whined Rose, spreading his hands in a gesture that combined surrender with desperation, 'but I didn't think I was doing anything wrong. It's very easy to lose customers in this game, you know. One likes to oblige.'

'Well, you can oblige me by telling me the names of the men you introduced to Kim Light, otherwise Scott, or Gloria as you called her.'

'I can't think of any immediately,' moaned Rose.

'Why, because there were so many?'

'This will ruin my business, you know,' Rose said.

'Not as badly as the Common Serjeant will,' commented Dave, looking up at the ceiling as though possessed of some inside information.

'What? Who's he?' Mystified by Dave's interruption, Rose stared at him as though he was the only common sergeant he'd come across.

'I'm surprised you don't know,' said Dave. 'The Common Serjeant's the second senior judge at the Old Bailey and he doesn't know any numbers under seven.'

'What Sergeant Poole means is that you're quite likely to be spending a year or two in the nick for living on immoral earnings,' I said, declining to offer this overweight pimp any comfort.

'I don't know, Mr Brock, really,' said the anguished Rose. 'I never asked their names. It doesn't do to know too much in this business.'

'And it doesn't do for you to know too little in mine,' I said. 'What about Andrew Light? Did he part with fifty pounds to be introduced to Gloria? For the purposes of prostitution.'

'I told you, the name means nothing,' whined Rose miserably.

'Oh dear!' I said. 'Well, in all probability the Vice Squad at West End Central will be popping in to have a word with you, Mr Rose.' Dave and I stood up. 'Don't bother to see us out. We know the way. But doubtless we'll be seeing you again.'

'Any time, Chief Inspector, any time,' said Rose. But he spoke with an ill-disguised desperation rather than a desire to renew our acquaintanceship.

The crowd of paying voyeurs had increased by the time we walked back through the main area of the club. A strobe light cast a sequence of the colours of the rainbow on two naked girls who were alternating between entwining themselves around the chromium pole and around each other. At least three other girls, wearing nothing but banknotes stuffed into a garter high on the thigh, were gyrating on tables, their neatly trimmed pubes within inches of their salivating admirers.

'Going so soon, gents?' enquired Tony the bouncer. 'You'll be missing the best part of the show.'

'What's that, then, a demonstration valeta?' asked Dave casually. But I knew that his interest was aroused.

'No,' said Tony, taking Dave seriously, 'it's Sonia on the trapeze. She's something else, is that one.'

'I understand that you were Gloria's pimp,' I said quietly.

'What?' Cutting through the small talk and the jokes, my statement clearly stunned Tony, who, until that moment, thought we were nice, friendly policemen. 'Whoever told you that?' he asked, moving his right shoulder under his dinner jacket like a boxer recovering from a winding blow.

'A man who paid you twenty quid for Gloria's mobile-phone number so that he could pop round to her drum in Notting Hill and have it off with her, Tony, that's who.' And then I hazarded a guess. 'And she sent you a little present for your trouble, didn't she?'

'I didn't know that's what he wanted,' said Tony. 'He told me he was a friend and he wanted to get in touch to invite her and her husband to dinner.'

'I hope you're not taking the piss, Tony,' said Dave menacingly, as he moved a pace closer to the bouncer.

'I think what my sergeant is attempting to convey to you, Tony, is that the roof's about to cave in. The man who paid you twenty pounds for Gloria's phone number is prepared to swear on a stack of Bibles that you *personally* are actively engaged in pimping for a prostitute. And that is an offence that could well qualify you for some serious porridge. With me so far?'

Tony Lambert had rapidly assumed a hunted look. Casting a glance over his shoulder, he said, 'I get a break at nine, guv'nor. If you can meet me at the pub on the corner of Lavenham Street, I'll tell you all I know.'

Tony had swapped his jacket for an anorak, but still wore the same furtive look. He inspected the other customers closely before crossing to the end of the bar where Dave and I were drinking.

I bought him a pint. Well, it was the least I could do, and it turned out to be a good investment.

'I didn't like to say anything in front of Mr Rose,' Tony began. 'He worries a lot, you know, but there was a guy who took what you might call an unhealthy interest in Gloria.'

'Any idea who he was?'

Tony smiled. 'I wouldn't hold down my job if I wasn't on top of it, sir,' he said, preening himself slightly as he plucked a small notebook from his hip pocket. He thumbed through it and looked up. 'His name was Dent, Robert Dent, and he always enquired if she was appearing when he came in. Gloria told me that he followed her home one night. I'd called her a cab, as usual, but apparently he'd got his own car somewhere nearby. She didn't realize it until she got back to her place but then she saw him driving by, slow like, looking. Anyway, she mentioned it to me the next evening, and I had a word with this Mister Dent the next time he turned up asking after her.'

'And what sort of word would that have been?' Dave enquired.

Tony grinned broadly and cracked his knuckles again. It seemed to be a habit. 'Probably better you don't know, sir, but let's say that he decided not to patronize the club any more. Mr Rose wants the job done, but he don't want to know *how* it's done, if you take my meaning.'

'Any idea where this man lived?' I asked.

'No, but Kim copped his car number and passed it on to me.' Tony tore a page from his notebook and scribbled the details on it. 'There you are, guv'nor,' he said, handing me the slip of paper.

'How long ago was this?'

'Must have been, what, a year ago.'

'D'you happen to know where she was living at the time?'

'No, sorry, sir, I don't.'

'Doesn't matter,' I said, realizing at once that it really didn't matter. It was just my mania for collecting trivia. Sometimes it came in useful; most times not. But I did wonder if Kim had kept a flat in which to entertain 'clients', away from Durbridge Gardens where the Coopers said she and her husband had lived for about two years.

'You won't need to mention any of this to Mr Rose, guv'nor, will you?' pleaded Tony.

'Your secret's safe with me, Tony. And now we've got the bullshit out of the way, you can tell me what's really going on. As I told Rose, I've got witnesses who claim to have bribed him to provide toms, and to have bribed you too. So, don't forget what I said. When the chips are down, Tony, there'll be quite a little party at the Old Bailey.'

'And you'll be invited,' said Dave, and ordered three more pints.

Tony pulled out a packet of cigarettes and offered it to us while he engaged in a bit of in-depth soul-searching. 'Look, guv'nor,' he began eventually, 'I can tell you a lot about what goes on, but there's some very nasty people involved.' He cast another furtive glance around the pub.

'Well, the choice is yours, Tony. Tell me what you know and I'll work out how we can safeguard you.'

There was another long pause while Tony took several mouthfuls of his beer. 'Mr Rose keeps a book in his safe. It lists all the clients he's introduced to the girls.'

'What for?' I asked innocently, but I knew the answer.

Tony let out a derisive scoff. 'So's they can screw 'em, of course.'

'And is he in this on his own, or is there someone else pulling the strings?'

'Christ, guv'nor!' said Tony. 'You don't know what you're asking.'

'You've gone this far,' I said. 'You might as well go for the five-card trick.'

Tony lowered his voice and cast another furtive glance around the pub. 'It's a guy called Danny Todd, a really nasty piece of work.'

'Does he use the club?'

'Yeah, comes in most nights.'

'And what's his interest?'

'I don't know exactly, but Mr Rose is dead scared of him.'

And that was that. For the time being. But it was confirmation that the lap-dancing Kim Light, formerly Scott, sometime Gloria, had doubled as a call-girl. And she had attracted the attention of an unsavoury character who had been given the 'warning formula' by Tony the bouncer.

But the really interesting lead, according to Tony, was that Rose was running a vice ring and, it appeared, was being leaned on by a character called Danny Todd. I decided it was time to take a great interest in Mr Danny Todd.

Six

There had seemed little point in working on Sunday and, in the interests of the overtime budget, I had given most of the squad the day off. I'm nothing if not generous. Well, that was my view, but the troops were a bit choked at being deprived of the extra money. Anyway, it'd give me a chance to take my girlfriend Sarah Dawson out for a meal.

Monday morning's most important job was to lay hands on the book in which Tony Lambert said John Rose kept details of the call-girls he was hiring out.

Anticipating that there might be an element of resistance on Rose's part – particularly if Tony's story about the mysterious Danny Todd was true – we took the precaution of obtaining a search warrant.

'We're not open yet,' said Tony as he answered the door in response to our knocking. 'Oh, it's you, sir. Want Mr Rose, do you?'

'Yes, I do,' I said firmly. The expression on Tony's face indicated that he was probably regretting what he had told us in the Lavenham Arms on Saturday evening.

Although it was not yet eleven o'clock, a couple of girls in leotards were rehearsing in the main arena of the club. 'Bit of new talent learning the ropes,' Tony said as we walked through.

'Oh, you've got ropes as well,' said Dave.

John Rose was sitting at his desk poring over a pile of papers as we entered. Struggling to his feet, he said, 'Chief Inspector, how nice to see you,' in such a way that it was obvious that he had started lying immediately.

'I have a warrant to search these premises,' I said,

placing his copy of the document on the desk in front of him.

Rose sat down again, suddenly, and stared at the warrant as though it might jump up and seize him in a stranglehold. 'This is a respectable establishment, Mr Brock,' he said. 'I don't know what you want to do that for.'

'Because I don't think this *is* a respectable establishment, Mr Rose,' I said. 'And we'll start with that, shall we?' I pointed at a small, somewhat old-fashioned, steel safe in the corner of the office.

Pulling a bunch of keys from his pocket, Rose opened the safe. There was a confusion of paperwork inside, but on a shelf at the top was a small leather-bound book that proved to be a five-year diary. I opened it and flipped through the pages. Each week showed the names of girls Rose had supplied to 'clients'. Among the many listed were Danny Todd – frequently – and, going back a way, Andrew Light and Jonathon Wheeler. Gloria's name appeared fairly often and with different men's names against it, including, I noted, Danny Todd's.

'It seems to me, my friend,' I said, 'that this puts you in the frame for procuring women for the purposes of prostitution.'

'I was doing a favour for friends.'

'More than you were doing for yourself,' commented Dave.

Rose shot a nervous glance in Dave's direction. He obviously hadn't got the measure of my sergeant. I knew how he felt.

'Of course, it might help your case, if you could show that you were acting under duress,' I said.

'Duress?' Rose savoured the word as though it was new to his vocabulary.

'I have heard from my informants, who are many and various, that you're paying protection money to this Danny Todd' – I tapped the book with a forefinger – 'and that he has any of your girls that he fancies, free of charge. Added to which, he gets a cut of what your girls make when you sell them to any other punter who wants them.' All of which was pure speculation.

Although the office was quite cool, Rose began to sweat profusely. 'Mr Brock, I'm running a legitimate business here,' he said, exposing the palms of his podgy little hands in my direction. 'I don't have to get involved in anything like that. Who told you all those wicked lies?'

'You did, Mr Rose,' I said. 'You've written it down in this book. At least that's what I shall tell Mr Todd when I interview him. Unless you care to co-operate.'

'This'll be the death of me,' Rose whined.

'It certainly will if Todd gets to hear of our conversation. So, if I were you, I'd stay shtum about it. Anything you tell me won't go any further.' Well, it was half right.

Rose's chin sunk on to his chest and it remained like that for some seconds. 'All right,' he said, looking up at last, 'I do pay Mr Todd a small fee for making sure that there aren't any problems here. This is a very competitive business and he guarantees that no one else's heavies will come in here and make a nuisance of themselves.'

'Bit like a claque, I suppose,' commented Dave.

'What does this Todd do for a living?' I asked.

Rose swallowed hard. 'I've no idea, Mr Brock. Perhaps he's in import and export.'

'Well, that'll do for the time being, Mr Rose. I shouldn't say a word to Mr Todd about our little talk if I were you.'

'You don't have to worry about that, Mr Brock. It's more than my life's worth.'

'Very likely,' said Dave as we left behind us one very distressed club owner.

A girl carrying a feather boa and wearing nothing but high-heeled sandals, crossed in front of us as we walked down the stairs. She blew Dave a kiss.

'Looks like your luck's in, Dave,' I said.

'More than his is,' said Dave, cocking a thumb in the direction of Rose's office.

Before going to Rose's club, Dave had telephoned the Stows, the couple who lived next door to the Lights, to check that they were back from their holiday and were available for interview that afternoon. They were.

That part of the roadway outside twenty-seven Durbridge Gardens had been coned off. With a muttered oath, Dave got out of the car and moved one of the cones on to the pavement so that he could park. The PC standing in front of the house crossed the pavement in two strides, a look of terrifying officiousness on his face. 'Why d'you think we've put those cones there, Sunshine?' he demanded.

Dave loved jousting with petty authority, particularly when it came from his own stable. 'To stop people parking there, I suppose,' he said mildly.

'Exactly. So move it.'

Dave placed his warrant card so close to the policeman's face that I thought he was going to insert it into one of his nostrils. 'DS Poole, Murder Squad,' he said. 'And next time you get all puffed up with piss and importance, find out who you're talking to first, *Sunshine!*'

The PC mumbled an apology and retreated to his safe haven at the foot of the steps leading to the Lights' house.

Peter and Gill Stow looked to be in their late thirties and were what the glossy magazines would doubtless call 'an attractive couple'.

Their sitting room was as pleasingly furnished as the one in the Lights' house next door, although not as lavishly.

'It was a terrible shock to get home on Saturday to hear the news,' Peter Stow began. 'What a dreadful thing to happen.'

'It quite took the edge off our holiday,' Gill Stow added.

But obviously not the suntan: both were a deep walnut.

'I understand that you knew Mr and Mrs Light quite well,' I said. That should be enough to get them going, I thought. Once you start people talking about their neighbours, it's very difficult to stop them. Thank God!

'We were quite friendly for a while, yes,' said Peter Stow slowly.

I sensed a reluctance. 'Does that mean the friendship cooled?'

Gill Stow was not as reticent as her husband. 'It most

60

certainly did,' she said firmly. 'After the holiday.'

'Do go on.'

'They moved in about two years ago' – Gill glanced at her husband for confirmation and received a nod – 'and we hit it off right from the start. They came to dinner here, and we dined with them next door, quite regularly. He's a lawyer of some sort, I think. A barrister, I believe.'

'That's why he's so filthy rich,' muttered Peter Stow enviously.

But there again, the Stows didn't seem to be exactly on the breadline.

Ignoring her husband's interruption, Gill carried on. 'We got back on Saturday and found a policeman standing next door. No sooner had we got indoors than Debbie Wilson opposite was across the road telling us all about it. We thought that *both* the Lights had been murdered – Kim *and* Andy – but then we found out that she'd been found with someone called . . .' She paused.

'Duncan Ford,' I said. It was no secret. It had been in all Friday's newspapers, the tabloids screaming 'LOVE NEST KILLING IN NOTTING HILL', which must have delighted Andrew Light.

'Yes, that's the name.' Gill looked up at me. 'What was he doing there?'

'I was hoping you might be able to tell me that,' I said, despite knowing bloody well what he'd been doing there. 'But can we get back to the holiday? Am I right in thinking that something happened that put a damper on your relationship with the Lights?'

The couple looked at each other, seemingly unwilling to go into details.

'I can assure you that anything you say will be treated in the strictest confidence,' I lied.

'It was Kim who was the cause of the trouble,' Gill began hesitantly.

'In what way?'

'We'd hired our usual villa near Aljezur in the Algarve

– we always go to Portugal for our holidays – and last year we invited the Lights to join us. It's a beautiful spot, very secluded, very comfortable and with its own swimming pool. And it was the pool that created the problem.'

'Did it leak?' I asked innocently, doing my dense police-man impersonation again.

'Oh no,' said Gill Stow, taking me seriously, 'it was Kim Light. On the very first morning, she came out of the villa for a swim and she was stark naked. Peter, Andrew and I were already there, and admittedly I was topless' – she contrived to look slightly embarrassed at this admission – 'but I would never have dreamed of going any further, not with another man there. But Kim didn't seem to care. She just walked across to the pool and dived in. She wasn't at all inhibited. It was as though she was quite accustomed to walking about with nothing on.'

'She was,' Peter Stow chimed in. 'She told me so.'

'Told you what, Mr Stow?'

'She told me she used to be a lap-dancer.' Stow laughed. 'To be honest, I think that's a euphemism for a stripper. We saw a programme about lap-dancing clubs on television once. The girls dance in the nude. To be honest,' he continued, 'I sensed that Kim was a dangerous woman and the less I had to do with her, the better. She was a marriage-breaker if ever I saw one.'

'What Peter means is that Kim was clearly making a pass at him, particularly if he was by the pool on his own,' said Gill. 'And then out she'd come, starkers.'

'Didn't her husband have anything to say about it?' I asked.

'Not in as many words, but then he didn't seem to care anyway.' Gill spoke pensively. 'As a matter of fact, I don't think he'd've been averse to playing the field himself. I got the distinct impression that he was a womanizer and if I'd given him the slightest encouragement, he'd have followed it up.'

'Were you at the Christmas drinks party that the Coopers gave last year?'

'Yes, we were,' said Gill. 'Kim put a few backs up there, I can tell you. But I recognized it for what it was. It was the same old routine that she'd adopted on holiday.'

'You mean she arrived naked?' asked Dave with a bogus look of concerned enquiry on his face. I always knew when his interest was aroused. And I knew when his sense of humour was breaking out.

Peter Stow laughed. 'Not quite, but she might just as well have done. Her dress couldn't have amounted to more than about one square yard in total.'

'The only redeeming feature is that it must have cost her husband a fortune,' said Gill savagely, 'and serve him right.'

'Presumably she was making a play for the men who were there,' I said, wishing to confirm what the other neighbours had told Frank Mead's team of house-to-house officers.

'Yes,' said Gill, 'and working very hard at it she was, too.'

'Did she get any takers?' I asked.

'I don't know.' Gill shrugged. 'But I wouldn't be at all surprised.'

'Have a look at this,' I said, producing a copy of the photograph of Duncan Ford that we'd taken from his flat, 'and tell me if you ever saw this man calling at the Lights' house.' I enunciated the last two words slowly: I knew that one day I would slip up and call it 'the lighthouse'. I'd said as much to Dave and he'd suggested that if it was a lighthouse it would have had a red light, but Dave was always ahead of the game.

Gill Stow took hold of the photograph first and studied it carefully. 'It's possible,' she said. 'I saw someone calling there a few months ago who looked a bit like him. He was certainly good looking, but I couldn't swear to it being this man.' She looked up. 'Is it the man who was murdered?' she asked, handing the print to her husband.

Peter Stow gave the photograph a cursory glance and shook his head. 'Never seen him,' he said.

'Yes,' I said, 'that's the murder victim. You didn't happen to see what sort of car he arrived in, did you?'

'No, I'm afraid I'm not very good at cars,' said Gill. 'You ought to have a word with Debbie Wilson, across the road. She's very – how shall I put it? – observant.' She smiled and glanced once more at the photograph that her husband was still holding. 'Was Kim having an affair with him, then?' she asked.

'I suppose it's possible,' I said, not wishing to give too much away. But Gill Stow appeared to be quite a shrewd woman and must have guessed, particularly knowing what she did about Kim Light. 'I take it you didn't have much to do with them after the holiday.'

'We certainly weren't as close as we had been,' said Stow. 'We tended to hold them at arm's length.'

'We were still polite, of course,' put in Gill. 'Passed the time of day whenever we saw them, but there were no more dinner parties. In fact the only time we really talked to them at any length was at the Coopers' Christmas drinks party, but then it was only the usual small talk. I was going to make damned sure she didn't get her claws into Peter.'

'You needn't have worried on that score,' said Stow.

'Says you!' Gill laughed and gave him a playful dig in the ribs with her elbow.

'Did Kim Light ever give the impression that she knew her behaviour on holiday had gone too far, and it was that perhaps that had soured your friendship?' I was beginning to get the gut feeling that these two weren't being too open about their relationship with the Lights and I wondered why. A damage-limitation exercise, perhaps? If so for what reason? Dissociating themselves from an unsavoury scandal was the most obvious conclusion. There again, maybe the Stows had something to hide about their own conduct.

'If she did, she made no reference to it,' Gill replied. 'Personally I think she had a skin like a rhinoceros. She probably carried on like that all the time. As a matter of fact, I said to Peter that if she wasn't careful she'd finish up one day with her throat cut.' She paused, curiosity getting the better of her. 'Was her throat cut?' she asked.

'No,' I said. 'She'd been shot.'

'What date did you go on holiday this time?' asked Dave, looking up from his notes.

'It was three weeks ago,' said Stow, 'the twenty-fifth of May. We usually have three weeks if I can get away from my job that long.'

'What is your profession, as a matter of interest?' Dave asked.

'I'm in advertising.'

'Very nice,' said Dave, in tones only just short of sarcastic.

Having told the Stows that we might need to speak to them again, although I couldn't immediately think of a reason, Dave and I crossed the road to the Wilsons' house. From what Frank Mead and the Stows had said, Mrs Wilson was exactly the sort of woman I needed as an informant. As if to confirm it, we were just in time to see a woman retreat rapidly from an upstairs window.

After a short delay, commensurate with the time it would take for her to come downstairs, plump up the cushions and check her hair in a hall mirror, the door was opened.

Debbie Wilson was a well-built, ash blonde of about forty. I explained who we were, not that I needed to: she was the sort of woman who worked such things out. And sometimes even got them right.

'What an awful thing to have happened,' she began as she ushered us into her sitting room. 'This is such a respectable neighbourhood, you know. Nothing like that ever happens around here.'

I felt like telling her that double domestic murders weren't exactly run-of-the-mill anywhere in London, even in these days of widespread lawlessness.

'I understand that some months ago you saw a man arriving at Mr and Mrs Light's house, Mrs Wilson,' I began.

'D'you know' – Debbie Wilson edged forward on the sofa and spoke confidentially – 'I thought that he was up to no good. He was sort of furtive, you know.'

This was entirely the wrong start. Mrs Wilson obviously believed that the mysterious caller was the murderer. God preserve me from women who believe themselves to be amateur detectives. I blame Agatha Christie.

'Perhaps you'd just tell me what you saw, Mrs Wilson.' *And let me make up my own mind.*

'It must have been three or four months ago. Andrew Light – such a nice man – was off on a trip—'

'How did you know that?' I asked.

'It was obvious. He had a suit carrier and one of those holdall things. You know, like a sports bag but made of leather. It looked very expensive.' Debbie gave me a glance that suggested that such a deduction was perfectly logical. 'Well, he got into a taxi, to take him to the airport I suppose, and off he went. Then, about an hour later, along comes this Range Rover and a young man got out. Tall and good-looking, he was, and casually dressed.'

'And what happened next?'

'It must have been about nine o'clock, when he arrived, and he was there for at least four hours.'

'Were the bedroom curtains drawn during this time?' asked Dave, more out of devilment than a need to further the investigation.

'Oh yes. In fact they were closed for most of the day.'

'And when did you next see Mr Light?' I asked.

'Three days later,' said Debbie promptly.

'And you didn't see him in between those times.'

'Oh no. I knew he'd been away because he was carrying the same suit carrier and the same holdall. And he looked quite tired, as though he had that jet-lag that people get when they go to America.'

I produced the photograph of Duncan Ford. 'Do you recognize this man?'

'That's him,' said Mrs Wilson without hesitation. 'Yes, that's definitely him.' She sat back in her chair, a look of satisfaction on her face.

'Did you, by any chance, see him going into the Lights' house any day last week, Mrs Wilson?'

Debbie Wilson adopted a thoughtful look, gazing up at the light fitting in the centre of the ceiling. 'Possibly,' she said after some time.

'When?'

'I'm not sure. Maybe on Tuesday, or perhaps it was Wednesday.' She raised the photograph from her lap. 'Yes, I think so.'

'You think so, what?'

'I think I did see him, but I couldn't be sure which day it was.' There was a pause before Debbie Wilson spoke again. 'Mind you, I've seen all sorts of men popping in and out over the two years since the Lights moved in.'

I was surprised that she didn't keep a diary of events, but we had to leave it at that. I'd already written her off as a useless witness, and one probably motivated by jealousy. Maybe Kim Light had made a pass at Debbie Wilson's husband along with all the others.

'I'd love to put her in the box, Dave,' I said as we left the house, 'just to see her taken down a peg or two.'

'She'd be more use to the defence than the prosecution, guv,' said Dave. And he was right. She was the type of witness who has a great desire to assist the police, but whose testimony so often turns out to be counter-productive. Such people are seekers after limelight, and just can't wait to see a press photograph of themselves emerging from the Old Bailey, captioned 'VITAL WITNESS'. However, Mrs Wilson had, more or less, confirmed what we'd already learned: that Kim Light had operated as a call-girl.

'What did you think of the Stows, Dave?'

'Apart from the fact that she was a sexy bird, d'you mean?'

'Yes, apart from that. I got the distinct impression that they weren't being entirely truthful, that their whole performance was sort of rehearsed. I think the neighbours got to them before we did, and for some reason they're distancing themselves from the Lights. I wonder why.'

'Probably because Gill Stow was having it off with Andrew Light, and Peter Stow was shafting Kim,' said Dave. 'Right up until the Stows went on holiday this time.'

Seven

Back at the incident room, I gave Frank Mead the enquiry about Robert Dent, the man that Tony Lambert told us had followed Kim Light home from the club one night, but told him that I would interview Dent once he'd been traced.

'Could be a stalker, I suppose,' I said, 'even though this incident took place a year ago.'

'Stalkers are persistent bastards, Harry. We might just be dealing with a guy who'd bided his time. Someone who'd been watching her for years.'

'Thanks a bundle,' I said.

I don't know how it can happen. When I was in the sixth form at school one of my mates had a sister who was being pestered by some smarmy bastard of about twenty-five who used to hang around outside her school gates waiting for her. She was an attractive kid of sixteen, I seem to recall, but looked about twenty, and she didn't want anything to do with this guy. So one night her brother mustered the rugby-football first fifteen and shanghaied him to the local park, pointed out his mistake, stripped him naked and left him tied to a tree. He never bothered her again.

'I've got the result of the search for the Lights' marriage, guv,' said Dave. 'DC Appleby went through St Catherine's House with a fine toothcomb.'

'Get a result, did he?' I asked.

'Of sorts,' said Dave. 'There was no trace of Andrew Light's marriage to Kim,' he said. 'To make absolutely sure, he checked every entry from Andrew Light's sixteenth birthday right up to the present day. Twice. And nothing.'

'Don't worry about it,' I said. 'They may have been married in Scotland or even abroad somewhere.'

'But there was a previous marriage recorded,' Dave continued. 'About eight years ago he was married to a Lorna Richards, and divorced her about three years later.'

'Thanks, Dave,' I said. 'Probably not important.'

'Of course, Andrew and Kim might not have been married at all,' said Dave. 'That'd give Debbie Wilson something to crow about. Unless she's not married either,' he added. 'Funny place, Notting Hill.'

I turned to Colin Wilberforce's desk and picked up the full lab report. 'That's what I was looking for,' I said, finding the list of property that the SOCOs had found at Durbridge Gardens. 'Passport in the name of Kim Light.' But there was a note saying that an entry in the passport showed that she had changed her name from Scott by deed poll. So the Lights weren't married after all. Not that it mattered. 'What about Duncan Ford, Dave? Anything on him?'

'The most likely candidate that Appleby picked out is a Duncan Ford, born thirty-six years ago at Westminster Hospital, the son of Richard and Amy Ford. Richard Ford is shown as a company director.'

'Which doesn't tell us anything. Any luck with the theatres?'

'Not yet, guv, but I've got feelers out. The only one I've come across where they're putting on that particular Oscar Wilde play is a small theatre in Newcastle. I gave 'em a bell, but they'd never heard of Duncan Ford, and the guy playing John Worthing is about twenty-five and is called . . .' Dave paused and felt for his pocket book.

'Forget it,' I said. 'If you're satisfied that he's not our man, it doesn't matter. But keep at it.'

'Yes, sir,' said Dave gloomily. He was calling me 'sir' again.

'Have you ever thought about employing a criminal profiler, Mr Brock?' The commander, fiddling with his top-pocket handkerchief as he walked into the incident room, had obviously had a brainwave.

I knew what he was talking about. Profilers are cerebral wizards who study the scene of a crime and then ask a computer to tell them who'd committed it. Magic! Nevertheless I avoided risking a facetious reply: the commander's sense of humour – if indeed he had one – was certainly not on the same wavelength as mine. 'I can't say I have, sir, no.'

'Might be worth considering, you know. Particularly with a tricky case like this one.'

'I'll bear it in mind,' I said. Clearly there was less to the commander than met the eye. If he thought this was a tricky case, he should have seen some I've handled. God preserve me from senior policemen who imagine themselves to be detectives.

Worse still though are members of the public who think they are. I don't know why – perhaps it's the television – but all manner of people seem to think that they know more about coppering than the coppers themselves. My usual reaction is to ask such an 'expert' his profession and then tell him how to run his business. They don't like it. Funny that, ain't it?

As if reading my mind, the commander said, 'I was out to dinner with friends last night and we were discussing murders, only in general terms of course.'

'Of course, sir,' I murmured.

'One of them is a psychiatrist – holds a chair at one of the better universities actually – and he was telling me about a programme he'd seen on television. On satellite, as a matter of fact.' The commander brushed his moustache.

'Really, sir?' I got the point. Not only were the commander's friends highly qualified professional people, but they could afford satellite television, too. Mind you, so could most other people these days.

'The FBI use them quite extensively, it seems.'

'So I've heard, sir.'

'With a great deal of success, I understand.'

'Yes, but this isn't America, sir.' This was not the time to tell him that I thought FBI stood for Famous But Incompetent. 'I doubt I'd be any good at catching villains in, say, New York, any more than a New York detective would be much cop here, if you'll excuse the pun.' The commander didn't see the joke. 'I much prefer good old-fashioned methods of crime detection.'

'You must keep up with the times, Mr Brock.' The commander very nearly smiled as he wagged an admonitory finger. 'We are surrounded by a host of modern technology that's been developed at vast expense to assist the investigating officer. It's there to be used, you know.'

Any minute now, I thought, I'm going to get the standard Bramshill lecture about the officer in the case being the conductor of a vast orchestra but, mercifully, the telephone rang. 'Excuse me, sir,' I said, grabbing the handset.

The commander waved a hand of assent and wandered off to peer closely – as though he understood what it was all about – at the board bearing the photographs of the principal subjects featuring in my enquiry. I was only sorry that we hadn't been able to obtain one of Kim Light dancing in the nude. That would have made his eyes water.

The telephone call was from one of Frank Mead's team, a vivacious young DC called Nicola Chance. 'I've tracked down Duncan Ford, sir,' she said. 'In a manner of speaking.'

So, crafty old Dave Poole had laid off the enquiry. 'Which theatre?'

'It's not a theatre, sir, it's a small independent television company that makes programmes for the big networks.'

'Well done, Nicola.' Why the hell hadn't I thought of that? Tunnel vision again, I suppose. Just because I'd found the script of a play at Ford's flat, I'd automatically assumed that he was reading for a theatre production. Television hadn't even occurred to me.

'Let's have the details, then.'

'Don't you want me to make further enquiries, sir?' asked Nicola.

'No, leave that to me. Just tell me where I can find this outfit.'

*   *   *

The television company was in a tiny office on the first floor of a drab building in London's Soho, the natural habitat of those associated with the media, however tenuous that connection.

It's no good denying it – critics of the police wouldn't believe me anyway – but I am predisposed to assume that everyone connected with the entertainment industry dresses outrageously, is as queer as a nine-bob note and goes around calling his colleagues 'luvvy'. I couldn't have been more wrong.

The managing director was immaculately suited, wore polished black brogues and had hair that was trimmed to a decent length.

We introduced ourselves.

The managing director told us his name was Charles Winters. 'I thought you might be from the police,' he said. 'You look like policemen.'

This is the usual response from those who, until the moment we told them, hadn't the faintest idea that we were Old Bill.

'I'm enquiring into the murder of Duncan Ford,' I began.

'Who?'

'Duncan Ford. I believe that he was due to take part in your production of *The Importance of Being Earnest.*'

'Should I know about this?' asked Winters, a puzzled expression on his face.

'I understand that one of my officers, a DC Chance, recently made enquiries here and that it was confirmed.'

'Oh yes. A rather attractive young lady. Yes, I do recall that.' Winters extracted a file from among a pile of others on a side table. 'Ah! "*Importance*",' he muttered. I'd forgotten that film-makers always abbreviate the titles of their productions. 'But it foundered,' he added.

I glanced at Dave, willing him not to ask if Winters's company had ever produced a version of *Titanic*. 'So, it's not going ahead, is that what you mean, Mr Winters?' I asked.

'We put out a few scripts, but then we found that one of the big companies – it might even have been the BBC

72

– was doing a remake of it. There was no way we'd have been able to sell it in the face of that sort of competition, so we abandoned it.'

'I see. But Duncan Ford was reading for it, was he?'

Winters flipped over a few pages of his file. 'Yes, he was one of several auditioning for the part of John Worthing, but we told him that it was off some weeks ago. At least we told the casting agency, according to this.' He prodded a finger at the page he was reading and then looked up. 'There's a note here that says it's doubtful that he'd've got the part anyway. Hadn't got what it takes.'

I outlined the circumstances of Ford's death before telling Winters the real reason for us being in his office. 'We're having a great deal of trouble finding out anything about his background. There was nothing to talk of in his flat, or in his car.' Then I remembered the letter. 'I suppose the name Eve doesn't mean anything to you . . . ? An actress, perhaps?' It was a forlorn hope and I knew it.

Winters laughed. 'There are more so-called actors in this town than you can shake a stick at,' he said. 'And incidentally, the female of the species prefers to be called an actor these days, rather than an actress. It's this equality thing. But to answer your question, no, the name Eve doesn't mean anything to me. In any case, we don't hire actors directly. We just ring a casting agency and they do the donkey work for us. I suppose they might be able to help you. I never met this Ford guy personally. It's just a name on a piece of paper.'

Fortunately, the casting agency's offices were only a street away. A cramped waiting room bulged with a number of would-be actors *and actresses* – I don't care what Winters said – reading newspapers and magazines, *The Stage* predominant among them. We fought our way through this mass of doubtful talent to a girl sitting behind a computer screen.

'You'll have a long wait,' she said. 'She's not seeing anyone until after dinner.'

I assumed she meant lunch. 'We are police officers,' I said quietly, 'and we need to see the person who runs this place. Urgently.'

'Hang on, then.' The girl disappeared through a door, returning moments later. 'Go in,' she said. There was a distinct mumbling from the waiting hopefuls.

A middle-aged woman with horn-rimmed glasses and hennaed hair sat behind a cluttered desk. She had a cigarette in her mouth, and an open packet of Consulate and an overflowing ashtray within easy reach. There was a pile of files on the floor and a few dog-eared theatre posters on the wall opposite a wire-meshed and firmly closed window.

'Duncan who, dear?'

'Duncan Ford,' I said. I was beginning to weary of this already.

'One of hundreds, dear. Believe me, we get them trooping in here all day and every day. Well, you saw them outside, didn't you? All looking for the big break. Hollywood here I come.' She laughed scornfully and blew ash all over the papers on her desk. 'Sod it,' she added, and made an attempt to brush it off.

'I was told that you placed him for a part in *Importance*,' I said, quickly adopting the theatrical shorthand.

'Quite likely.' With an obvious effort, the woman pushed down hard on the arms of her chair and forced herself into an upright position. She pulled her woollen cardigan more closely around her overweight body and, with an even greater effort, knelt on the floor and shuffled through the heap of files. 'Here it is. Yes, so we did. I remember him now.' With a sigh of relief, she sat down again. 'Personally I didn't think he'd be much good. He was gay, you know. Not exactly what they're looking for, not for John Worthing's part, but he'd've done a lovely Lady Bracknell. He was no actor though, and frankly, I told him that he'd do better behind the counter of a burger bar rather than wasting his time in the profession. But apparently they took him on. For an audition anyway.'

'Did he have an agent?' I asked.

'Now you're asking,' said the woman.

'Indeed I am,' I said.

'Here we are. Oh yes. This bloke's sent us some crap over the years, I can tell you.' It seemed that nothing and nobody would satisfy this harridan.

'Who is he?'

'Name of Mark Light.' The woman reached up to a toilet roll suspended above her desk on a long piece of string, tore off a sheet and scribbled down the address.

That Duncan Ford's agent bore the same surname as the dead woman and her husband was too much of a coincidence to be ignored. However, I determined that some background enquiries would be made before we went blundering in. I just hoped that the woman at the casting agency wouldn't ring Mark Light and tell him we were interested in him. That was always the detective's dilemma: if you told anyone not to tell the subject of your enquiry you were asking about him, you could bet they'd be on the phone the moment you left their office. You just had to trust to luck that they were so busy they'd forget about it. If we now left Mark Light alone for a few days, he'd probably think we weren't interested in him anyway.

Frank Mead rang me on my mobile as Dave and I left the casting agency.

'We've tracked down this Robert Dent, Harry, the guy who followed Kim Light home about a year ago. Lives at fifteen Pepper Lane, Richmond.'

'Any idea what sort of man he is? What he does for a living?'

'He's an IT consultant and he works from home, which is a detached two-storeyed cottage not far from the river. Probably worth a bob or two. Incidentally, the car he used to follow Kim isn't the car he's got now, for what that's worth.'

'Thanks, Frank. You never know, he might be the bloke we're looking for.'

'Yeah,' said Frank, 'and pigs might fly. By the way,' he continued, 'the coroner has released the bodies of Kim Light and Duncan Ford.'

'Does Andrew Light know yet?'

'I don't know. Want me to find out?'

'No, leave that to me, Frank. I'd like to know when the funeral is to take place. Might be worth keeping obo from a distance, just to see if anyone interesting turns up.' It was a vain hope. Although beloved of crime series on television – in fact, it's usually the opening scene – I've rarely found it to be of use. But right now we were clutching at straws.

I told Frank about Mark Light and asked for enquiries to be made. 'And I reckon now might be a good time to talk to this Dent guy,' I said, glancing at my watch. 'Should have finished work by now.'

'Lucky bloke,' said Dave mournfully.

Eight

Pepper Lane was one of those tiny – almost rural – backwaters that I'm always surprised to find in a suburb like Richmond, less than nine miles from the centre of London. The façade of Dent's house was covered in ivy and, unsurprisingly, bore the name River Cottage.

'Yes, what is it?' The man, dressed in jeans and a blue denim shirt, had the aggressive demeanour of someone constantly plagued by door-to-door salesmen selling anything from useless household items to time-share apartments in Spain. About forty, he had the handsome features of a man who would undoubtedly have shared a mutual attraction with my estranged wife, and a full head of hair that showed no signs of greying. I was cynical enough to think that he'd succumbed to television adverts for hair dye.

'Mr Robert Dent?'

'Yes.'

'We're police officers, Mr Dent. We'd like a word with you.'

'What about?' Dent showed no signs of inviting us in.

'We can either discuss it on the doorstep or inside.' I didn't intend to waste any time on this suspect. 'It's up to you.'

'Tell me what it's about and I'll decide.' Dent pointedly put his hands in his pockets.

Clearly a guy labouring under the misapprehension that an Englishman's home is his castle. Well, if that's the way you want it, sport, that's fine by me. 'It concerns your association with a lap-dancer called Gloria,' I said, perhaps

77

not loudly enough for the neighbours to have heard, but certainly loud enough for Dent's wife to have heard. If he had a wife, and if she was at home. 'She worked at Rose's club in Soho.'

'Er, you'd better come in,' said Dent hurriedly. Had he not been inhibited by the offence of assaulting a police officer, I think he would have dragged us bodily through the door. As it was he couldn't get us into the sitting room at the front of the house fast enough.

He waved a hand at a black leather sofa, which we took as an invitation to sit down. Then he left the room, closing the door behind him. Moments later, he returned and sat down in an armchair opposite us. 'Now, what's this about? I don't know anyone called Gloria, and I certainly don't frequent lap-dancing clubs.'

'Stalking is a criminal offence,' said Dave mildly, by way of opening the proceedings.

'What on earth are you talking about?' demanded Dent, managing to combine indignation with an ill-concealed expression of slight panic.

'About a year ago, Mr Dent,' I said, 'you followed a lap-dancer called Gloria from the club where she worked in Lavenham Street, Soho, to her home address. She informed the management of that club and the chief security officer explained to you that your presence at the club was no longer welcome. And it was not the first time, was it?' I added, guessing wildly.

'This is outrageous,' blustered Dent. 'That woman and the people at the club got it all wrong.'

'So you did frequent this particular club?'

'What if I did? Hundreds of people go to those places.'

'Why then did you follow Gloria home?'

Dent plucked briefly at the arm of his chair. 'I'd been with her a couple of times,' he said quietly.

'Meaning?'

'For sex,' said Dent even more quietly.

'And presumably you paid her for her services.'

'Of course.'

'Why, then, should she have complained to the people at this club that you'd been following her?'

'She told me that she didn't want to see me any more.'

'Why? Did you want a freebie?' Dave asked.

'Certainly not. I always paid her. Well, on the two occasions I went with her.'

'And where did she take you on those occasions?'

'To a flat in Pimlico.'

That was an interesting coincidence but, I suspected, nothing more. I asked nevertheless. 'Does the name Duncan Ford mean anything to you, Mr Dent?'

'No, should it?' But then Dent paused, suddenly realizing that a long time had elapsed since his confrontation with Tony Lambert. 'Are you telling me that you're investigating this ridiculous business a year after it was supposed to have happened?'

'Mr Dent, I am Detective Chief Inspector Brock of the Serious Crime Group at New Scotland Yard, and I am investigating the murder of Mrs Kim Light, who you knew as Gloria.'

'My God!' said Dent, paling visibly. 'You're not suggesting that I had anything to do with that, surely? I haven't seen her for a year. Not since that bloody man at the club—'

'Told you to get lost?' asked Dave.

'D'you blame me? That damned bouncer told me that if I didn't back off, he'd telephone my wife and tell her all about it.'

'Where were you on Tuesday and Wednesday the eleventh and twelfth of June, Mr Dent?'

'Manchester,' said Dent without hesitation.

'Doing what?'

'I'm an IT consultant – information technology – and I was advising a company on the installation of a new computer system. In fact I was there all that week.'

'You seem very sure,' I said. Dent's answer had come out much too quickly, and it made me suspicious. Suspicious that he'd said the first thing that had come into his head.

'Of course I'm sure. It was a lucrative contract, and there

79

aren't many of them about these days. It's a cut-throat business, believe me.'

'I take it that someone there can vouch for you.'

'I imagine so, but I don't see why I should have to prove it to you.'

'In a murder enquiry, Mr Dent, I check everything that I'm told. Who did you see there?'

'A chap called Donald. We don't go in for surnames much in our business. But surely you can't think I had anything to with this, can you?' Dent asked again.

The door opened and a woman stood on the threshold. 'I wondered if your visitors would like a cup of tea . . . or something stronger, Robbie,' she asked. She smiled at Dave and me.

'Oh, er, this is my wife, Holly,' said Dent, obviously embarrassed by her intervention. She was, like Dent, dressed in jeans and a denim shirt, but barefooted, and wore her long, brown hair loose to just below shoulder level. She was slim and attractive and I wondered why, with a wife like that, Dent needed to consort with a prostitute.

Dent glanced at us. 'Would you care for something, gentlemen?' he asked. But the look on his face indicated that he hoped we would refuse.

I rescued him, but only because we'd more or less finished. 'No thank you, Mrs Dent,' I said.

'If you're sure, then,' said Holly Dent. 'I do hope my husband can help you out,' she added, smiling again, before leaving the room and closing the door behind her.

I raised my eyebrows and glanced at Dent.

'I told my wife that you were from the police and needed some help over a computer problem,' he said ruefully.

'Oh, I see.' I stood up. 'Well I don't think we need to take up any more of your time, Mr Dent. If you can tell my sergeant the name of the company you visited in Manchester last week, that should be all. Oh, and where your own offices are.' Frank Mead had told me he worked at home, but I love confirmation.

'I don't have any. I work from here,' said Dent.

*   *   *

80

'Before you go, Dave,' I said, when we arrived back at Curtis Green, 'get a message off to the Greater Manchester Police and ask them to make enquiries ASAP about Dent's visit to that company. I'm not too happy about him. For one thing, why should Kim Light have given him the elbow? After all, she was in the trade, and money's money.'

'Perhaps she didn't like the way he did it. From what we've heard of her so far, she was a bit oversexed and Dent might not have come up to par. On the other hand, despite his denial, he might just have wanted it for nothing.'

'Or she'd put up her prices and he couldn't afford it,' I said. 'Especially if Rose was taking a cut.'

'I can see you've got your finger on the pulse, guv,' said Dave as he reached for the telephone.

While Dave was doing that, I rang Andrew Light. 'I don't know whether you were informed direct, Mr Light,' I said, 'but I've just heard from the coroner's officer that the body of your wife has been released for burial.'

'Yes, I was informed, Mr Brock, but thank you for telling me anyway.'

'Perhaps you'd let me know where and when the funeral is to take place,' I said.

There was a pause. 'Well, yes,' said Light slowly, 'it's tomorrow afternoon at Kensal Green, but may I ask why you want to know?'

'A double murder in a fashionable part of London attracts huge media interest,' I said. At least it had when it happened, but as my old man used to say: today's news is tomorrow's fish-and-chip paper. 'I'll arrange for the local police to ensure that the press don't become too intrusive.'

'Thank you. That's very kind of you. It's been a very trying time for me.'

I toyed with the idea of asking him whether he had a brother Mark, and if he'd be at the funeral, but decided that that question would be better posed face to face, and I wanted to see his reaction – rather than hear it – when I told him.

*   *   *

81

The result we got from the police in Manchester the next day came as no surprise.

The company that Robert Dent claimed to have been advising – during the week commencing the tenth of June – did not exist.

'So what do we do about that, guv?' Dave asked.

'We nick him, Dave, that's what. Or at least Mr Mead's merry men will. Is he about?'

Dave returned a few moments later with Frank Mead. And a tray of coffee.

I told Frank that I'd not been happy about our interview with Dent, and in view of what we'd heard from the Greater Manchester Police, it was obviously time to bring him in for a serious talk.

'Reckon he's your man, Harry?' Frank asked.

'Nothing to point to it at the moment, Frank,' I said, 'except gut feeling.'

'Usually been good enough for you in the past,' observed Frank drily.

'There's one other thing,' I said, ignoring his sarcasm. 'This guy's into information technology so get a warrant to do the computers he's got down at Richmond, tomorrow morning. Never know what you might find. Then bring him in and I'll have a go at him. Dave and I are off to Kim Light's funeral this afternoon, just to see if there's anything useful.'

The funeral was due to be held at three o'clock at Kensal Green cemetery. After fighting our way through the traffic from central London, we only just made it. And it was blisteringly hot.

The only mourners, apart from Andrew Light himself, were Peter and Gill Stow, the neighbours from Durbridge Gardens with whom the Lights had once been so friendly, and Debbie Wilson, who, I suspected, would not have missed a funeral for all the tea in China.

My request for a police presence – grudgingly provided by the local superintendent – had resulted in the attendance of one very bored PC who had not even managed to struggle out of his car.

The hordes of television cameras and journalists that I'd promised Andrew Light had materialized, but not for Kim's funeral. There was some sort of a celebrity interment going on at the same time; there were certainly a few B-list television faces among the huge crowd gathered around the graveside, but I suppose I'll have to wait for tonight's television news to see who it was they were planting.

Dave and I watched from a safe distance. Andrew Light, I'm sure, did not see us.

'I wonder, Dave,' I said, on the way back to Curtis Green, 'what's happening about Ford's funeral. It'll be interesting to find out if any arrangements have been made for it.'

'I'll have a word with the coroner's officer when we get back, guv,' said Dave. 'If no one's claimed the body, I suppose it'll be buried at public expense. But if anyone has come for it, it'll be a firm of undertakers. We can make a few enquiries there.'

I gave Dave a sideways glance, and he corrected himself. 'Yeah, all right, guv, *I'll* make a few enquiries there.'

Colin Wilberforce had a message for me when we got back to the office.

'A guy called Tony rang for you, sir. He said that the man you're interested in is at the club now. Does that make sense?'

'Yes, it does, Colin,' I said, 'and I'm just in the mood for sorting out a nasty bastard.'

With our second visit to Rose's tawdry dive I began to understand why some officers pleaded to be returned to ordinary duty after a spell on the Vice Squad. The constant sight of bare female flesh ceased to be a turn-on and actually started to have the opposite effect.

'Is your friend Danny Todd here tonight by any chance?' I was not going to admit that I already knew that he was.

Rose's face was suddenly beset with a look of great alarm and he mopped ineffectually at his face with a colourful handkerchief. 'This'll ruin me,' he whined.

'Quite possibly,' I said, 'but is he here tonight?'

Rose walked to the window of his office and drew back the curtains. 'That's him.' He pointed to a bald-headed thug in his fifties who was sitting alone at a table slightly behind the main horseshoe. In front of him was a glass and a bottle of whisky. 'That's Danny Todd, but for God's sake don't tell him I told you.'

'Of course not,' I said, not meaning a word of it.

'I'm surprised this place is still open, guv,' commented Dave as we walked down to the arena.

'I haven't mentioned it to the vice lot yet,' I said. 'I don't want them shutting it down until this enquiry of ours is well and truly wrapped up. Then they can do what they like.'

'Danny Todd?' Dave leaned forward and whispered in the man's ear.

Todd glanced briefly at the warrant card Dave had thrust under his nose. 'So?' he said, before returning his gaze to the nearest nude.

'I'd like a word with you,' I said.

'And supposing I don't want a word with you?' said Todd truculently.

The moment I'd spoken to Todd, I sensed villainy. 'Either here or at the nick,' I said. 'Please yourself.'

Todd rose to his feet and followed us, his glance lingering on a shapely gymnastic blonde who looked as though she was in training for the naked Olympics.

'What's this all about?' Todd demanded once I'd steered him into the darkness at the very rear of the room.

'Gloria,' I said.

'Gloria who?' Todd fidgeted with a button on his jacket. 'I don't know no Gloria.'

'What a shocking memory you've got. She was a dancer here up to about two months ago. And you had the pleasure of her company several times. I doubt somehow that it was to listen to your collection of classical CDs.'

84

'I don't remember nothing about her. I've had lots of toms. Ain't no law against it.'

'That's very true.' Dave was on my left, leaning against the wall. 'It is unlawful to murder them, though.'

'What the bloody hell are you talking about, copper?' sneered Todd. Dave's throwaway line had not disturbed him in the slightest. 'This is a bloody stitch-up. I know your game. Just because I've got a bit of form behind me, you think you can fit me up with anything.'

As I said, from the moment I saw him, I guessed that Todd had a criminal record, and although I hadn't bothered to check it out yet I was pleased to receive confirmation.

'What's your date of birth?' asked Dave, pocket book at the ready.

'What d'you want to know that for?' But Todd knew why we wanted it. 'You're breaching my civil rights,' he added.

Dave slowly withdrew his handcuffs and dangled them on the forefinger of his right hand. 'You ain't seen nothing yet,' he said quietly, abandoning his proper English in favour of a bit of criminal argot.

Todd promptly furnished us with his date of birth.

'And is your name Danny, or Daniel?'

'Daniel, but everyone calls me Danny. Anyway, why all the questions? I never done no murder.'

'The body of Gloria, otherwise known as Kim Scott, or Kim Light as she was known by then, was found in the bedroom of her house in Durbridge Gardens on the thirteenth of this month.'

'And what makes you think I had anything to do with that?'

'The fact that you slept with her a few times,' I said.

'I told you, I've never heard of her. And even if I had, it don't mean I topped her.'

'Did you ever go to Durbridge Gardens?' asked Dave.

'Don't even know where it is,' said Todd.

'When did you last see her?' I persisted.

'How many more times do I have to spell it out? I've never heard of no Gloria.'

'Where d'you live, Danny?' asked Dave.

'Docklands. I've got a flat there.'

That reckoned. Todd was a villain who clearly made his money out of villainy, and obviously thought it would enhance his status to live among the rich and famous.

'Where were you on Tuesday the eleventh of June?' I asked.

'I haven't a clue. I don't keep a diary.'

'Doing a blagging somewhere, perhaps?' said Dave.

'No I bloody wasn't,' said Todd with a predictable expression of outrage. 'I'm going straight now.' At that point the sort of knowledge that criminals acquire came into play. 'If you think I was anywhere near that bird when she got topped, you prove it. I don't have to say a bleedin' word.'

He was right of course. The trouble is that people know too much about their rights these days. It's all these damned police programmes on television.

'All right, you can go,' I said. 'For the moment.'

'And if John Rose happens to have an accident, we'll come looking for you,' Dave added, assuming that Todd would have guessed where our information had come from.

'Is that a threat?' jeered Todd.

'No,' said Dave, 'a promise.'

I never ceased to be amazed at the speed with which Frank Mead resolved enquiries.

'I sent young Appleby to St Catherine's House to look up Mark Light's birth certificate, Harry. He's thirty-three and the son of Edward and Martina Light. And snap, the same set of parents as Andrew Light.'

'Well, there's a surprise,' I said.

'I made a few enquiries about Mark Light's agency and from what I learned it seems to be a bit of a one-man-and-his-dog set-up. Curiously though, none of my informants in the business seems to have heard of him. But I'm told that there are a lot of these agencies – many of which don't last five minutes, they said – so that doesn't necessarily mean much.'

Nevertheless, I decided that I would wait a while before going there myself. Sometimes when a person has been alerted to police interest in him, he will make the first move. If the woman at the casting agency had indeed telephoned Mark Light and told him about our call there, he might just decide to drop into a police station. If only out of curiosity.

Nine

'You're going to love this, Harry,' said Frank Mead.
'I am?'

'I took a computer expert from the Yard with me, and we turned over Robert Dent's drum first thing this morning, and guess what?'

'Surprise me, Frank.'

'He had some very dodgy pictures on his computer.'

'He's not a bloody paedophile, is he?'

'No, but we found about a thousand very graphic images of naked women, and of men and women engaged in sexual intercourse.'

'But that's not an offence,' I mused, 'unless he's flogging them.'

'Oh, there were some floggings as well.'

'Meaning?'

'Well, they weren't all stills. He's got some video stuff on his computer, too. And flogging was among them. Men whipping women and women whipping men. And that wasn't all. There was a load of obscene stuff you'd find on the worst blue movies that come in from the continent.'

'Did he have any of Kim on there, by any chance?'

'I didn't look at them all, but I suppose it's possible. The problem's going to be who do we get to have a look. We can't ask Andrew Light, or the Stows.'

'Mrs Wilson might fancy a free viewing, guv,' Dave put in.

Frank and I ignored him. 'What did he have to say about these pictures, Frank?' I asked.

'Nothing. I've got him banged up at Charing Cross

nick, but he refuses to say a word until his solicitor's there.'

'Very wise of him,' I said. 'Dave and I will sally forth and talk to him.' But I stopped at the door. 'One other thing, Frank, get the lads digging on Danny Todd. I want to know as much as there is to know.'

Dent's solicitor was already jousting with the custody sergeant when we arrived at Charing Cross police station. Needless to say, his attempts to secure the release of his client had been unsuccessful.

I identified myself to the sergeant and arranged for Dent to be brought up from his cell.

'This is scandalous,' said the solicitor as we made our way to the interview room.

'Yes, isn't it just?' I said, being deliberately ambiguous. I'd met lawyers like this one. Many times. Their ploy is to go on the offensive immediately, but he wasn't going to have any luck with me.

'What the hell's the meaning of this?' Dent demanded as we entered. 'I was dragged out of bed at some unearthly hour this morning. My wife was upset by policemen swarming all over the house, and my privacy was violated. And for what?'

Once Dave had completed the business of switching on the tape recorder and telling it who was in the room, I settled down in a chair opposite Dent and his mouthpiece. Dave sat beside me.

'When I spoke to you on Tuesday evening, Mr Dent, you told me that you'd been in Manchester all last week. A consultation with a firm considering the installation of a new computer system, I think you said.'

'So?'

'The Manchester police have never heard of this company, Mr Dent. In fact they say that such a company doesn't exist.'

'It's hardly my fault if they don't know their way round Manchester,' said Dent dismissively. 'I told you, I saw a

89

guy called Donald there.' I was sure he was lying, but I suppose he was naïve enough to have thought that we wouldn't check.

'Perhaps you'd tell me the name and address of this company again then.'

Dave looked up from his notes. 'That's the one, sir,' he said, once Dent had repeated it.

'So where were you, Mr Dent? I'd remind you that I am investigating the murder of a woman with whom you admitted having had sexual intercourse. She was murdered on either the Tuesday or Wednesday of last week. You can't account for your whereabouts on those days, and that makes me justifiably suspicious.'

'My client is under no obligation to account for his movements, Chief Inspector,' said the solicitor mildly, 'unless you can produce strong evidence that connects him in some way with this crime.'

'My evidence,' I said, keeping my gaze on Dent, but talking to the solicitor, 'is that he's a sexual pervert.'

'I hope you intend to substantiate that, Chief Inspector,' exclaimed the solicitor with a convincing display of professional outrage, presumably to indicate to his client that he was earning his fee.

'When officers searched your house earlier today, Mr Dent,' I continued, 'a large number of obscene images were found on your computers. Images that, according to the detective inspector who found them, undoubtedly breached many of the obscenity laws.' I wasn't too sure about that. In fact, I wasn't too sure that we'd got any obscenity laws left.

Fortunately the solicitor didn't know either, and from his bemused expression it was also clear that he knew nothing about the collection of erotic pictures that Frank Mead's team had found. I do love it when a solicitor is caught wrong-footed.

'So what?' snapped Dent truculently. 'They're for my personal use, and if you think I'm trading in them, I suggest you try to prove it.'

Dent seemed to be doing quite well on his own, and I wondered why he'd bothered to engage the services of a solicitor at all.

'However,' I continued, 'that still doesn't account for your whereabouts on Tuesday and Wednesday of last week.'

'I've already said, Chief Inspector,' the solicitor began, 'that—'

'I was with a call-girl,' said Dent, cutting across his legal adviser's lame intervention.

'Really? Who was she?'

'Her name was Trixie.'

'Trixie who?'

'I haven't the faintest idea,' said Dent.

'Where did you pick her up?'

'I got her name from one of those cards they put in phone boxes.'

'So you'll remember the telephone number, won't you?'

'No. I threw the card away once I'd rung her. I didn't want my wife to find it.'

'No, I'll bet you didn't,' I said. 'However, I shall require you to furnish me with a set of your fingerprints.'

'What for?' Dent obviously didn't like the sound of that.

'For elimination purposes. We have several unidentified sets found at the scene of Kim Light's murder.'

'Well, I'm not giving you mine.' Dent sat back in his chair and folded his arms, a truculent expression on his face.

'As is his right,' chimed in the solicitor, but he obviously wasn't too clued up on the law relating to the taking of fingerprints. In fact, I was slowly coming to the conclusion that he wasn't too clued up on the law. Period.

'Very well,' I said. 'I shall now seek a superintendent's authority for those prints to be taken on the grounds that I reasonably suspect you of being involved in the death of Kim Light.'

The detective superintendent at Charing Cross didn't bat an eyelid, and promptly signed the form. 'Reckon it's down to him, Harry?' he asked.

'I'm not sure, guv,' I said, 'but right now he's a front runner.'

Having admitted Dent to police bail, Dave and I, somewhat despondently, returned to Curtis Green.

'What d'you think, guv?' Dave asked.

'Could be,' I said, 'but we're going to have one hell of a job proving it. Unless his dabs turn up at Durbridge Gardens.'

The revelation that Mark Light was Andrew Light's brother was interesting, but enquiries into their respective backgrounds took second place to the activities – current and previous – of Danny Todd and Robert Dent, in my view much more interesting prospects.

Dave had not been idle. 'Got Todd's list of previous, guv,' he said, appearing in my office with a printout.

'Let's have it, then.'

'Armed robbery, malicious wounding, living on immoral earnings, and handling stolen property, to name but a few. He was also suspected of being involved with a protection racket a few years ago, but nothing was ever proved. He's fifty-five now and has spent about fifteen of those years in the nick. Came out about five years ago.'

'I'm beginning to fancy him for these two murders, Dave,' I said. 'I think we shall look more closely at Mr Todd's activities.'

Then came another revelation – two in fact – but detective work's like that.

'We got an interesting result from one of our searches of records, Harry,' said Frank Mead, as he wandered into my office and settled into my armchair.

It is standard practice in any major enquiry that searches are made of every government agency's records. 'Which one?' I asked.

'Customs and Excise. It seems that they've got Duncan Ford's Range Rover on their suspect list. For bootlegging.'

'What's the SP, then?' I asked. SP is another piece of police jargon culled, as is so often the case, from the racing fraternity. Although it stands for 'starting price', a policeman using it is actually enquiring the strength of the information. Don't ask me how it came about, but it does save a lot of time.

'He got turned over a fortnight ago at Dover on suspicion of smuggling large quantities of cigarettes, but nothing was found.'

'So why's he on their suspect list, Frank?'

Frank shrugged. '"Information received" is the best I could get out of them, but they weren't willing to disclose the source of that information. Probably some operation they've got running, but it seems they still don't trust the police.'

In a way I could understand that. In the past some very bent policemen have recycled drugs seized from prisoners or, in furtherance of some professional turf war, have completely buggered up a customs operation. But that's all changed. We're now an incorruptible police *service*. The Commissioner says so, so it must be true. 'Did these bright sparks at customs say whether the driver was Duncan Ford?'

'Not in as many words. They were a bit cagey, but they said they'd done a check with the vehicle licensing people at Swansea and found it was registered to him.'

'So we don't know for sure that Ford was driving the vehicle at the time it got turned over.'

'No, but I doubt that customs would have done a turn-out without having a look at the driver's passport, so we have to assume it was him.'

'And we didn't find his passport,' I mused. 'But none of that gets us any further forward. Smuggling cigarettes and booze doesn't exactly make him unique, does it, Frank? Incidentally, where is the vehicle now?'

'Still at Lambeth and I suppose it'll stay there until such time as someone claims it. I've left instructions that if someone does turn up, they're to hold the vehicle, send for a policeman and give us a bell.'

'Be interesting if it was Mark Light.'

'Wouldn't it just?' said Frank.

'I think it's time I went and had a chat with young Mr Light,' I said.

Mark Light's office was in that part of Fulham that the residents love to call Chelsea. I suppose it impresses their impressionable friends.

There was an intercom box next to a dirty green door. On it was a handwritten label that said 'Light Agency'. The uninitiated could be forgiven for thinking that Mark Light was, perhaps, something to do with illumination. I hoped that he might turn out to be. I pressed the bell-push.

'Hello?' said a female voice.

'Mr Light, please.'

'Who is it?'

I don't like showing out before I can see who I'm talking to, but there was no alternative. 'Police officers,' I announced.

I can only assume that the receiver at the girl's end distorted my message. 'He's not taking on any more policemen,' said the girl's voice. 'He's got dozens on his books already. Try *The Bill*. They sometimes take direct. They're down at Merton somewhere.'

'I am a police officer, miss,' I said clearly, slowly and in my best constabulary voice, 'and I wish to see Mr Light on official business.' Beside me Dave smirked.

There was a buzzing noise as the lock was released and we were in. Not that it did us much good.

We ascended the rickety uncarpeted staircase to the first floor and were treated to the sight of a nubile young woman of about twenty-two sitting behind a very small desk. On the desk was the inevitable computer, but it was turned off and the girl was reading a copy of *Hello!* magazine.

'He's not here, you know,' said this vision. For some reason she stood up and stepped around the desk. She was wearing a knitted crop top that left her midriff bare, a pair of low-slung, tight leather trousers and high-heeled shoes.

Presumably she wanted us to admire the piece of glass glued to her navel.

'Ah! A womb with a view,' muttered Dave in an aside.

'Where is he, then?' I asked.

'Gone abroad. Went this morning.'

'What for, a holiday?'

'Dunno. He just said he was going and he'd be back on Monday.'

'Whereabouts has he gone, d'you know?'

'France, I think. He never says much.'

'So what do you tell people who call here on business?'

'What I just told you.'

'Is there any way of getting in touch with him?' I asked.

'He's got his mobile.'

I didn't need to know his mobile number because I had no intention that my first conversation with him would be through that unreliable medium, but I collect things. 'What's his mobile number, then?'

'I'm not allowed to say,' said the girl.

I knew it would be pointless to ask for his home address. 'Thanks,' I said. I was annoyed that we hadn't been able to get hold of Mark Light before this young lady warned him, as I was sure she would. Not that he could possibly know what we were going to ask him, but it's always helpful to maintain an element of surprise. I had no intention of mentioning Duncan Ford's name to she of the bare belly because I only had the word of the woman at the casting agency that Light was Ford's agent. 'We'll be back on Monday, then. What time does he get in?'

'About ten usually.'

We went back to our car in time to see an officious traffic warden in the act of putting a parking ticket on the windscreen.

Dave carefully removed the ticket from its plastic shroud and took a pen from his pocket. Then he wrote 'Cancelled – D. Poole, Det Sgt, New Scotland Yard' on the ticket and handed it to the warden. 'Have a nice day,' he said.

'Here, you can't . . .' The outraged warden was still waving his desecrated ticket as we drove off.

'By the way, guv,' said Dave, 'I picked this up off that bright young thing's desk when she wasn't looking.' He handed me a business card with Mark Light's name and agency address on it, and his telephone numbers, one for the office, the other for his mobile. 'Silly cow,' he added.

Ten

In the policing business interruptions that cock things up rapidly become the norm. On this occasion it was the arrival of Frank Mead.

'Robert Dent's fingerprints, Harry.'

'What about them?'

'They match a set found in Kim Light's bedroom.' Frank tossed the relevant paperwork on to my desk.

'That's more like it,' I said. 'Get someone to go and nick him.'

'A couple of the lads are on their way to Richmond as I speak,' said Frank, dropping into my armchair. 'But there's more.'

'What, about Dent?'

'No, about Danny Todd.'

'Don't tell me it's all coming together,' I said. This was too much to hope for.

'Beginning to look that way. First of all the facts. Like he said, he's got a place in Docklands – he owns a penthouse in a block called The Heights – and he has a top-of-the-range Mercedes.'

'Where does he get all his money from then, Frank, as if I didn't know?'

'I put the feelers out among a few of my more reliable snouts, but they weren't too happy talking about him. It seems this guy Todd is bad news. Anyway, I eventually persuaded them' – Frank looked up and grinned – 'and apparently he's got his fingers in all sorts of pies, not least of which is John Rose's club.'

'That much I gleaned from Tony, and Rose eventually admitted it.'

'But it's heavy,' said Frank. 'He's made it plain to Rose that unless he pays up, he gets shut down, so violently that it's unlikely that Rose would escape without serious personal injury. And there's a bonus, for Todd that is. Any of Rose's girls he fancies, he gets. No arguments and free of charge. And he takes full advantage of the arrangement. Any of the birds he likes the look of get sent down to his penthouse in a limo . . . at Rose's expense.'

'I'm looking forward to sorting this guy,' I said. 'And we might start by doing his place for dabs. Wouldn't it be nice if we found Kim's fingerprints there?'

'It's a possibility. He might be so cocky that he's got careless. Or contemptuous. Another of my snouts confirms what you discovered, that Rose is running prostitution big-time from the club, and Todd gets a rake-off from their take in addition to his "protection" fee.'

'Any whispers about Todd bootlegging?' I asked hopefully.

'I was coming to that,' said Frank. 'The word is that he's got a hand in that, too, although there's nothing on record. I checked with customs but he's not come to their notice. Perhaps he thinks that he's not likely to go down as heavily for tobacco and alcohol – if he's caught – than if he was nicked for smuggling drugs. If that's the case, he hasn't read the papers lately.'

'I wonder if he was tied up with Duncan Ford, Frank,' I mused, 'given that customs have got Ford on their magic machine. Could be a reason. Try this for a scenario. Todd and Ford are in the bootlegging game together. There's a falling out and Todd tops him. I said at the start that those murders look like an execution, and the method points to a professional. Straight shot to the head in each case.'

'Yes, but surely Todd would've used a contract killer, Harry. He could've afforded it, and he wouldn't want to get his own hands dirty.'

'Maybe that's why he wore rubber gloves,' Dave commented drily.

'And,' I went on, 'when he gets there, Kim recognizes him because he's shafted her previously, and so she gets topped as well.'

'Nice theory, Harry,' said Frank, 'but why the Lights' place? Why not Ford's Pimlico flat? Anyway, we've no evidence for any of it.'

'In that case, we'd better start looking,' I said. 'First of all, I want an obo put on Todd so that we have some idea of his movements, and I want to know that he'll be at home when we hit him.'

'We haven't got anything like the manpower we'd need for an observation of that sort, Harry,' Frank said, 'and Criminal Intelligence Branch won't want to know. Todd might be well bent, but I doubt if he falls into what they'd call the target criminal category.'

'Leave it to me, Frank,' I said, tapping the side of my nose. It was sheer optimism.

I walked down the corridor to the commander's office. He was there. Of course he was.

'Ah, Mr Brock.' The commander took off his glasses and looked up expectantly. 'You've made an arrest in the Notting Hill murders?'

'No, sir, but I do need your help,' I said. That ought to do it. Any suggestion that a seasoned detective like me might be seeking the commander's help would almost certainly flatter him into doing something he wouldn't otherwise have done.

'Fire away.' The commander leaned back in his chair – a chair of superior quality to mine, but then he was very senior – and waved a hand indicating that I should sit down.

'I need some more men, sir,' I began.

'Ah!' The commander leaned forward again.

I told him all that we'd learned about Danny Todd and outrageously embroidered the reasons I fancied him for the murders. 'And so you see, sir, we must be absolutely sure of our facts before we go in. If Todd's our man, I want him absolutely bang to rights because he'll be able to buy the best mouthpiece in the business.'

'Mouthpiece?' The commander seemed to be under the impression that I was talking about some part of a musical instrument.

'A lawyer, sir.'

'Oh, I see. You're right about Todd, of course.' Appearing to give the matter deep thought, but in reality playing for time, the commander picked up his letter-opener and spun it in the centre of his blotter. It stopped with the point towards me: not a good sign. 'I'll have to speak to the DAC. Leave it with me.'

Well, that reckoned. The commander would never make a decision if he could persuade the deputy assistant commissioner to make it for him.

'Time is of the essence, sir,' I said in a vain attempt to get him moving.

'Of course, of course,' said the commander smoothly. 'I'll let you know as soon as I have some news.'

'All fixed up, Harry?' Frank Mead greeted me with a mocking smile when I returned to my office.

'I hope so,' I said. 'I think I frightened him into thinking that if it all went pear-shaped, it'd be down to him.'

'Dent's at Charing Cross police station,' said Frank. 'Arrived about ten minutes ago.'

'Good,' I said. 'I feel like venting my wrath on someone.'

'No solicitor?' I asked, as Dave and I entered the interview room.

'No,' said Dent without enlarging further. Given yesterday's incompetent performance by his lawyer, Dent probably thought he was an unnecessary expense. I certainly did.

'You're entitled to have one present. Do you want one?'

'No.'

'Those are your fingerprints?' I said, placing a scenes-of-crime photograph on the table.

'Am I supposed to be surprised?' asked Dent sarcastically. 'You took them when I was here yesterday. Against my will, I may say, which will be the subject of a complaint to the

100

European Court of Human Rights.'

'You can cut the crap, Dent,' said Dave. 'They're your dabs all right, and they were found in a bedroom at twenty-seven Durbridge Gardens, Notting Hill, not six feet from the dead body of Kim Light, who you knew as Gloria the stripper.'

Dent didn't seem surprised. 'All right, so I did go there.'

'You said that on the two occasions you went with her, she took you to a flat in the Pimlico area.'

'So I lied.'

'Why?' I asked.

'Because I'd read about the murder in the paper, and I guessed it wouldn't take you long to track me down.'

Well, well. It's not often I get a compliment like that from a suspect.

'Let's get back to the night of Tuesday the eleventh of June.'

'I told you yesterday where I was. I spent the evening with a girl called Trixie whose name I picked out of a phone box.'

'How long were you with this woman?' Dave asked.

Dent thought about that for a moment. 'I'd been in London for a meeting—'

'Not in Manchester?'

'No.'

'Another lie then. Go on.'

'The meeting broke up at about six. I took one of the firm's IT guys out to dinner, to try to sweeten him up a bit, and we parted at about eight thirty.'

'And then?'

'When I got to Waterloo station, I rang Holly, my wife, to say I was on my way, but the answerphone was on and I remembered that she was staying the night with her sister in Molesey. This card caught my eye and I thought, well, why not? So I gave this Trixie a ring and she told me to come round to her place.'

'And where was this place?' I was doubtful about Dent's story. He was well into information technology, and yet he used a public phone, not a mobile. The answer, of course, was that he was actively looking for a tom that evening, and he didn't want her number showing up on a cellphone bill that his wife might see and query.

Dent ran a hand through his hair. 'God! I can't remember. Somewhere in Kennington, I think. Anyway, I got a taxi. It wasn't far from Waterloo.'

'To get back to my previous question, how long were you with her?' Dave asked.

'All night.'

'*All night?*' I was surprised. The sort of prostitutes who advertised in Waterloo phone boxes were at the rougher end of the market, and it was usually a case of a quick bang-bang and out again. 'How much did that cost you?'

'A hundred quid.'

'You must be in a good way of business if you can afford to lash out a hundred pounds.'

'I survive,' said Dent. 'But I had nothing to do with Gloria's death,' he added vehemently. 'What would have been the point?'

'Why did Gloria – Kim Light – tell you that she didn't want to see you any more?'

'She said she was giving up that sort of life. Well, I didn't believe her, but I didn't follow her. I knew where she lived – I'd been there – and I knew what time she usually finished, so I waited for her to get home.'

'When was this?' I asked, although I knew what Tony the bouncer had said, and I recalled what Dent had said the last time we spoke. But I wanted to be sure.

'About a year ago. But I told you that.'

'Did you speak to her?'

'Yes, I asked her when we could meet again. But she got quite angry. She told me again that she'd finished with all that, and that if I didn't get lost she'd call the police. As it was she must've told the guy at the club, the one who threatened me.'

'If we were to take you to Kennington,' said Dave, who lived in that part of London, 'would you recognize this place where you say you spent the night with this Trixie.'

'I'm not sure. Probably not. It was dark by then.'

'What, at nine o'clock at night?' said Dave. 'I don't think so.'

'Well, I can't remember.'

'Only ten days ago, and you can't remember,' said Dave acidly. 'And what does your wife think about all this?' he asked, more out of devilment than anything else.

'For Christ's sake,' Dent protested, 'she doesn't know. At least, not about Gloria and the others. As it is I think she'll be leaving me. Thanks to you lot searching our house the other morning.'

'It wasn't our fault you had all those images on your computer,' I said. 'However, I shall renew your police bail to return to this station one month from now. Should we not require your attendance, you'll be notified.'

And there we had to leave it. The law says that Dent doesn't have to prove his innocence: we have to prove his guilt.

'What d'you reckon, Dave?' I asked as we walked down Whitehall, back to Curtis Green.

'Load of bullshit, guv. His statement's shot full of holes. Even so, I don't think he did it. I don't think he's bright enough.'

'It's only those who aren't bright enough who get caught, Dave,' I said.

Frank Mead had good news. 'The commander's given us enough people to do a round-the-clock surveillance on Todd, Harry,' he said.

'Bloody hell! So when do they start?'

'Ten o'clock tonight.'

'I hope you've briefed them well. Todd's a seasoned villain and he'll spot a tail a mile off.'

'I've cracked it, Harry,' said Frank. 'I've issued them all with gorilla suits. Todd won't suspect a thing.'

'Sorry, Frank,' I said. I knew when I'd been given a mild bollocking.

*　　*　　*

That afternoon, I began getting to grips with the inevitable paperwork that builds up with an enquiry like the deaths of Ford and Kim Light. But I was interrupted almost immediately by Colin Wilberforce.

'I've tracked down the Trixie that Dent said he was with on the night of the murders, sir,' he said. 'One phone call did it. The guys at the Yard who deal with this sort of thing collect these cards from phone boxes, do a subscriber check on the number and put them in an index.'

'So what's the SP?'

'Her name's Patricia Hunter, sir, and she lives at fifteen Turnley Street, Kennington,' said Colin. 'I've written it down for you,' he added, handing me a slip of paper.

'Well done, Colin, but I think I'll make that a Monday morning job.'

I decided it was time to tackle Andrew Light about his brother, not that I thought there'd be much profit in it.

But it was now nearly four o'clock and being a Friday it was almost certain that he would have left the office. And despite his promise, he still hadn't given us the name of the hotel he was staying at. There again, I'd forgotten to ask him when last we spoke.

As I'd anticipated, Light wasn't at work but his secretary was. 'I'm afraid Mr Light is abroad on business,' she said. 'May I say who's calling?'

I told her. 'Do you know when he'll be back?'

There was a pause and I could hear the riffling of pages, presumably of Light's appointments diary. 'On Monday,' said the woman. 'Is there anything I can do?'

'Not really. Where's he gone, as a matter of interest?'

'Paris.'

I wondered if Mark Light had gone to Paris too, although I was not sure that the young woman in Mark Light's office actually knew where he was. She hadn't struck me as being super-efficient.

'I understand Mr Light's staying at a hotel while his house is being sold,' I said. 'D'you happen to know which one?'

'That's news to me,' said the secretary. 'As far as I know, he's still living at Durbridge Gardens.'

And there we had to leave it.

I decided to take Sarah Dawson out to dinner. At last!

Eleven

My relationship with Sarah, a doctor of science at the laboratory at Lambeth, had become more relaxed over the months since we'd met and we were now much easier in each other's company. Our first date had not augured well for the future: she'd told me that she'd been engaged once, to an army captain called Peter Hunt, but he'd been killed a few years previously on some damn-fool exercise on Salisbury Plain. And I'd told her about Robert, our only son, who had drowned in a pond at a friend's house where my German wife Helga had left him for the day while she went to work. That was the beginning of the end of our marriage and our divorce was, at long last, going through.

That, of course, would pose another question: whether I should ask Sarah to marry me. These days a permanent unmarried partnership was not exceptional, but I didn't think that Sarah would be very happy with that arrangement. Although we had slept together once – a fit of unrestrained passion that was as much at her instigation as mine – I always got the feeling that Sarah had regretted it afterwards.

She was always unduly concerned that I might be in danger, but she was a girl who understood the vicissitudes of a detective's job and the detrimental effect it had on our social life: dates cancelled at the last minute, takeaways instead of dinner at a decent restaurant, to say nothing of her constantly apologizing for turning up alone at a party to which we'd both been invited.

This time, however, we made it and enjoyed a pleasant and uninterrupted dinner at our favourite bistro in Chelsea, a short taxi ride over Albert Bridge from her Battersea flat. Sarah looked particularly gorgeous this evening. Her long black hair shone like polished ebony and her simple, silver-coloured dress moulded to her figure without being overtly provocative. Although it was to me.

Afterwards, we strolled along Chelsea Embankment. To hell with the job, I thought, and switched off my mobile. It was a lovely June evening – the sort of June evening that I often believed was a thing of the past – and we stopped to gaze at the river.

'Wouldn't it be nice,' said Sarah, leaning against me, 'just to get on a boat here and see where it took us?'

'There are plenty there,' I said, pointing at the house-boats.

'Silly!' she said. 'You wouldn't get far in one of those. I was thinking of some deserted South Sea island.'

The setting seemed ideal to pose the question of marriage, but I had long ago determined that I would wait until my decree absolute came through. I was sure that if ever I married again, it would be Sarah I chose for a wife. But right now, I put an arm around her slender waist and steered her to the comparatively safe cover of a tree before kissing her passionately, a kiss to which she responded with an equal fervour. Why the tree? To be honest I'm always scared that a passing copper will recognize me and relay all the salacious details to a gossip-hungry canteen. Not that passing coppers are all that plentiful these days.

She shivered slightly and pulled away from me. 'Harry, it's nearly eleven o'clock,' she said. 'I really think we ought to be getting back. I've got an early start in the morning.'

'What, on a Saturday?'

'I'm afraid so. Two of our people are off sick and the work's piling up.'

'I suppose that means no coffee, then,' I said.

'No coffee,' she said sternly and laughed.

I hailed a taxi and delivered her to her flat. I gave her one last gentle kiss in the recesses of the doorway before wending my way back to Wimbledon, to an empty house. Of Helga there was no sign. I assumed her favourite doctor was shagging her again. We're cynical bastards, us coppers.

But any ideas of having the whole weekend off were shattered by a telephone call that I received in the early hours of Saturday morning.

'Andrew Light's been arrested, sir,' said Detective Sergeant Gavin Creasey, the night-duty incident-room manager at Curtis Green.

'Where and for what?' I asked, switching on my bedside light.

'He was nicked at Heathrow Airport in possession of a quantity of diamonds, sir.'

'Bloody hell! What's the SP?'

'No idea, sir,' said Gavin. 'We've just got the bare facts at the moment. Came from Special Branch at the airport. They knew that Light's wife had been murdered and thought it might be of interest to you.'

'Damn' right it is,' I muttered. 'What time is it?'

'Twenty to four, sir.'

I yawned and debated whether to go out to the airport now or wait until the morning. 'Where's he being held?'

'He was charged at Heathrow nick and is now in the custody of customs . . . at the airport, sir.'

'And what? Court appearance in the morning?'

'Then or Monday, sir. At Uxbridge Magistrates Court, anyway.'

'Are they BBC magistrates?' I asked.

'Yes, sir,' said Creasey, fully conversant with CID parlance for a lay bench comprising the butcher, the baker and the candlestick-maker.

'So he'll probably get bail,' I mused.

'Seven-to-four-on, sir.' Creasey clearly shared my cynical view of the whims of magistrates.

I decided against rushing out to Heathrow. It was, after all, a customs knock-off and there was no way that I could interfere. At which point I realized that there was nothing I could ask him anyway.

I did, however, ring Dave Poole.

The gorgeous Madeleine, Dave's ballet-dancer wife, answered the phone. 'Hello, Mr Brock.' She was all bright and sparkly, and I wondered if she and Dave were up early. Or up to something. Whatever, it was certainly unusual for a detective's wife to respond so civilly to a duty call in the small hours, even from a senior officer.

Dave came to the phone and I explained about Light's arrest and told him that we would be making a visit to Heathrow later that morning to find out the form.

At first, the duty customs surveyor seemed a little loath to tell me anything, but once I'd explained my interest in Andrew Light and assured him that I was not there to make a nuisance of myself, he came across.

'I suppose he was unlucky,' the surveyor began, 'but his aircraft went "tech" at Zurich and the flight was delayed. Didn't touch down here until two thirty. During the day there's more passenger traffic than we have the manpower to cope with. But a single flight in the middle of the night, well the night watch thought they'd have a blitz on the green channel. Even to start with, Light was a bit evasive, but then he got on his high horse. Started banging on about being a barrister and how he was going to contact the chairman of the Board of Customs and Excise to make a complaint about being treated like a common criminal, and so on and so on.' The surveyor smiled. 'In our experience that usually warrants a turn-out and, guess what, these were secreted in false heels on his shoes.' He showed us a collection of small diamonds.

'Was he known to you?' I asked. 'I mean was he a customs suspect?'

'No, never come across him before. He certainly wasn't on CEDRIC.'

'On *what*?' I hate acronyms and I suspected that CEDRIC was some sort of computer. The combination of the two makes me irritable. Dave reckons it makes me downright bad-tempered.

'It stands for "Customs and Excise Departmental Reference Information Computer",' said the surveyor with a cunning grin.

'Didn't know you sent your people to the Police College,' I muttered, referring to the cloning factory at Bramshill in the wilds of Hampshire. 'Did he say anything?'

'Not a word. Refused to make a statement – which is his right – and wouldn't tell us where he worked either.'

'Well, I can tell you that,' I said, and gave the surveyor the address of the merchant bank that employed Light.

'Interesting,' mused the surveyor. 'This guy Light will appear before the beak on Monday morning and probably get weighed off there and then. We're only really interested in the duty avoided, and that's probably in the region of five thousand, but we've referred it to our National Investigation Service just in case there's more to this than meets the eye.'

'Anyone in particular at NIS?' I asked.

The surveyor glanced at his notes. 'A guy called John Fielding.'

'Will he be on duty this morning?'

'Of course,' said the surveyor. 'You coppers aren't the only ones to work weekends.'

Dave and I made our way direct to Lower Thames Street in the City, the Custom House headquarters of NIS.

'A barrister with a merchant bank, eh?' said Fielding, once we'd introduced ourselves and told him of our interest in Andrew Light. 'Give me a moment or two.' He skimmed rapidly through the brief routine report that the Heathrow customs people had emailed to him, and looked up. 'So what's he up to?' He looked thoughtful and drummed a tattoo on the arm of his chair.

'Skulduggery,' said Dave, summing up the situation in a single word.

Fielding looked askance at Dave and then laughed. He was probably having the same problem with Dave's sense of humour that most people had. Including me. 'And some, I should think.'

110

'I was thinking about having a word at this guy's bank,' I said. 'Is that likely to tread on your toes?'

'No, it looks like a straightforward job from our point of view. Mind you, if you pick up anything that's likely to be of use to us, perhaps you'd let me know.'

'Certainly, John,' I said. 'Incidentally there's a link in my murder enquiry between Andrew Light's brother Mark and Duncan Ford, the male murder victim, who, I'm told, was of interest to you. Duncan Ford, I mean.'

'Really? For what?'

'Bootlegging apparently. I'm told that Ford was turned over at Dover about a fortnight ago, but nothing was found.'

'Curiouser and curiouser,' said Fielding and turned to his computer. 'Yeah, he's on here, right enough. Anonymous information that he was smuggling cigarettes on a large scale.' He turned to face me again. 'Mind you, we get a lot of this stuff, but we usually find there's nothing in it. More often than not it's a neighbour wanting to work off a grudge.'

'I'm also interested in a Daniel Todd whose name's come up in my murder enquiry, and there was a hint he might have been up to a bit of smuggling. But I understand that he's not come to your notice.'

Fielding turned to his keyboard again and tapped in the relevant details. 'Well we've got him on here now, but we knew nothing about him until a couple of days ago. A DI Mead rang us. Is he one of yours?'

'Yes, Frank Mead's on my team. But to get back to Andrew Light, John. Any idea of the value of the diamonds that he had in his possession?'

'Not yet.' Fielding fingered the hard copy of the email report which, so far, was the sum total of his information on the case. 'The senior officer at Terminal Two took a cockshy at about thirty grand.' He shrugged. 'Could be more, could be less. We shall see when a proper valuation's been done.'

*　　*　　*

111

But just before noon on Monday John Fielding telephoned to say that Light had been fined ten thousand pounds – twice the duty avoided – by the Uxbridge magistrates that morning and had left the court at about eleven o'clock. The diamonds had been forfeited to the Crown, and customs, Fielding continued, had no further interest in the matter.

I now wondered if Light's smuggling offence impinged in some way on my murder enquiry. My first thought, that the killings had been executions, might yet prove to be true. Had Duncan Ford been involved in what could be a smuggling ring involving Andrew Light and Danny Todd – and perhaps even Mark Light – and had he been guilty of some double-cross that resulted in his death?

But of the three it was Danny Todd about whom I harboured the gravest suspicions. His list of previous convictions proved that he was a vicious bastard, and the sort of executions exacted on Kim Light and Duncan Ford would be quite in character for him.

The whole affair could turn out to be much more complex than I had originally thought.

In the circumstances I could see no alternative but for Dave and me to have a word with a senior director of the bank where Light worked. Having told him why we wished to see him, I made an appointment for half past two that afternoon.

Rather than waste the morning, I decided to check Robert Dent's alibi with Trixie.

If I'd been Dent, I'd've taken one look at Trixie's house and done a runner. It was a terraced dwelling in one of the poorer parts of Kennington – and that's saying something – with dirty windows and even dirtier curtains hanging at them. The front door probably hadn't seen paint for a good twenty years and the brass doorknocker was black with grime.

In terms of maintenance, the woman who half opened the door was no better. I guessed she was in her mid-twenties, had unkempt, peroxide-blonde hair, and wore a faded blue candlewick dressing gown. A hand with chipped nail varnish briefly removed the cigarette from her mouth.

'D'you know what bloody time it is?' she asked.

'Half-past ten, give or take a few minutes,' said Dave.

'Well, what d'you want?'

'Are you Patricia Hunter, known in the trade as Trixie?' Dave continued.

'Oh, bloody coppers. Well, what is it this time?'

'D'you want to talk here or inside?' I asked.

'You'd better come in then,' said this vision. Leaving us to close the street door, she led the way into the front room.

It was a tip. A broken-down settee, an armchair from which the stuffing was attempting to escape – and who'd blame it – and dirty clothing all over the place. The carpet had obviously seen better days, and those days were probably thirty years ago. And the smell . . . !

'Well?' Trixie lit a fresh cigarette from the butt of the first.

I told her who I was. She didn't like the sound of that. Prostitutes are accustomed to sergeants from the Vice Squad, not detective chief inspectors from the Serious Crime Group.

'I'm investigating the murder of a prostitute,' I said.

'Christ! What, round here?'

'No, in Notting Hill.'

Trixie sighed with relief. 'What are you doing here, then?' she asked.

'On the night of eleventh–twelfth of this month – that's almost a fortnight ago – I understand you entertained a man called Robert Dent. This man claims to have telephoned you from Waterloo station, having found one of your cards in a phone box there.'

'Now just you hang on. I never put them cards there.'

'I don't care whether you put them there or your ponce did, Trixie,' I said. 'I'm investigating a murder. So, did a man called Robert Dent come here on those dates?'

'Bugger me, I don't know. I don't keep a list of tricks. Anyway I never ask their names. It only complicates things.'

'This man says he spent the whole night with you and paid

113

you a hundred pounds for the privilege.' Frankly, looking at the woman and her place of business, I thought she ought to have paid him.

'I seem to remember a bloke who spent the night, but I don't remember when it was. Probably was about a couple of weeks ago, though. Don't often get a taker for an all-night session. Not complaining, is he?'

'I didn't enquire whether he was satisfied with the service,' I said. 'I'm only interested in whether he was here.'

'Well, I don't know. He might have been. I don't remember the date.' Trixie walked across to a table laden with dirty crockery and old newspapers. Pouring herself a substantial measure of gin, she downed it, neat, at a gulp. 'You reckon he done this murder then?'

'It rather depends on what you tell me,' I said.

Trixie gave a shrug. 'I can't remember all the tricks I have,' she said.

'Business that good, is it?' put in Dave.

'Supposing I showed you a photograph of this guy,' I asked. 'Would you remember him then?'

'Might do. Why? You got one?'

'Not yet, but I'll get one.'

It was a bloody nuisance, but I still had a hunch about Robert Dent. That a man who lived in a nice house in Richmond with a glamorous wife should resort to having sex with the likes of Trixie made him something of an enigma. But the pictures that Frank Mead had discovered on Dent's computer, coupled with his visits to lap-dancing clubs and his use of prostitutes, indicated a man who was living a double life.

It all shouted 'sexual pervert' in capital letters, and I knew from experience that sexual perverts commit sexual murders. But with a gun? Somehow, for all his bravado, I thought that Dent was a little too lily-livered for that sort of violence. And my mind went back again to Danny Todd.

'We shall be seeing you again, Trixie,' I said.

'I don't doubt it, love,' said Trixie.

114

Twelve

On our arrival at the prestigious banking house where Andrew Light worked, we were ushered into the senior director's office without delay. A secretary appeared and dispensed coffee. Waiting until the door was closed behind her and introductions had been effected, I recounted fully the circumstances that had led to Light's arrest.

'This is all very disturbing, Mr Brock,' began the director, who told us his name was Klein. 'I can't say that I ever recall a senior executive of this bank being arrested before.'

'I take it that Mr Light is not here this afternoon.'

'No, he telephoned earlier to say that he was unwell. But I never thought . . .' Clearly worried about the whole affair, Klein allowed his sentence to tail off. 'I wonder if it was some sort of mental aberration resulting from the death of his wife,' he mused.

'I suppose that's a possibility,' I said, 'but I assume that Light's illegal importation of diamonds has nothing to do with the bank.'

Klein stirred idly at his coffee and then replaced the spoon in the saucer. 'I'm not so sure about that,' he said 'The moment you telephoned me this morning with news of his arrest, I caused an examination to be conducted.'

'What sort of examination?'

'I won't weary you with the details,' said Klein, 'but suffice it to say that we have uncovered an extremely disturbing discrepancy.'

'Oh?'

'My chief accountant found that last Thursday Andrew

115

Light transferred a sum of thirty thousand pounds electronically to a numbered account in Switzerland.'

'And of course you don't know the identity of that account holder,' I said resignedly. The secrecy of Swiss bankers was well known.

'On the contrary, Mr Brock, we in the banking world have our contacts, otherwise we couldn't operate.' Klein was clearly distressed at what he had discovered. 'I'm afraid the account was in the name of Andrew Light,' he said quietly.

I'd spent a few years on the Fraud Squad and I was fairly certain that I knew what Light had been up to. If I was right, it wasn't unique. 'I wonder,' I speculated, 'if having purchased those diamonds in Switzerland, it was Light's intention to bring them home and sell them for more than he paid? And that he would then have paid the proceeds into his Swiss account, transferred the original amount back again to this bank – adding the appropriate amount of interest – and would then have expunged the entire transaction from the computer system.' I leaned forward and picked up my cup of coffee, wondering how often he'd done it before, successfully. 'Unfortunately for him, it would appear that he was arrested before he could complete the fraud and leave the profit in his Swiss account. Assuming I'm right, of course.'

'Yes, I think that you probably are right.' Klein stared at me with a jaundiced eye. 'Have you ever thought about taking up banking, Mr Brock?' he asked. 'You have just the sort of suspicious mind I could use.' He took a sip of coffee.

'From what I've seen of his house in Notting Hill, he has an opulent lifestyle,' I continued, 'and I got the impression that no expense had been spared. His wife's wardrobe would certainly have cost a small fortune, and as far as I know, she had no income of her own.' I wasn't about to tell him that she'd been a lap-dancing prostitute. Poor old Klein had enough on his plate.

'Really?' said Klein despondently. That information seemed only to add to his depression.

116

'I understood from Mr Light's secretary, when I phoned her on Friday, that he'd gone to Paris on business and was not due back until today.'

'It's true he left on Thursday, but not on business, although that's maybe what he told Sheila. No, he'd taken a couple of days off. A long weekend in Paris, he told me. But instead it seems he went to Switzerland.'

'Yes,' I said. 'Zurich actually.'

Klein shook his head. 'My God, what a mess,' he said. 'Was the bank mentioned in court, d'you know?' It seemed that he was more concerned with the bank's reputation than with the fate of Andrew Light.

'I don't know, 1 wasn't there.'

Klein looked glum and drank some more coffee.

'Perhaps I could have a word with Light's secretary, Mr Klein.'

'Of course. I'll have my secretary show you to Sheila's office,' said Klein, flicking down a switch on his office intercom.

'Incidentally, does Light's secretary know of this fraud?' I asked.

'Good heavens no. At the moment only a few senior people know of it.'

'In that case I shan't mention it, but it will be necessary for me to tell her of Light's arrest, just to see her reaction,' I said. It briefly crossed my sceptical mind that Sheila might have been Light's willing accomplice.

Sheila – Miss Sheila Corbett to be exact – was a stern but presentable and well-groomed woman of about forty, and I immediately dismissed the idea that anything sexual was going on between her and her boss. One never knew though. Perhaps beneath that severe exterior she was an absolute wow in bed.

'We spoke on the phone last Friday, Miss Corbett,' I began, having introduced myself and Dave Poole.

'Indeed we did,' said Sheila.

'And you told me that Mr Light had gone to Paris on business.'

'That's correct.'

'But Mr Klein told me that Mr Light was not away on business. He'd apparently taken leave.' I could have said 'taken leave of his senses', but this was no time for jokes.

'That's what Mr Light gave me to understand, that it was a business trip. But if it was a holiday, well, after the loss of his wife in such tragic circumstances, I suppose he deserved a break.'

'Did he, by any chance, leave a contact number in Paris?' I asked, knowing damned well that he wouldn't have done.

'No,' said Sheila without hesitation. 'He said he wasn't quite sure where he would be staying, but that he would ring me when he was settled.'

'A little unusual, wasn't it, Miss Corbett? Presumably you would make a hotel booking for him in advance whenever he travelled on business.'

'Usually, yes,' said Sheila curtly, giving the impression that she was somewhat piqued at not having been asked to do what efficient secretaries normally do.

'And did he telephone you to say where he had settled?' I asked, pursuing my original question.

'No, he did not. And may I ask,' Sheila continued frostily, 'why you are asking all these questions about Mr Light?'

'Mr Light was arrested on Saturday morning at Heathrow Airport, Miss Corbett,' I said, 'on his way in from Zurich.'

'Zurich?' Sheila Corbett spoke the word calmly, with just a slight lift of the eyebrows. There was no gasp, no hand put to the mouth, no tearful utterance of 'how awful' at the news of his arrest. She appraised each of us in turn. 'Whatever for?' she asked eventually.

'Smuggling.'

'How ridiculous,' said Sheila. 'A couple of bottles over the limit, was he?'

'No, it was a little more serious than that.'

'Oh! Not naughty videos again, surely?'

'You said "again", Miss Corbett. Was he in the habit of importing pornographic material?'

'I've no idea,' said Sheila haughtily. 'All I can tell you is that there was an occasion when I went to his briefcase to look for some papers – it was just after he'd returned from a trip to Amsterdam – and there were two pornographic videos in it. But he is a man, after all,' she added scathingly.

'How did you know they were pornographic?' asked Dave, his face feigning innocence. I think he was hoping that she'd confess to having viewed them herself.

'The titles did not leave very much to the imagination, young man,' said Sheila, giving Dave a piercing stare before dismissing him from the conversation. I got the impression that Miss Corbett might have been a racist. 'I didn't mention them to him and he didn't mention them either,' she continued, redirecting her gaze to me. 'After all, Mr Light's private life is none of my business.' But then she negated that assertion by adding, 'Mind you, he did marry a stripper a few years ago.' She wrinkled her nose.

'How did you know that?' I asked.

'A man has very few secrets from his secretary,' said Sheila dismissively.

I believed her, and silently thanked a parsimonious Commissioner that I didn't qualify for a secretary.

'And what did you make of all that, Dave?' I asked when we'd adjourned to a nearby coffee shop.

'I think your guess was right, guv. It was a grand fraud, and if he hadn't been nicked at Heathrow, he'd probably have got away with it.'

'Where the hell would he have unloaded thirty K in diamonds at short notice? Presumably he would have wanted a quick return before the bank found out about the illegal transaction.'

'Simple, guv,' said Dave. 'If you know where to go in Hatton Garden there are traders who'll give you cash for them immediately, no questions asked. And the stones would more than likely be out of the country within twenty-four hours. Amsterdam probably.'

And Sheila Corbett said that Light had been to Amsterdam before.

119

'How the hell d'you know all that, Dave?' I asked, amazed, yet again, at the knowledge my sergeant had acquired over the years.

'I've got a mate who works in Hatton Garden,' said Dave, tapping the side of his nose with a forefinger. 'He's ex-Job.'

'The girl in Mark Light's office said Mark was in France this last weekend, didn't she?' I said. 'The same time Andrew was in Zurich.'

'If Mark *was* in France,' said Dave. 'For all we know he might have been in Zurich too.'

'Ironic, isn't it, Dave? There was I thinking that Mark was the bent one of the family.'

'Perhaps they're both bent,' said Dave drily.

'But we'll have to interview Andrew Light now. I'm sure the commander's not going to let me separate the fraud from the murder of Kim and Ford, even though Light's not in the frame for them.'

Andrew Light had been in Stockholm at the time of the killings at Durbridge Gardens, a story that was supported by the Swedish businessman he'd been to see, right down to the dinner that Light had with the man and his wife, and the sightseeing trip the following day. And so, having thought about it, I decided that there was nothing to be gained by talking to Andrew Light just yet.

Instead, Dave and I returned to Mark Light's Fulham office. This time he was there.

'Is this about Andrew's spot of bother?' Mark Light asked, once we were settled in his spartan office.

I had to admire his nonchalant dismissal of so serious an offence. 'A spot of bother' was hardly how I'd've described getting nicked for the attempted smuggling of diamonds worth thirty grand.

'You've heard about that, then,' I said.

'Sure,' said Mark. 'He rang me this morning. Of course, it was all a huge mistake.'

So it was, but the mistake was Andrew's.

'No, it's nothing to do with that offence. I'm investigating the murder of Andrew's wife. And Duncan Ford.'

'So I believe.' Light unscrewed a bottle of mineral water and poured some into a glass.

'I believe Duncan Ford was a friend of yours, Mr Light.' I didn't know any such thing, of course, but it was worth floating.

'No, he was a client. An actor. But not a very good one, I'm afraid.'

'How long had he been on your books?'

'About a year, I suppose,' said Mark Light thoughtfully. 'But I'd only managed to place him twice during that time. Once for a non-speaking walk-on part in some costume drama, and once in a short television advert. I'd advised him to give up acting. He was never going to get his name in lights.'

Which was more or less what the woman at the casting agency had said. 'Was he a homosexual?'

'I believe so, but that's not unusual in the acting profession. Man or woman.'

'You didn't go to your sister-in-law's funeral,' I said. Having met him, I was now sure of that.

'No, I didn't. I couldn't stand the bloody woman, and I'm not one of those people who would forgive and forget just because she's dead. Kim was a whore before she married my brother, and carried on being one afterwards.'

'Where were they married?' I asked, being fairly sure from the note in Kim's passport that they weren't.

Mark Light smiled. 'They weren't actually married,' he said. 'Not that anyone cares a damn about that these days.'

Light's brother was beginning to irritate me. He was a little too confident for my liking but there again, perhaps he had nothing to hide. 'Have you any idea why Duncan Ford should have been found in your brother's house along with Kim?'

Light spread his hands and laughed. 'Now, how on earth d'you expect me to know the answer to that?'

121

'Did Kim ever mention him?' I persisted. 'Or did Ford ever mention Kim?'

'I haven't spoken to Kim for at least two years, Mr Brock. And no, Duncan Ford never mentioned her.'

'You said just now that Kim carried on being a whore after she went to live with Andrew. Would you care to elaborate on that?'

'I can only tell you what Andrew told me. He and Kim went on holiday with some neighbours—'

'Did he tell you their names?' I asked, but I knew. At least, I thought I did. Maybe the Stows hadn't been the only ones.

'No, he just said that they were next-door neighbours in Durbridge Gardens.'

'Could they have been called Stow?'

'I don't know,' said Mark. 'Anyway all four of them went to a villa in the Algarve that these people had rented – apparently they always went there – and Kim took to swimming nude in the pool the moment they arrived. Well, that turned out to be too much of a temptation for this other guy and Andrew caught them at it. He said he'd gone to bed and had woken up at about two in the morning. Kim was missing and, thinking she might have been taken ill, he wandered around looking for her.' Mark gave a twisted smile. 'And he found her, down by the pool, naked and wrapped around the equally naked other guy.' He gave a coarse laugh. 'Gives a whole new meaning to the expression "a night on the tiles", doesn't it?'

'What did your brother do about it?'

'Knowing Andrew, I don't suppose he could have cared less. He reckoned he went back to bed. That's what he said, anyway. In fact he hinted that he'd had an affair with the guy's wife, just to even the score. Some holiday.'

And there we left it. For the time being. If what Mark Light had told me was true, the Lights had enjoyed playing mixed doubles on holiday in the Algarve just as much as the goody-goody Stows. And that perhaps added another dimension to the murder of Kim Light.

But how did that involve Duncan Ford? Wrong place, wrong time, perhaps? What was certain was that I would now have to interview the Stows afresh. Had their respective affairs got so out of hand that Gill Stow was intent on leaving her husband for the well-heeled Andrew Light, the impediment having been Kim who refused to give up Andrew, despite their not being lawfully wedded?

Maybe Peter Stow had murdered Duncan Ford thinking that he was Andrew. Such a mistake could easily have been made in the dark. And if Kim Light had witnessed it, or at least been aware of it, that would explain her murder.

I expounded my theory to Dave as we drove back to the office.

'The Stows were on holiday at the crucial time, guv. We had to wait until they got back before we could talk to them, remember?'

'We've only got their word that they were on holiday, Dave,' I said.

Dave gave me a baleful look, like I'd just kicked him in the stomach. 'I know, sir,' he said. 'Find out.'

'Got it in one, Dave,' I said, 'but I think we'll have a word with Andrew Light first. I'd rather not interview the Stows again until we've got some confirmation of what Mark Light told us, and I reckon that Andrew Light might just be persuaded to provide that for us.'

Thirteen

The next day, having established that Andrew Light was still not at work, I telephoned him at home and made an appointment to see him at eleven o'clock. He didn't mention his brush with customs and nor did I. Not immediately, anyway.

The carpet in the sitting room at Durbridge Gardens was new, although I would have thought that a competent firm of professional cleaners could easily have removed the bloodstains from the old one. The hole in the wall made by the bullet that killed Duncan Ford had been filled and the entire room redecorated with expensive wallpaper. I wondered if the bed in the master suite had been replaced, along with the damaged wardrobe door. Money seemed to be no problem to Andrew Light, although it might now have become one following his hefty fine.

'You've not sold your house yet,' I said.

'No, I've decided to stay,' said Light, but didn't elaborate. 'So, how can I help you, gentlemen?' he asked when we were all seated. Relaxed, and in his own home, Light was the confident barrister and I knew that he would weigh every one of my questions before giving me an answer.

'I have to be honest with you, Mr Light,' I lied, 'but it's now a fortnight since the murder of your wife and Duncan Ford, and I'm struggling.'

'I imagine so,' said Light. 'It must be a very difficult investigation.'

'Consequently, I'm obliged to follow every line of enquiry, no matter how tenuous.'

'Of course,' Light murmured. 'So how can I help?'

'You can start by telling me about Kim.'

'Why?'

I thought that would have been pretty obvious to a lawyer. 'Because the sort of woman she was, the sort of friends she had, where she went, what she did, may all help me to discover the identity of her killer.'

Light leaned forward and aligned a magazine with the edge of the coffee table. 'She was a stripper when I met her, Mr Brock,' he said, looking up. 'I used to visit a lap-dancing club in the West End some years ago.' He gave no appearance of embarrassment at his admission. 'I took her out to dinner a few times and we became quite close. And after a few months—'

'You were married?' I wanted to see what he would say to that. But he surprised me.

'No, we never got married. To be honest, I'd been married before but it didn't work out, and I wasn't going to risk it again. Two years ago, I invited Kim to come and live with me, here, and she jumped at it. The only condition I made was that she gave up stripping.'

I found it hard to believe that Light didn't know that Kim had continued lap-dancing until at least two months ago and, more to the point, that she was a practising, professional whore. But perhaps he did know and was ashamed to admit it. Or the spectre of immoral earnings was hanging over him. 'And your first wife?'

'I'm sorry to say that she was killed in a road accident shortly after the divorce. We were still good friends.'

'If Kim had given up her career,' I said, 'how did she occupy her time?'

There was a lengthy pause and I knew instinctively that Light was about to fabricate his answer. 'Notting Hill is a very sociable area,' he said. 'She used to go to tea with friends quite regularly, and shopping for clothes in the West End –' he sighed, but I suspect it was contrived – 'and I think she even got involved with some charity or other.'

From what I'd heard about Kim Light, belonging to the Notting Hill set, frequenting Harvey Nichols and playing the

125

lady bountiful were the last things that she could be accused of. Mrs Wilson's claim that she had seen a man, several in fact, calling at the house during Light's absence – and that one at least had stayed a few hours – coupled with Mark's account of what his brother had told him about the holiday with the Stows gave the lie to that. But most telling of all was the discovery that Jonathon Wheeler had paid Kim for sex, an admission that had led me to John Rose's little book that listed all Kim's sexual trysts. There again, Andrew Light might have known and condoned it.

'Peter and Gill Stow.' That should stir things up, I thought.

Light smiled. 'I wondered when you'd get around to them, Mr Brock,' he said. 'We went on holiday with them last year. To the Algarve. I suppose you've spoken to them.'

'Yes, we've interviewed all your neighbours. It's something we always do in enquiries like this one, just in case they might have seen something.'

'And did they?'

'Unfortunately no.' *Not as far as the murder enquiry was concerned, that is. I wasn't about to tell him the rest. Yet.*

'You know that the Stows were on holiday when Kim . . .' Light looked down at the carpet, a sad expression on his face.

'So they said.' But I wasn't going to reveal my suspicions of Peter Stow for fear of boosting Light's hopes that we might be on the brink of finding his wife's killer.

It seemed, however, that Andrew Light had arrived at a similar conclusion. 'You don't think that Peter Stow could have had anything to do with it, do you?' he asked, frowning as he looked at me.

'What makes you ask that?'

'May I offer you a drink, Mr Brock?' Light rose to his feet. 'Or you, Sergeant?'

Hello, he's playing for time. I wonder why.

'No, thank you,' I said, speaking for Dave and me.

'You won't mind if I do, will you?'

'Not at all. It's your house.'

Light crossed to the satinwood table and poured himself a stiff Scotch. 'As I was saying,' he continued as he sat down again, 'we went on holiday with the Stows last year, but I'm afraid there was a falling out. We hardly ever spoke again after that.'

'Would you care to tell me what happened?'

'It was Kim's behaviour that created the problem.'

'What sort of problem?' Mark Light had told me the story – a different one from the Stows' version – but I wanted to hear what Andrew Light had to say.

'Kim had never worried about nudity. After all, she'd made a career of it before we started living together.' Light smiled at that. 'The first day we were there, she just stripped off and went for a swim. It was a very secluded villa, with just the four of us, and it seemed the most natural thing in the world. But Gill – Gill Stow, that is – took exception to it, even though she was topless herself.'

'And that caused a row, did it?'

'Not that, no. Although from then on Kim wore a G-string whenever the Stows were by the pool. It was what happened on the fourth day. The fourth night, actually. It must have been about two in the morning and I woke to find Kim missing. She always was a bit of a martyr to insomnia, but even so, I was a little worried and went to look for her. I found her lying on an airbed by the pool, and I called out, something like "Are you all right, darling?" She scrambled to her feet and ran towards me, and threw her arms round me. It was quite dark without the pool lights switched on, and I didn't see Peter Stow at first, but then I noticed him, sitting on one of the sun-loungers.

'When we got back to our room, Kim told me that she'd gone for a swim, *au naturel*. The Portuguese nights are very hot at that time of year, and I suppose she thought that the other two wouldn't be about. Anyway, she said that Peter had suddenly appeared just as she got out of the pool, and he was naked too.' There was a long pause as Light shook his head and pinched the bridge of his nose. He looked up with a distraught expression on his face. 'It was then that she told me that Stow had raped her,' he said in a whisper.

But I was not wholly convinced of his distress despite the faltering histrionics. And the story didn't hang together either. The girl claimed she had just been raped and yet Light found her reclining on an airbed while her attacker was sitting on a sun-lounger.

'You're a lawyer, Mr Light, why didn't you do something about it?' I asked.

'Precisely because I am a lawyer, Mr Brock,' Light said coldly. He'd recovered very quickly. 'To put one's wife through court proceedings – and in a foreign country at that – would have been traumatic in the extreme. And you must know that in such cases, it would have been her word against Peter Stow's.'

Light was quite right in what he said. I'd seen enough rape trials to know that it was a lottery and that, unfairly, the woman often emerged from court more tarnished than the man.

It did, however, reveal a different Peter Stow from the one I'd met. Perhaps there was more to the holiday than had, at first, been apparent. Had there been one hell of a row, with Andrew Light threatening to kill Peter Stow, or vice versa? More to the point, had Peter Stow returned to Notting Hill a fortnight ago and murdered Ford believing him to be Andrew? Or was Mark Light's account of what his brother had supposedly told him the true version: that it was Kim who had been the prime mover in her sexual liaison with Stow, and had perhaps told Andrew that she was leaving him for their neighbour? It really all hinged on whether the Stows had an alibi for the time of the murders.

As with every other aspect of the enquiry, I had to take my questioning to its conclusion: to go down every street until it became a dead-end before returning to the crossroads and starting again. 'Did you have an affair with Mrs Stow, Mr Light?' I asked.

'No, I bloody well didn't,' said Light vehemently. 'Whatever gave you that idea? Is that what the Stows said?'

'No. In fact the Stows denied any sort of impropriety, other than to mention Kim's habit of swimming naked. Something to which both Peter and Gill Stow said they took exception.'

'Well, that's bloody rich, I must say. He couldn't take his eyes off her.'

'I understand that you were arrested by customs on Saturday, Mr Light,' I said, abruptly changing the subject.

Light expressed no surprise that I knew about that. Nor did he ask how I knew. 'I'm afraid it was my own fault really,' he said. 'I'd bought some diamonds abroad and for security reasons I'd secreted them in my shoes. I was so bloody tired after the flight that I completely forgot about them and went into the green channel. I'm afraid I got fined rather heavily at Uxbridge Magistrates' Court yesterday.'

'Presumably you'll appeal?' I didn't bother asking him why he'd told his secretary he was going to Paris. That was obvious.

'No point,' said Light. 'The Crown Court won't believe it was a foolish mistake. I was perfectly prepared to pay the duty, but by then it'd gone too far.' He crossed to the drinks table and had begun replenishing his glass when I posed a crippler.

'How long have you known Danny Todd, Mr Light?'

Light's reaction was more than I could possibly have hoped for. His whisky tumbler fell from his grasp and smashed to pieces on the table.

'What?' Ignoring the broken glass, he turned, white-faced. 'How the hell d'you know about him?' he gasped.

'I know quite a lot about him, Mr Light, but I'm more interested in what you know about him.'

Disregarding the whisky that was now dripping from the edge of the table on to his new carpet, Light picked up another tumbler and half-filled it with scotch. Then he came and sat down again, his hand visibly shaking. 'That man's made my life a misery,' he said.

'In what way?'

'He had a relationship with Kim when she was a dancer,

129

and he wanted to continue it after she came to live with me.'

'But you warned him off, presumably?'

'I tried to, but he's a violent criminal, Mr Brock. He threatened to kill Kim if I didn't make her carry on seeing him.'

'And so you let him continue?'

'What else could I have done?'

'You could have gone to the police, Mr Light. You, as a lawyer, would know better than most people that they would have dealt with him.'

'He told me that if I did, he would kill us both. I don't think you've any idea what sort of man he is.'

Now I knew he was lying, in part anyway. Here was a barrister who, on the face of it, was being terrorized by a professional villain, but claimed to have done nothing about it. There had to be another reason, and I was now more sure than ever that it had some connection with smuggling.

'I do know,' I said. 'I've interviewed him.'

'You have? Why?'

'Because he is conspiring with Rose to run a stable of prostitutes, of which, almost to the time of her death, your wife was one.'

'What d'you mean by that?' Light demanded angrily.

'Rose keeps a book in which he lists all the girls at the club and who they've been with. Your wife's name appeared regularly.'

'I don't believe it,' said Light.

But I didn't believe him.

'I'm afraid it's true.'

'D'you think it was Todd who killed her, Mr Brock?'

'It's a possibility I'm looking into,' I said. I didn't tell him that it had now become a very strong possibility.

Dave had not interrupted during this tense questioning of Andrew Light, realizing that I had carefully planned what I would ask him.

I stood up. 'I'll keep you informed of any developments,' I said.

* * *

The latest interview with Andrew Light had started to bring together the disparate elements of what we had learned so far. Andrew Light, a convicted smuggler, knew Danny Todd. Todd had regularly had sex with Kim. Light's brother Mark was Duncan Ford's agent. And Duncan Ford was on the Customs and Excise suspect list.

The investigation would now have to be concentrated on Todd, the leading suspect for the murder of Kim Light and Duncan Ford. Despite what we had thought at first – that Ford was the target – the fact that the killings had taken place at Durbridge Gardens and not at Ford's flat in Pimlico did not really bear out that theory. But if Kim had been the target whom Todd had threatened to kill, then it all started to make sense. Duncan Ford had just picked entirely the wrong time to get his end away. Or Todd had mistaken Ford for Andrew in carrying out his threat to kill both the Lights.

However, that did not mean that other loose ends could be left loose.

Although I hadn't much doubt that the blustering Jonathon Wheeler was telling the truth about his week at the races, I was still going to check it with his secretary Fiona Squire. Not only for the hell of it, but because he might just have been lying. People who have committed murder rarely admit to it immediately, tending instead to say the first thing that comes into their head. Like I was in bed with my secretary. Then they'll telephone her and ask her to tell the same tale to the police. But it doesn't work very often, mainly because secretaries object to having their names hawked around as being an easy lay. Even if it's true.

As Wheeler had said that he was rarely in his London office, I decided it was safe to speak to Fiona Squire there.

I could quite see why Wheeler had taken his secretary to the races. And even if he hadn't, it was obvious why he'd've wanted to. Anyone would've wanted to. She was a svelte thirty-year-old, tall and good looking, bulged in all the right places, had straight blonde hair that curled gently under at

131

shoulder level, and a come-on smile. What baffled me was why *she* would have wanted to go to the races with *him*.

'My word,' she said brightly as we were shown into her office. 'It's not often that we have the police here. How exciting.'

'Mr Wheeler tells me that you're his secretary, Miss Squire.'

'It's *Mrs* Squire,' she said with a confident smile, 'and I service all the part-time directors. Not just him.'

'I see. We're investigating a murder, Mrs Squire. Two murders in fact.'

Fiona's eyes opened in astonishment. 'D'you mean that Mr Wheeler is somehow . . . ?'

'No, not at all.' I didn't really think so, but one never knew. 'He tells me that you and he spent the week beginning the tenth of June this year at Epsom races.'

A deep flush rose on Fiona's cheeks. 'What else did he say?' she asked nervously, her initial confidence rapidly ebbing.

I got the impression that Jonathon Wheeler was about to get a very disturbing phone call, and would probably be looking for a new secretary, to say nothing of a different partner for his next race meeting. 'Did you in fact spend that week at Epsom with him?'

'Well, yes, I did,' she said, slowly and with some reservation.

'Is there anything else you want to tell me, Mrs Squire?'

'No. There's nothing wrong in spending a week at the races, is there? I was due some leave and I took it. If I care to spend it with Mr Wheeler watching horses run round and round, I don't see that that's anyone else's business.'

'Mrs Squire, I haven't come here to pry into your private life. Frankly, I don't care what you do, but this is important.'

'Why? What's so important about it?'

I was going to have to tell her. 'Mr Wheeler knew the murdered woman.'

'Oh my God! Then you *are* saying that he may have had

something to do with it, aren't you?' Fiona reached for a glass of water and took a sip. In a wild leap of imagination, she was probably seeing herself as his next victim.

'That rather depends on what you tell me.'

It was then that the tears began. She took a tissue from the open drawer of her desk and dabbed gently at her eyes, being careful to avoid smudging her mascara. 'Does this have to go any further?' she asked.

'I shan't rush round and tell your husband, if that's what you mean.'

'My husband and I lead separate lives,' she said tartly.

'You were saying . . . ?' I continued.

'Jonathon and I spent a week at a hotel near the race-course,' she mumbled.

'And presumably you—'

'Yes,' said Fiona, 'and we slept together, if that's what you want to know.' She shot me a glance full of hatred. Funny that, the way people who have been caught out want to blame the person who forced them to reveal their dark secrets. On the other hand, she might have been ashamed that her association with the overweight, pompous Wheeler had been discovered. She must have had better offers than that. I could only surmise that she had been impressed by Wheeler's Bentley and the money that he had undoubtedly lavished on her.

'And how did you explain that to your husband?' asked Dave, his prurient curiosity getting the better of him.

'If it's any concern of yours, I told him I was away on a business trip. It happens quite often.'

And looking at the girl, I could quite believe that it did. Perhaps there was a wider meaning to her claim that she serviced all the directors.

Fourteen

'Interesting couple of days, Harry,' said Frank Mead.
'Not particularly,' I said.

'It was a statement, not a question,' said Frank, flourishing the surveillance log. 'Todd spent most of Saturday afternoon at Rose's club, but didn't stay for the evening performance.'

'So where did he go?' I asked.

'At about five o'clock, he took a taxi from the club to Tothill Street junction of Matthew Parker Street.' Frank looked up. 'That's a turning running round behind Central Hall and into Storey's Gate.'

'Yeah, I know,' I said. 'I walked it when I was a probationer PC. But what the hell was he doing there? It's usually as dead as a dodo on a Saturday evening.'

'He wasn't doing anything there. He waited a couple of minutes and then hailed another cab that took him to Wandsworth.' Harry glanced down at the log. 'He was then seen entering a warehouse near the river, just west of Wandsworth Bridge.'

'D'you reckon he'd spotted the tail?'

'No chance. It was just the natural caution of a villain. He spent about half an hour in this warehouse before taking another taxi to Lower Richmond Road, Putney, where his Merc was parked. He then drove to his penthouse in Docklands, arriving at five past eight.'

'That it?'

'As far as his own movements are concerned, yes. But at nine o'clock, a limo turned up and a leggy blonde got out and made her way up to Todd's penthouse. She stayed until eleven o'clock the following morning, Sunday, when she was collected by the same limo and taken to an address in Clapham.'

'No prizes for guessing what she was doing in Todd's penthouse all night,' I said.

'Advising on interior decoration perhaps,' said Dave, slowly peeling a banana. 'Ceilings in particular.'

'We ran the number of the limo and it goes out to a chauffeur-driven car hire company,' Frank continued. 'I sent one of the lads round on Monday morning to see what the SP was. It's a legit outfit and they said they'd had a call to take a fare from Rose's club to Docklands on the Saturday evening and to collect her again at eleven on the Sunday morning. The guy at the car-hire place said it was a regular booking, and the tab was picked up by Rose. Apparently he's got an account with them.'

'What about this warehouse, Frank?'

'That'll take a bit more time, Harry, but if it's anything to do with Todd, it's bound to be bent. And the fact that he took precautions getting there tends to prove it. Enquiries are in hand, but I think it's a case of softly-softly.'

'What about Monday and yesterday, Frank?'

'Nothing. The guy never moved from his penthouse.'

'Who's the leggy blonde? Do we know?'

'Not yet, but I'll get someone to make some enquiries at the Clapham address.'

'Don't bother. I'm sure John Rose will be delighted to tell me this evening.'

There was always the risk that Todd would be in the club, but I took a chance on his having other things to do at six o'clock on a Wednesday evening.

'On Saturday evening you sent a girl down to Todd's place in Docklands,' I said, as Dave and I entered Rose's office, 'where she stayed the night. Who was she?'

Rose sat down again, suddenly. 'I don't know what you're talking about, Mr Brock.'

'You seem to have forgotten that I've seen your little

135

black book, John, old son.' For some reason, my use of Rose's first name seemed to disconcert him. 'You're running a cathouse takeaway service, and a limousine, paid for by you, took a girl from here to Todd's penthouse at nine o'clock on Saturday, and collected her at eleven on Sunday morning. Now who was she?'

'Penny Harper.'

'And did she get paid?'

'I hope you're not suggesting—'

'Did she get paid?'

'Yes.'

'By whom?'

There was a longish silence before Rose said, 'Me.'

'And she works here as a dancer, yes?'

'Yes,' said Rose.

I had no intention of mentioning Todd's warehouse at Wandsworth. Rose might well know what it was used for, but I didn't want him to tell Todd – as I'm sure he would – and thus alert him to the surveillance.

'Let me see that book of yours again, John,' I said.

Rose handed it over without a word of protest. I looked at the page for the eleventh of June, the date of the murders. The entry showed that Todd had 'entertained' Penny Harper at his penthouse.

'D'you think I'm bloody stupid?' I snapped. I was tempted to nick him there and then, but it suited my purpose to leave him where he was. For the time being.

'What d'you mean?' asked Rose nervously.

'That date was blank the last time I looked at that book. Now, mysteriously, there's an entry that shows that Todd was having it off with Penny Harper. Again. She one of his favourites, is she?'

'I think you've made a mistake there, Mr Brock,' said Rose, panicking.

'Where's Penny Harper now?' I asked.

'She's in the club somewhere.' Rose, caught in the crossfire between Todd and me, moved to the window that gave a view of the arena, and drew back the curtain.

136

His hand left a sweat mark on the cloth. 'Yes, she's on stage now,' he said with a resigned sigh.

'Then get her up here. And tell her to put some clothes on before she does,' I said, a request that undoubtedly disappointed Dave.

Rose tapped out a number on his telephone and issued an instruction. A few moments later we saw another girl appear on the microscopic stage beneath us and whisper in the ear of a nude blonde dancer with whom she then changed places on the greasy pole.

Five minutes later a girl who could have been no more than nineteen appeared in Rose's office. Her idea of getting dressed amounted to donning a gold lamé bra and thong, and a flimsy negligee. Her heels were a good six inches high.

'You wanted me, Mr Rose?'

'These gentlemen are from the police, Penny. They want to talk to you.'

A frisson of fear flitted briefly across the girl's face as she glanced nervously at Dave and me. It was a glance that told me she was a frightened pawn in the unsavoury world populated by Todd and the equally odious John Rose. And her revealing outfit might have been because she'd thought that Rose wanted her for an entirely different purpose.

She sat down on the banquette beneath the window and crossed her long legs.

'Do you recall where you were on the night of Tuesday the eleventh of June, Penny?'

The girl shot a furtive glance in Rose's direction and received a nod.

'I was with Mr Todd at his penthouse at The Heights in Docklands.'

'What time did you get there?'

'Eight o'clock.'

'And when did you leave?'

'Ten o'clock on Wednesday morning.'

'And how did you get there?'

Penny glanced nervously at Rose again and then said, 'Mr Todd sent a car to take me there and bring me back.'

'And did you sleep with him?'

Penny looked down at the floor and nodded. 'Yes,' she whispered.

'So you were with him all night?'

'Yes,' said the girl again. Then she looked up. 'I'm not a prostitute, if that's what you're thinking,' she protested defiantly. 'Mr Todd's my boyfriend. I didn't get paid or anything like that.'

'I don't care what the arrangement was,' I said. 'I'm investigating a murder, not the vice trade.' But the implication that I didn't believe a nineteen-year-old to be the girlfriend of an ageing villain seemed to discomfit her even further. 'I'll just get my sergeant to take a statement from you, and that'll be that.'

The girl was not happy, but she made a statement.

'What did you think about her, Dave?' I asked as we made our way to the exit.

'Bit of all right, wasn't she, guv?' said Dave enthusiastically.

'I wasn't talking about her vital statistics, Dave, I was talking about her statement.'

'Rehearsed, guv. Frankly, I don't believe her. I reckon Todd got to her before we did and put the fear of Christ up her. He's got form for malicious wounding, don't forget, and the threat of a blade across that pretty little face of hers would've persuaded her to do anything and say anything he wanted her to.'

'But when would he have had time to set that up?'

'He must have sussed out that we'd got him in the frame when we saw him here a week ago,' said Dave. 'Sometime between then and now, Todd scared the living daylights out of the girl and put the frighteners on Rose to make that entry in his book.'

'I reckon you're right, but what are we going to do about it?'

'Talk to her again, on her own and away from the club. But I doubt we'll break her story, unless we promise her all sorts of things. Like the witness protection programme.'

As I have often said, Dave Poole is a very shrewd detective.

'Tony,' I said, when we reached the door, 'what time does Penny Harper usually turn up here?'

Tony sucked through his teeth, an obvious aid to thinking. 'Usually about five in the evening, sir,' he said. 'Unless she's doing an overnighter,' he added with a wink.

I knew damned well that Penny Harper had lied to us about spending the night of the murders with Todd, and much as I felt sorry for her, I knew that I'd have to disprove her claim if I was going to justify arresting Todd for killing Kim Light and Duncan Ford. Not that it would be absolute proof, but at least it would be a start.

My first inclination was to leave it for a day or two until we'd had a chance to interrogate Todd, but the following morning I changed my mind.

'Oh!' said Penny Harper when she opened the door. 'It's you.' It was very apparent that she'd hoped not to see us again.

The flat in which she lived was tastefully furnished, and the girl herself was attired in designer jeans with a white belt, and a black roll-neck sweater.

'You told me yesterday,' I began, once we were seated in her living room, 'that you were not a prostitute.'

'I'm not,' she exclaimed indignantly. 'I'm a dancer.'

'Look, Penny, I don't really care what you are. As I said before, I'm investigating a murder. But that apart, I saw the book that Rose keeps of girls he supplies to clients, and your name appears fairly regularly over the past six or seven months. Admittedly you visited Todd quite a few times, but there were at least four other, different men that you've spent the night with on a fairly regular basis. They can't all be "boyfriends", can they?'

Penny looked at me defiantly, but said nothing.

'You didn't spend the night of Tuesday the eleventh of June with Todd at all, did you?'

'Of course I did. Why don't you believe me?'

'Because when I posed the question, you came out with the answer immediately. There was no hesitation. Now, if someone asked me what I'd been doing a fortnight ago, I'd have to stop and think. But you didn't. So who told you to tell me that story? Todd or Rose?'

'I'm not saying anything.'

'Yesterday evening you made a written statement in which you said that you *had* spent that night with Todd. You also signed a caveat to the effect that it was a true statement. If it's proved to be false you could be open to prosecution.' I regretted having to make the threat, but the girl was being stubborn.

'You don't understand,' said Penny miserably. 'Danny forced me to say that. He said that if I didn't, he'd . . .' She broke off and burst into tears.

'He'd what?' I asked, having given her time to recover slightly.

'He said he'd cut me.'

'We shan't let that happen, Penny,' I said. 'We can always protect a witness.'

'*Witness!*' Penny looked up, despair on her tear-stained face. 'You surely don't think that I'd go to court and give evidence against him. I might as well commit suicide now.'

'So you didn't spend the night with him.'

'No.'

'There may be a way out of this, Penny.'

'How?' asked the girl hopefully.

'Where were you really that night?'

'I can't remember. I'll have to look.' She took a small diary from her handbag and riffled through the pages until she found what she was looking for. 'I spent the night with a man called David Moore.'

'Where?'

'At his flat in Chiswick.'

'Address?' asked Dave, notebook and pen at the ready.

'Have you been there before?' I asked as Dave wrote down the details.

140

'No, that was the first time.'

'And Rose sent you down there in a limo, I suppose.'

'Yes. He always does.' The girl suddenly broke down and sobbed uncontrollably. Taking a tissue from her bag, she dabbed gently at her eyes. 'He makes me do it,' she said suddenly.

'Who makes you?'

'Mr Rose. I'm not a prostitute. Really I'm not.' She looked up, imploring me to believe her.

'Go on.'

'I always wanted to be a dancer, and my father paid for me to go to dance school. But when I left there, I couldn't get a job. Then I met one of the girls I'd trained with and she told me that she was working as a lap-dancer at Mr Rose's club. She introduced me and I got taken on. That's when it all started to go wrong.'

'In what way?'

'One night Mr Rose told me that one of the clients wanted to take me to dinner. It turned out to be Danny Todd. Mr Rose sent me down to his place in Docklands in a car. It wasn't until I got there that I realized what Todd wanted me for.'

Oh, you poor naïve little bitch, but hers was not a unique story by any means.

'And?'

There was another bout of tears before Penny spoke again. 'He raped me,' she whispered. 'And he told me that he would have me whenever he wanted me, or he'd scar me for life.'

I knew there would be little point in asking the girl whether she wished to prefer charges against Todd and Rose. That would come later when they were both in custody. Maybe.

'Did you get paid for your services?'

'No I didn't. Mr Rose said I was getting paid as a dancer, and I was getting the garter as well. So that was it.'

'The garter?'

'Yes, it's what the girls call the tips they get. The

141

clients tuck money into our garters if we perform on their table.'

'And the same thing happened when you went with other men, did it?'

'Yes. Mr Rose said that I had to have sex with them otherwise Danny would make trouble for him. And for me.' There was a pause while Penny dabbed at her red-rimmed eyes again. 'What'll happen about that statement?' she asked tearfully.

The girl had been terrorized by Todd and Rose, and I didn't intend to add to her fears. 'Nothing,' I said. 'I'll tear it up. Provided what you've just told me is the truth.'

'It is, I swear it,' said the girl.

'I'm really looking forward to having those two bastards in the nick, guv,' said Dave as he drove us back to central London.

'Promise not to hit them, Dave,' I said. I was joking. I knew that he'd never struck a prisoner in his life.

'No need to,' said Dave. 'Once they're banged up in Wormwood Scrubs or wherever, a quiet word to the screws and the whisper'll go round about what they're in for. They'll be taken care of. Anyway, that said, are we any further forward?'

'Depends on what David Moore has to say. But if he bears out Penny Harper's story, it gets her off the hook without risk to her. We'll tell Todd that we made independent enquiries and have disproved his alibi. I may even let slip that Rose told us.' I laughed at the thought of the mayhem that could cause. 'Todd needn't know that Penny gave us the lead, or even that we've interviewed her. I know she's a reluctant tom, maybe, but that's no reason for her to be carved up.'

'I should hope not,' said Dave wistfully. 'She's got a beautiful body, that girl.'

'All of which, if it's kosher, puts Todd well and truly back in the frame.'

'Unless he was up to something else he didn't want us to know about, guv.'

142

'Such as?' I asked.

'Todd could have been doing a run across the Channel on that night.'

'Possible,' I said, 'but by the same token, he might just have been murdering Kim Light and Duncan Ford.'

'Possibly, guv. But Todd's got a warehouse in Wandsworth we don't know anything about. Why not top Ford there, or in Ford's own drum in Pimlico? Why do him at Durbridge Gardens where he might have been spotted by neighbours and run the risk of meeting up with Andrew Light?'

'Or Kim Light.'

'Exactly,' said Dave. 'But we still don't know if Todd and Ford knew each other.'

'We're going round in bloody circles,' I said gloomily.

'Never mind, guv. *Tempus omnia revelat.*'

'And what the bloody hell does that mean, Dave?' I asked, shooting a sideways glance at my sergeant.

'Time reveals all things . . . sir.'

'Smart-arse,' I said.

Fifteen

There were now several matters vying for my immediate attention. The obvious one was Danny Todd and his association with Andrew and Kim Light, and Kim in particular. And Todd's warehouse. Then there was the disparity between the stories told me by the Stows and Andrew Light about what had actually occurred on the infamous Algarve holiday. And finally there was the question of where exactly Peter and Gill Stow had been at the time of the murders.

First of all, I instructed Frank Mead to tell John Fielding, the surveyor at the Custom House headquarters of the National Investigation Service, what we had learned. I hoped that Fielding could be persuaded to mount an observation on Todd's Wandsworth warehouse. I certainly didn't have the manpower, and I reckoned that the warehouse might be of more interest to customs than to police. If anything turned up regarding the murders, then I would reap the benefit without having made the effort. Perhaps.

But before I got carried away with too much theorizing, I decided to speak to the Stows again. The answer might still be right next door. Next door to the Lights, that is.

It was therefore of paramount importance to check whether the Stows had in fact been on holiday in Portugal at the time of the murders.

But I knew from previous investigations that enquiries through airlines and holiday-villa agencies would probably take a week at least, and I didn't have that sort of time. That left me with no alternative but to rely on copper's cunning to persuade the Stows that I knew more than I did.

*   *   *

It was six o'clock when we pulled up outside twenty-nine Durbridge Gardens. The sun was still high in the sky and the temperature well into the eighties. After some delay, Peter Stow answered the door. His surprise at seeing us on his doorstep was matched by mine at finding him in a dressing gown so early in the evening.

'I wonder if we might have a few words with you and your wife, Mr Stow?'

'It's not really very convenient' – Stow was clearly unhappy at our unexpected arrival – 'but I suppose . . .' He stepped back and opened the door wide. 'I'll just call my wife. She's upstairs.'

A few moments later we were joined in the sitting room by a flushed Gill Stow clad in a cerise kaftan.

'I'm sorry to trouble you, but it is rather important,' I began, accepting Stow's invitation to sit down. 'You know DS Poole, of course.'

The Stows each nodded in Dave's direction and mumbled some sort of greeting.

'When I came to see you on Monday of last week, you told me that you'd been on holiday to the Algarve . . .'

'Yes, that's right,' said Peter Stow.

'But that wasn't true, was it?'

'Er, no, it wasn't, but how did you know?' Well, that was easier than I thought. 'So where were you?'

'We'd gone to Dorset.'

'Really?' That sounded unlikely: the couple had been deeply tanned when Dave and I first saw them. 'Is that where you and your wife got that suntan?'

Stow laughed. 'We've got a sunbed upstairs,' he said.

'I still don't understand why you said you'd gone to Portugal. Why not admit you'd been to Dorset?'

'Is this relevant?' demanded Stow.

'It may be. I'm investigating the murder of your next-door neighbour's wife, and a man called Duncan Ford.'

'But surely to God you don't think we had anything to do with that, do you?' Stow's face displayed shock at the implication.

145

'Look at it from my point of view, Mr Stow,' I said. 'The last time I saw you, you told me that you'd been on holiday in the Algarve, but now you tell me that you'd been to Dorset. Exactly where in Dorset?'

'Chard St Mary. It's very close to Chesil Beach.'

'Then I'll ask you again. Why did you tell me that you'd been to Portugal?'

The Stows glanced guiltily at each other.

'You'd better tell him,' said Gill. She was blushing now and I anticipated some tasty revelation. I wasn't wrong.

'We didn't think you'd see the need to check up on us, Mr Brock,' said Peter Stow accusingly, 'and I'm afraid we're a bit embarrassed about it.'

'What, about going to Dorset?' I began to wonder whether this was a keeping-up-with-the-Joneses thing. That the Stows were terrified that their rich Notting Hill neighbours might find out that they could no longer afford a foreign holiday. Mind you, in my experience, holidays in England now cost more than those abroad.

Gill Stow, who must have known what was coming next, suddenly stood up and ran from the room. I heard an upstairs door slam.

'We like to go on holiday with other couples,' said Stow.

'So do a lot of people,' I said.

There was a lengthy pause before Stow spoke again. 'We usually find them through a magazine, which is what we did this time.'

'What sort of magazine?' I asked, but I had a bloody good idea what sort of magazine it was. Beside me I could almost hear Dave licking his lips.

Stow leaned forward, elbows on knees, hands loosely linked between them. He stayed like this for some time before eventually looking up. 'We're into sexually liberated holidays,' he mumbled.

Why was I not surprised? It certainly explained Gill Stow's sudden departure: discussing such intimate arrangements with two policemen could not have been to her liking.

146

'We find it keeps our marriage fresh,' said Stow, attempting to justify what he and his wife had indulged in. It didn't sound convincing. 'We have a very good sex life, but a bit of variation once in a while is a real stimulus. We spent two weeks with this couple in Dorset. They were a very active pair and totally uninhibited, even suggesting that all four of us always did it in the same room. Group sex is much easier with complete strangers. Shirley was a real goer –' he smiled at the recollection – 'and Gill and Jamie were unbelievably inventive. Not that I had much time to watch them.'

In the absence of his wife, Peter Stow had become much more open. Even so, I was surprised, once again, at how candid some people can be when describing their sex lives to complete strangers.

'And the address of this couple, Mr Stow?'

That slowed him down. 'You don't mean that you're going to talk to them, surely?' he asked nervously.

'How else do you suppose I'm going to confirm your story?'

'But . . .' Stow ran a hand through his hair. 'Oh God! What will they think?'

'You originally told me that you were in the Algarve,' I said, 'which you now admit was a lie. Why should I believe this second story, that you and Mrs Stow went on a sexual holiday with two people you'd never met before, and whose names you say you obtained from a contact magazine?'

Suddenly Peter Stow was back in the frame. It was a damned sight easier to get to Notting Hill from Dorset and back again in one night, than it would have been to travel from Portugal.

'But it's true,' pleaded Stow.

'Mr Stow, I'll remind you again that I'm investigating a double murder that took place a fortnight ago, right next door. I have a duty to pursue every possible lead.'

'But you can't honestly believe that Gill and I had anything to do with Kim's death,' Stow said again.

'I shall be more inclined to believe that if the two people you say you stayed with can vouch for you,' I said.

147

'I told you their names were Jamie and Shirley,' said Stow quietly, 'and they live at Storm Cottage in Chard St Mary.'

Dave looked up from his pocket book. 'What's their surname, Mr Stow?'

'I don't know. We didn't ask and they didn't tell us. And we didn't tell them ours, either, or where we lived. It saves complications. We were there for a fortnight and then we left. End of story. I don't suppose we'll ever meet again.'

'Now, about your holiday with the Lights,' I said, just when Stow thought I'd finished.

'What about it?'

I could see that Stow was beginning to tire of my questions, but if he wanted to be awkward, I had enough justification now to arrest him and continue the interview at the nick.

'Would you care to tell me about it?'

'I told you last time you were here.' Stow's answer was belligerent.

'Yes, but you didn't tell me the whole truth before, did you?'

Stow sighed. 'We got together with the Lights just after they moved in, and we started dining together on a regular basis. It didn't take long to work out that we were kindred spirits. Andrew and Gill were mutually attracted, that was obvious, and as for Kim and me, well, I could see straight away that she wouldn't need any persuading. Gill and I discussed the possibilities and decided that we'd invite them to join us in the Algarve. We made it quite clear to them what form the holiday would take and they were all for it. They knew what was going to happen between us.'

'So your wife wasn't telling the truth when she said she objected to Kim swimming naked.'

'No, of course not, but she was too embarrassed to tell you what sort of holiday it'd really been.' Stow gave a humourless laugh. 'The truth is Gill swam naked as well, the entire time we were there. We all did. But the whole thing turned out to be a ghastly mistake.'

'How so?'

'To do what we did with Jamie and Shirley was one thing. A wild fortnight and then finish, never to meet again. But when we got back from the Algarve, Andrew wanted to carry on seeing Gill, and Kim kept pestering me to spend time with her when Andrew was away. Quite frankly it was beginning to get messy, and Gill and I decided to draw a line under what had been a very bad idea.'

I don't know how long Gill Stow had been standing outside the door, or how much she had overheard. 'Why don't you tell Mr Brock the truth, Peter?' she demanded angrily as she strode into the room. 'We didn't draw any lines at all.' Rather than rejoin her husband on the sofa, she pointedly sat down in a chair at right angles to him, and to Dave and me. 'We carried on our respective affairs until we went to Dorset. When Peter was at work, Andrew would come in here or I'd go in there.'

'When Kim was out presumably.'

'Not always,' said Gill. 'And I'll let you work out what used to happen on those occasions,' she added with a sly smile. 'And Peter continued to screw that slut Kim.'

'But wasn't Andrew bothered about it?' I asked.

'He was hardly in a position to object, was he?' said Gill scornfully.

'So Andrew's statement that you raped Kim is untrue,' I said, looking at Peter Stow.

'Is that what he told you?' A look of shocked incredulity crossed Stow's face.

I saw no harm in putting a wedge between Andrew Light and the Stows: the three of them were thoroughly unsavoury, immoral people and in my book deserved to reap what they had sown. 'Yes,' I said. 'Andrew Light said Kim told him that on the fourth night of the holiday, at about two in the morning, you raped her by the swimming pool.'

But Peter Stow didn't get the chance to rebut that allegation.

'What absolute rubbish,' said Gill, her initial embarrassment having passed through various stages to reach bravado.

149

'Kim was more than willing. And I should know because Andrew and I were screwing right next to them.'

'And that was as far as it went, was it? Just swapping wives?'

'Too bloody true,' said Peter Stow vehemently. 'I hope you're not suggesting that I'm gay. I don't think I've ever met anyone who was so violently opposed to homosexuals as Andrew. He hated them.'

It was obvious to me now that the Stows *had* colluded with Andrew Light to concoct a story about their holiday in the Algarve, but they hadn't got the finer details quite right. I wondered why they'd bothered. But sure as hell I intended to find out.

We returned to Curtis Green at about eight o'clock, but I decided to call it a day. 'We'll chew it over on Monday, Dave,' I said.

Dave looked delighted, delighted enough for me to presume that Madeleine had got a night off from being a swan in *Swan Lake* or whatever.

On Monday morning I got in at about nine, my usual time, come what may. The commander was already poncing about in the incident room.

'Ah, Mr Brock, this fraud thing that Light was involved in . . .'

'Allegedly involved in, sir.'

'Yes, yes, but I don't think there's much doubt about it, do you?'

'No, sir, not really.'

'Well, as you're mixed up with the murder of Mrs Light and this other person . . . what's his name?' This despite the fact that his name was in large letters next to Kim Light's on the whiteboard.

'Ford, sir. Duncan Ford.'

'Exactly. I think you should take on the fraud enquiry too. You've interviewed Light and you know about him. And this fraud doesn't look too complicated.'

150

God preserve me from fools like the commander. If he'd spent as much time as I had on the Fraud Squad – in fact if he'd spent *any* time on the Fraud Squad – he'd've known that fraud enquiries are among the most difficult to prove in court. Mainly because the average jury is so thick that they haven't got the faintest idea what prosecuting counsel is talking about. But in my experience, they don't talk much about juries at Bramshill Police College, which, to the commander, was the site of the police equivalent of the Holy Grail.

'Very good, sir. I'll try and fit it in with my double murder.'

The commander missed the sarcasm. Or chose to ignore it. 'How *is* the murder enquiry going?'

'Slowly, sir,' I said, 'but it's early days.' It wasn't early days at all – it was over a fortnight since the murders – and I was being bogged down in what seemed awfully like trivia. The reasons for the conflicting accounts given by Andrew Light and the Stows about what had happened in the Algarve last year were puzzling me.

The Stows had, somewhat belatedly, been staggeringly frank about the holiday – perhaps too frank to be credible – but Andrew Light had implied that he and his wife had been unwitting pawns in the Stows' sex-games holiday. But was Light the one telling the truth and really hadn't known what the Stows had got in mind for their fortnight in Portugal? Or was he, at this late stage, attempting to salvage something of his late wife's reputation?

More than once the thought had crossed my mind that Peter Stow was the killer, perhaps even Gill Stow, although firearms were only rarely a woman's weapon. I hadn't forgotten, though, that Gill Stow had referred to Kim as a slut, even after admitting that her own moral behaviour was not exactly beyond reproach.

'Incidentally, sir, it turns out that Duncan Ford was a bit of an iron,' I said casually.

Let's see what this pseudo detective makes of that piece of rhyming slang.

151

'An iron, Mr Brock?' The commander blinked. 'I don't think I, er . . .'

'Iron hoof, sir. Poof. A homosexual. At least he was until Mrs Light got hold of him.'

'Oh, I see.' The commander wrinkled his nose. He did not approve of CID jargon, particularly when used by senior officers who, mistakenly, he believed should be gentlemen. 'Well, good luck, Mr Brock,' he said, and wandered off, polishing his glasses with a colourful pocket handkerchief, doubtless to take refuge from reality in his office.

'I've been thinking about the Stows, guv,' said Dave, as he peeled a banana. He saw me looking at it, and added, 'Madeleine says they're good for me. They contain potassium and they give you instant energy.'

So Madeleine was a dietician as well. 'Good,' I said. 'Energy you'll need.' It was certainly an improvement on the oranges to which Dave was so addicted. I couldn't stand the smell of oranges. 'What *have* you been thinking about the Stows?'

Dave dropped the banana skin into the wastepaper basket and wiped his fingers on his handkerchief. 'They said they'd spent a fortnight in Dorset with two sex maniacs, but when we saw Peter Stow the first time, he said they'd left for their holiday on the twenty-fifth of May, and Mrs Stow told us that they'd got home on the Saturday after the murders. That's three weeks, not two. So where were they for the other week?'

'Why the hell didn't you mention that while we were there, Dave?'

'Two reasons, guv. One, I wasn't sure about it until I'd checked my notes, and two, I thought you'd want to hear what Jamie and Shirley had to say first.'

'So there's a week adrift, but we don't know which one. Bugger it! That means we'll have to go to Dorset.'

'I thought we'd have to anyway, guv,' said Dave. 'We can't take the Stows' word for it, and even if they were there at the crucial time, one of them could have returned to Notting Hill, done the business and gone back to Dorset again. All in a matter of hours.'

Which was exactly what I'd thought when Stow admitted to lying about having gone to Portugal. 'And d'you think one of them *might* have been responsible, Dave?'

'They lied the first time, and then they told a highly unlikely story about capers in Dorset. And don't forget that the Stows' story about what happened in Portugal was virtually denied by Light. Suppose that Stow did rape Light's wife and Light threatened to take him to court back here, which he could have done. That'd be a pretty good motive for Stow killing Andrew and Kim. I don't think Stow would much care for being banged up as a nonce.'

And that would serve him right, I thought. Nonces – sexual offenders in prison parlance – get a pretty rough time of it in the nick. 'But it was Kim and Ford who were murdered,' I said, 'not Kim and Andrew.'

'Yeah, I know that, guv, but you said yourself that the killer might have mistaken Ford for Light in the dark.' Dave chuckled. 'I like that: Light in the dark.'

'Well, how far is it to this Chard St Mary place?'

'A hundred and forty miles, sir,' said Colin Wilberforce promptly and looked up from his paperwork. 'Shall I ring them and make an appointment?'

'How can you ring them? We don't know their full names.'

'It's Jamie Pearson and Shirley Sanders,' said Dave.

'How did you find that out?'

'I'm a detective, guv,' said Dave without the trace of a smile.

'No, don't ring them, Colin. I want to surprise them.'

'Stow might have rung them already,' said Dave.

'You're a real bloody pessimist, Dave,' I said, 'but it's a chance I'll have to take. Anyway, Stow reckoned he didn't know their surnames.'

'He said a lot of other things that weren't true, too,' said Dave.

Sixteen

Dave and I had a quick bite of lunch before setting off for Dorset.

Chard St Mary was more of a hamlet than a village. Just a road with a few houses on either side and a pub. There was a winding lane that went up the side of the pub past a farm, and Storm Cottage was at the end. It was small – a farm-labourer's cottage probably – and not overlooked. The front door was a simple close-boarded affair with a Suffolk latch and a wrought-iron bell-pull to one side.

I'd made a point of arriving at about six-thirty, having assumed that Jamie Pearson and Shirley Sanders would have been at work all day. I gave the bell-pull a tug.

'Yes?' A bull of a man – probably in his mid-thirties – answered the door. Unshaven, he was stripped to the waist, apart from a red neckerchief, and wore moleskin trousers held up by a heavy leather belt with brass badges on it.

'Mr Jamie Pearson is it?'

'Who wants to know?' He was aggressive, but perhaps he'd mistaken us for passing evangelists.

'We're police officers, from London.'

'Are you really now?' Doubt was etched clear on his face.

Dave and I produced our warrant cards, which the man inspected closely.

'Are you Mr Pearson?' I asked again.

'I am that.'

'We'd like a word with you and your wife, if we may.'

'I ain't done nothing wrong,' protested the man.

'I'm not suggesting you have, Mr Pearson.' I imagined

154

that his only contact with the police would be because of some breach of the law on his part. And by the look of him it was probably poaching . . . or anything else he could lay his felonious hands on.

'You'd better come in, then.' Pearson turned abruptly.

The front door led directly into the living room. Pearson crossed to the television and switched it off.

'Here, I was watching that.' The woman was a blowsy blonde with an excess of make-up. Her red top, through which a black bra was clearly visible, had frills around a low-cut neckline that displayed her ample cleavage to the full, and a short, black, tight leather skirt. Her shapely, fishnet-clad legs were propped on a footstool.

'These gentlemen is policemen from London, Shirl. They want to ask us some questions.' Pearson turned to us. 'This here's Shirley, my woman.'

'You ought to put a shirt on, Jamie,' said Shirley.

'I don't want no shirt on, lover,' said Pearson.

Apart from the armchair in which Shirley was sitting, there was only one other and Pearson promptly sat in it leaving Dave and me to occupy a couple of wooden carvers.

'Now then, what's it you want to ask?' Pearson crossed his legs and reached across to take a pipe from a shelf beneath the television.

'I'm investigating a double murder in London,' I began. *That ought to concentrate their minds.*

'Murder?' Pearson took the pipe from his mouth, which was just as well because his jaw dropped. 'We don't know nothing about no London murders. Come to that, we don't know nothing about no murders full stop, do we, Shirl?'

'No, us don't,' said Shirley, putting her feet on the floor and taking a sudden interest.

This rough-looking couple both spoke with rich Dorset accents and I had great difficulty in visualizing the sophisticated Stows willingly indulging in group sex with them. Shirley certainly had a coarse allure that probably appealed to Peter Stow, but the thought of the genteel Gill and this gorilla . . . Well, it takes all sorts, I suppose.

'I'm not suggesting that you are involved, Mr Pearson, but our enquiries have led us to question a couple called Peter and Gill.' I deliberately omitted their surname because Peter Stow had told me that they had not revealed it to Pearson and his woman. 'They told me they spent a holiday with you, here at Storm Cottage, sometime between the twenty-fifth of May and the fifteenth of June.'

Pearson and Shirley glanced at each other. 'Never heard of 'em,' said Pearson.

'Did anyone stay here with you between those dates, Mr Pearson?'

Once again Pearson and Shirley glanced at each other.

'There was a couple what come down,' said Pearson, 'and I think they come from London. Leastways they had London accents. A bit hoity-toity as a matter of fact.'

'And what were their names?' asked Dave, opening his pocketbook.

'The girl called herself Sharon,' said Pearson, 'but I can't remember the man's name. You should though, Shirl,' he added with a lewd grin.

'He said he was called Kevin,' replied Shirley without hesitation, 'but I never believed neither of them. They never looked like no Kevin and Sharon. But so what? It don't matter.'

'And why did they choose to spend a holiday with you? Are they friends of yours?'

'Gawd, no!' exclaimed Pearson. 'We'd never met 'em afore.'

'Do you advertise holiday accommodation, then?' I asked, trying to lead them into confirming the Stows' story. But I needn't have bothered.

'Oh, don't beat about the bush, mister,' said Shirley. 'They must've told you why they was here. It were for sex. Jamie and me advertise for it in one of them magazines. Bit complicated it is. You gets put in touch through something they calls voicemail. Anyhow the long and short of it is them two answered and down they come. He were bloody good at it, that Kevin' – a dreamy look spread across her face – 'and that Sharon couldn't leave my Jamie alone. All over him like a rash, she was. Still, that's what they was here for and that's what they got. And we was glad to have 'em.'

I looked at Pearson, but he just laughed. 'S'right,' he said.

'How long were they here, then?' I was accepting, for the moment anyway, that Kevin and Sharon were names that the Stows had assumed.

Shirley at last stirred herself and walked through to what I imagined was the kitchen. She returned clutching a wall calendar. 'They come on the twenty-fifth of May, like you said, mister,' she said, 'but they was off on the eighth of June. Jamie and me only gets a fortnight a year, see. He works on the farm and I've got a job as barmaid at the Lord Chard pub down the road. You must have passed it on the way here.' She glanced at her watch. 'Glory be,' she exclaimed. 'An' I'll be late an' all if I don't get going. Is there anything else?'

'Oh, calm yourself and sit down, woman,' said Pearson. 'He can manage without you for a bit yet. Tell him we've had a couple of gents from Scotland Yard come a-calling. That'll quiet him.'

'Did either of them go out while they were here? On their own, I mean,' I asked.

'We all went down the pub most nights,' said Pearson, 'but that Kevin slept with her' – he nodded at Shirley – 'and Sharon was with me every night. Couldn't never leave me alone, like Shirl said,' he added with a lascivious grin.

'And we had a few friends in from time to time,' said Shirley. 'Just to spice things up a bit.'

I forbore from asking what 'spicing things up' meant. 'Did they say where they were going when they left here, Mr Pearson?'

'Said they was going home, wherever that is. Wish we knew. Wouldn't mind having them here again next year.'

A frown settled on Pearson's face. 'You reckon they done these murders, then?' he asked.

'Good heavens, no,' I said, by no means certain. 'It's what we call eliminating them from our enquiries.'

'Well, you never had to come all the way down here to do that, mister,' said Shirley. 'We'd've told you that on the phone.'

'Can you tell me what they looked like?' Dave, pen poised over his pocketbook, directed his question at Shirley.

'When they had clothes on, you mean?' said Shirley with a crude laugh, and gave a description that could have fitted the Stows. And a hundred others.

'And did they pay you for staying here for a fortnight?'

Pearson looked guilty and licked his lips. 'You ain't nothing to do with the Revenue, I hope.'

'Not bloody likely,' said Dave.

'That's all right, then. Aye, they give us three hundred quid, but that was to cover the food an' all.'

'Aren't we going to stay at a hotel, guv?' asked Dave, when we were back in the car.

'No, I want to get back to town tonight,' I said.

'Very good, sir,' muttered Dave crossly, and started the engine. The prospect of driving the return trip of a hundred and forty miles obviously didn't please him, but I could foresee an argument with the commander about expenses for what he would probably think was a totally unnecessary junket to Dorset.

Dave maintained an irritable silence until we turned on to the A354. 'So, we've a week to fill in, guv,' he said. 'If the Stows can't account for their whereabouts between the eighth and fifteenth of June, I reckon they're up for it.'

And so did I.

Having met Jamie and Shirley, I could quite understand the Stows' reluctance to admit having spent a fortnight of debauchery with such a repulsive couple, to say nothing of the spicing-it-up parties that their hosts had mentioned. But that didn't explain the missing week, a week during which

158

someone had entered the Lights' house and murdered Kim Light and Duncan Ford.

And from what Linda Mitchell, the SOCO, had said, that person, having gained entry, attempted to make it look as though they had broken in through the kitchen window. And that meant that they'd probably come through the front door, either having been admitted as a friend, or with a key.

Could it have been that Peter Stow returned from wherever he was during that missing week, and committed those murders?

Despite not reaching London until well after midnight – thanks to an excess of holiday traffic – Dave was in the office early the next morning.

'I suppose it's another visit to the Stows, then, guv,' he said.

'Yes,' I said, 'and this time we'll take a warrant, just in case they want to play any more silly bloody games.' I was fast losing patience with the two Notting Hill sexual socialites.

'I suppose that means waiting until he gets in from work.'

I thought about that for a moment. 'No, Dave,' I said. 'We'll catch Mrs Stow on her own. You never know what she might tell us when her old man's out of the way.'

Having gone via West London Magistrates' Court to get a warrant, we arrived at the Stows' house at about eleven o'clock.

'Oh, not again.' Gill Stow, wearing a clinging black dress, admitted us with an air of resignation. 'Peter's at work,' she said, once we were in the sitting room.

'It's you I want to talk to, Mrs Stow,' I said, when the three of us were seated. 'Or is it Sharon?'

Far from being surprised, Gill Stow laughed. 'You've been to Chard St Mary, then,' she said.

'Yesterday.'

'And now you're wondering how I could possibly have lowered myself to have sex with a rough like Jamie.' But before I could say anything, she added, 'Well, it may come as a surprise to you, Mr Brock, but some women do occasionally like a bit of rough, and I'm one of them.' She lifted her head and stared straight at me, as if defying me to contradict or criticize her.

'What you do is no concern of mine, Mrs Stow—'

'Then why are you here? I was beginning to think that you were taking an unhealthy interest in our sex lives.' She smiled and crossed her legs so that her skirt rose a few inches higher.

But I refused to be diverted by this woman's deliberately seductive teasing. 'When I first saw both of you, Mr Stow told me that you and he went on holiday on the twenty-fifth of May and you said that you'd returned on the fifteenth of June. But you later said that you'd spent a fortnight with Jamie and Shirley in Dorset. They confirm that it was only a fortnight.'

'I'm not denying it. We did spend only a fortnight with them.'

'Then where were you between the eighth and the fifteenth of June?'

'Since you ask, which you didn't before, we drove from Chard St Mary round to Bournemouth, left the car at the airport and flew to Amsterdam. And I'll leave you to work out what we were doing there.' Far from the demure woman that Gill Stow had pretended to be on our first visit, she was now not only flaunting her immorality, but obviously didn't see anything wrong in it. Not that her behaviour was likely to evoke much surprise in Notting Hill. 'We came back on the fifteenth and drove home here. There, does that satisfy you?'

'Where did you stay in Amsterdam?' asked Dave.

'In a brothel.' Mrs Stow was being deliberately provocative now, and shot an impish smile in Dave's direction. 'Well, to all intents and purposes it was. It was a remote country house just outside Amsterdam surrounded by chalets and a swimming pool, set up to cater for the sexual needs of both men and women. And very good it was too.

160

They're very liberated in the Netherlands, you know.'
With a seductive smile, she leaned towards Dave in such
a way that the scoop front of her dress riveted his attention.
'Give me your book, Sergeant,' she purred, 'and I'll write
down the address for you.'

I'd never seen Dave so besotted before. He handed her
his pocketbook and pen without a murmur.

Gill quickly wrote down the details and returned the book.
'It's called *Het Passie Huis*, Sergeant,' she said. 'That's
Dutch for "The Passion House".'

'I could definitely fancy that Gill Stow, guv,' said Dave, on
the way back to the office. 'I'll swear she hadn't got any
underwear on.'

'Why don't you and Madeleine go on holiday with her
and her husband, then?' I smiled wryly at the thought of
Madeleine's reaction to such a suggestion.

'That is not funny, sir,' said Dave, and promptly changed
the subject. Almost. 'So what do we do now? D'you want me
to go to Amsterdam to check out her story?'

'Don't be silly, Dave, you'd never get out of that place
alive. No, we'll get the Dutch police to check it out for us.
They're probably immune to temptation.'

'Not what I've heard,' muttered Dave.

'But in the meantime, while we're waiting for that to be
done, we'll go to Andrew Light's bank and get this fraud
thing off the ground. As if I haven't got enough to do.'

I asked Colin Wilberforce to make the appointment for
me. Klein, the director to whom we'd spoken previously,
agreed to see us at two thirty.

'One other thing, Colin. Would you telephone the police
in Amsterdam and ask them to check if Peter and Gill Stow
stayed at this *Passie Huis* place between the eighth and
fifteenth of June? Dave will give you the exact details.'

'But I don't speak Dutch, sir.' It was not often that Colin
looked disconcerted.

'They all speak English,' I said. 'You won't have any
trouble.'

After toying briefly with the latest paperwork that goes with a murder enquiry – reports and statements from here, there and everywhere – Dave and I grabbed a sandwich. Then we dropped back into the office so that Dave could pick up the plethora of stationery that is a necessary part of all investigations. The Job's paper bill would work out much cheaper if the Metropolitan Police had its own rainforest.

In order to get this thing off the ground it would be necessary to take statements from Klein and the computer whiz-kids who had discovered the discrepancy in the bank's funds. And anyone else whom the Crown Prosecution Service might wish to call as a witness at Light's trial. And on the basis of what we knew so far, I was in no doubt that there would be a trial. and I was in no doubt either that Light would plead not guilty.

Seventeen

'I was on the point of telephoning you, Mr Brock, when your sergeant rang to make this appointment,' said Klein when we were shown into his office.

'Yes, I'm sorry I haven't been back to you before now,' I said, 'but as you know, I'm also investigating the murder of Mr Light's wife.'

Klein nodded vacantly and fingered an impressive-looking sheet of paper, the only item on his desk. 'We at the bank have been thinking long and hard about this affair, Mr Brock,' he said, 'and the board has decided not to press charges against Mr Light.'

'But we're talking about thirty thousand pounds here, Mr Klein.'

A brief frown creased Klein's brow. 'I'm well aware of the amount involved, Mr Brock, but it was our money and it's a mere drop in the ocean. I can assure you that the bank's reputation is worth far more than that. If this affair reached the Old Bailey, and I assume that's where the trial would take place, the publicity could ruin us. Just imagine the reaction of some of our clients. If we can't safeguard our funds against one of our own employees, they would be wondering what sort of organization we were running here.' Doubtless he was thinking of other merchant banks that had gone under.

Although I agreed with him, and was relieved at not having to deal with a fraud case alongside the murders, the copper in me resented the thought that Light would be getting away with his dishonesty.

'You do realize, Mr Klein, that the diamonds Light was

163

attempting to smuggle are forfeit to the Crown, so there's no question of your being able to recover any of your losses from that quarter.'

'I'm aware of that, Mr Brock,' said Klein.

'Letting Light get away with it doesn't set a very good example to other employees, Mr Klein,' I said, my feelings for justice overcoming my desire to get shot of an enquiry I could well do without.

'Oh, he's not getting away with it, Mr Brock. We've terminated his employment and he'll never get another job with a bank, I can promise you that. He'll probably finish up in a betting office or an estate agency. But that's his problem.'

And there it was. Despite what Klein had said, Light *was* getting away with it. And working as an estate agent would, sure as hell, be better than doing six years in Wormwood Scrubs or wherever. Just about.

It was interesting, too, that Light's recent loss of his wife seemed not to have entered into the deliberations that had led to the board's decision. But the sympathy of bankers has never, in my knowledge, extended that far.

'The one thing we haven't done, Dave, is to check where Mark Light was at the time of the murders,' I said, once we were back at Curtis Green.

'D'you think he might have been involved, guv?' Dave gave me one of those looks that said the governor's gone off at a tangent again. 'And if so, why?'

'Got a better idea?' I asked.

'Look at it this way, guv. He made it quite clear that he'd no time for Kim Light – if you remember, he called her a whore – and he's not likely to have said that if he'd topped her, is he? Plus, I got the impression that he and his brother are hardly on speaking terms.'

'But we don't know that for sure, do we?'

'It's an inspired guess,' said Dave with a shrug.

He knew he wasn't going to win this one, but when – and if – he ever reaches my rank, he'll discover that the answer

164

is sometimes not only staring you in the face, but that every eventuality must be investigated.

'So we'll go and have another chat with him.'

Dave glanced pointedly at his watch. 'He'll have gone home, sir.'

He was calling me 'sir' again. 'You're probably right,' I said. 'To hell with it. We'll knock off for the day and go home and think.'

Back in my office, I rang Sarah and suggested dinner.

We went to our favourite restaurant in Chelsea, even though we were in danger of getting into a rut.

Sarah seemed a little tense this evening, and maybe she was thinking the same thing: that our relationship was getting too cosy and wasn't going to lead anywhere.

I waited until the first course was over before I told her my news. 'My decree nisi came through today, Sarah.' I patted the pocket containing the solicitor's letter. Helga hadn't argued – not that she had grounds for doing so – and was probably as pleased to be shot of me as I was to part from her.

'Oh!'

'Another six weeks and I shall be a free man.'

'And what are you going to do about Helga? You're still living with her, aren't you?'

'We're still living in the same house, but we're not living together,' I said. It was a fine difference that Sarah probably didn't understand. 'She says that she's going to move in with this doctor she's seeing.' I smiled grimly. 'When *his* divorce comes through.'

'It all sounds a bit messy.' Sarah dabbed carefully at her lips with a table napkin.

'Yes, but that's our problem. Helga's and mine. And the doctor's.'

'So you're going to stay at Wimbledon, are you?'

'That depends. The house is in joint names, so Helga's entitled to half. I probably won't be able to stay on. I'll have to find somewhere else, for the time being.'

I could see that Sarah was struggling with a decision. 'I'd

suggest you moved in with me. On a temporary basis, of course, but . . .'

I placed a hand on hers. 'No, Sarah, that's not a good idea.' I could see she was unhappy about it and the last thing I wanted was to upset the easy rapport that had developed between us. 'If we did that, I'd much prefer it to be on a formal footing.'

She knew what I meant, but took some time to respond. 'Is that some sort of proposal?' she asked hesitantly, and smiled.

'Well, I suppose it is.' I smiled too. 'I'm just a simple policeman, Sarah, and I'm not too good with words when it comes to things like that. I'm all right in the witness box, but the romantic stuff, well, that's a bit more difficult.'

'There's nothing simple about you, Harry Brock.' Sarah forced the gay little laugh that so beguiled me. 'I suppose I knew it would come to this eventually and if I'm honest I've been trying hard not to think about it. You see, I . . .'

The dilemma that was facing her suddenly hit me with all the force of a sledgehammer. She was still in love with Captain Peter Hunt, the fiancé who'd been killed on Salisbury Plain a few years ago. In her mind, I thought, anyone else would be second best.

'I'm not rushing you, believe me, but do give it some serious thought.' I forced myself to put into words what I'd known for some time now. 'I love you, Sarah Dawson, and you can't stay single for the rest of your life. Unless you want to, that is.'

'No, of course I don't, but to be honest, Harry darling, I don't really know what I want. Can we leave it for a while, so that I can get used to the idea and think about it? It's a big step.' She paused to toy with a fork before looking up again. 'And you're in a dangerous job.'

So that was it. She'd lost one man with whom she'd been in love and was terrified of the same thing happening again. I tried to reassure her, but I knew it was in vain.

'Harry Brock knows how to steer clear of danger, Sarah. These days I just send someone else.' I laughed, attempting to make light of her worries, but deep down I knew I'd failed. After all, coppers do get killed, all too often. I always knew that I was all right, but a policeman's wife, sitting at home, watching the clock, was worrying all the time. Usually being late meant being tied up with paperwork, but you try telling the womenfolk that.

'The Dutch police have been back on, sir,' was the first thing that Colin said when, next morning, I walked into the incident room.

'Christ, that was quick,' I said. 'They wouldn't like to send some of their guys over here to give us a hand, would they?'

'This *Het Passie Huis* place –' Colin stumbled over the pronunciation and smiled ruefully – 'is well known to them apparently, sir.'

'Thought it might be. And?'

'The Stows were definitely there the whole time between the two dates you mentioned, sir. And you were right about the language. The *commissaris* on the Amsterdam vice squad spoke very good English.'

'I said he would, Colin. I was once told by a Dutchman that because there are only about sixteen million Dutch speakers in the world, nobody bothers to learn their language, so the Dutch all learn English.'

'Fascinating,' said Dave, peeling another banana.

'The Amsterdam law reckon that this place is very popular with Brits,' Colin continued. 'The guests only have to call reception and order up a male or a female – straight, gay or lesbian – and one, or two if that's what they want, will arrive in their chalet within minutes. It costs a packet, but this Dutch copper said that the Stows made full use of the services.'

'I'll bet they did.' Dave took a bite of banana. 'Like Gill Stow said, they're very liberated in the Netherlands.'

'The *commissaris* did a thorough job too,' continued Colin. 'He even interviewed each of the girls who spent nights with Peter Stow, and the men who'd given Mrs Stow

167

a seeing-to. They were definitely there at the relevant time.' He proffered a sheet of paper. 'And the *commissaris* faxed through a copy of their bill. It includes the names of the men and women who provided the Stows with "personal services".'

'They don't give a toss, do they?' I said.

'Probably would if you asked them,' said Dave.

It was now almost three weeks since the bodies of Kim Light and Duncan Ford had been discovered and – with the Stows ruled out of the picture – I found myself once again in an investigative cul-de-sac.

'The killer was known either to Kim Light or to Duncan Ford,' I said for about the hundredth time. 'The kitchen window had been removed from the inside, so whoever committed the murders was admitted freely to the house. Or the killer had a key.'

'Do we know if Mark Light had a key?' asked Dave.

'No, we don't, but what motive would he have for killing Kim Light?'

'Dunno. But it was you who suggested interviewing him again, guv, to see where he was on the night of Tuesday the eleventh of June.'

'Right,' I said, 'we'll do it now.'

I didn't believe that Mark Light had had anything to do with the deaths of Ford and Kim, but one has to go through the motions. If only to stop the commander bitching and fretting over the report to the Crown Prosecution Service. If ever we got that far.

'How can I help you?' asked Mark Light confidently, having sent the girl with the bare midriff to get coffee.

'Do you have a key to your brother's house, Mr Light?' I asked. I saw no sense in skirting around the main reason for my visit.

Light looked puzzled. 'Why d'you ask?'

'Because one of the things I have to do in a case like this is to eliminate all the innocent parties.'

'And I'm an innocent party, am I?'

'You tell me.'

'Of course I am. I know I told you that I thought Andrew's woman was a whore, and she was, but I had no reason to kill the girl.'

I noticed that he avoided using the word 'wife' this time. 'As I said, Mr Light, it's a process of elimination.'

'No, I don't have a key. Thank you, Melanie,' he said, turning to his assistant as she brought in three cups of what I suspected – and later confirmed – was instant coffee.

'Where were you on the night of Tuesday the eleventh of June, Mr Light?' It was a straight question: no messing.

'Is this another bit of elimination?' Mark asked sarcastically.

'Yes.'

'I was in Paris for a few days.'

I affected a look of surprise. 'What sort of business takes a theatrical agent to Paris?'

'None that I can think of,' said Light. 'I was having a brief holiday.'

'Very pleasant,' I said, 'apart from the channel crossing. I always get seasick.'

'So do I,' said Light. 'That's why I always go on Eurostar. Very civilized.'

'I imagine so,' I said. 'I must try it someday.'

'I can thoroughly recommend it, Mr Brock.'

'And where did you stay in Paris?'

'What is all this?' demanded Light indignantly. 'First you tell me that I'm not a suspect, and then you cross-examine me about how I went to Paris and where I stayed.'

'You're under no obligation to reply,' I said, 'but it will make my job that much easier.'

Mark Light took out a pocket diary and thumbed through it. 'It was the Hotel New York,' he said. 'Funny name for a Paris hotel. I can't tell you the street other than to say it wasn't far from the British Embassy. I've a shocking memory for things like that.'

'And were you on your own?' It briefly crossed my mind that the bare-bellied Melanie might have accompanied him on his period of rest and recuperation. But from the look of her, I doubted that she would have afforded him much of either.

'Yes, I was.'

'That's all right, then,' I said, as I stood up. 'I don't think we'll need to trouble you further.'

'Arrogant little bastard, isn't he?' said Dave. 'D'you reckon he's kosher?'

'If he was in Paris at the time, Dave, that rules him out.'

'There is another possibility, guv,' said Dave thoughtfully.

'Which is?'

'That he was in France, but not in Paris. Suppose this theatrical agency is just a front for bootlegging and Mark Light was in the racket with Ford, a suspect smuggler. Don't forget that Mark said that Ford was a duff actor, and so did the woman at the casting agency. Could be that Light was doing a run. He was being a bit cagey, wasn't he? And then there's Todd. We know that Todd was screwing Kim and threatened Andrew Light. Coincidence? Or could it be that both the Lights and Todd are into smuggling big-time? There's a few motives for murder kicking about there.'

'You've cheered me up no end, Dave,' I said.

Back at Curtis Green we analysed what we'd got so far in the hunt for the killer of Kim Light and Duncan Ford. It didn't take long because we hadn't got much, apart from Dave's complicated theory. And speculation, which is no good without evidence.

'Are we near getting a result, Mr Brock?'

Just what I needed: the bloody commander on one of his taking-an-interest-in-the-troops walkabouts. I tried deflecting him.

'The bank has decided not to proceed against Andrew Light for the fraud, sir,' I said.

The commander fiddled with his glasses. 'Oh? And what

caused them to come to that conclusion, pray?' He always tried to sound educated.

'They took the view that a prosecution would be too damaging to the bank's reputation, sir.'

'Yes, I can understand that in a way.' The commander nodded sagely. 'One tends to overlook such commercial considerations in this closed little world of ours.'

It might be closed to you, sport, I thought, but it isn't from where I'm standing. Perhaps that's why they called him the eternal flame: because he never went out. I'd also heard that now he was nearing retirement age, he was actively touting for a security-director's job with a bank. I suppose he thought it would enhance his reputation among the snooty friends with whom, if he was to be believed, he and his lady wife dined on a regular basis.

'And what about the homicides?' he asked.

I loved the way he referred to a topping as a homicide. I suppose he was waiting for the jury's verdict, just in case they brought in manslaughter.

'Rather slow progress there, I'm afraid, sir,' I said. *Slow? We aren't making any bloody progress at all.* 'I think we'll have to go back to square one and start reviewing the evidence.'

'Yes, yes, always a good move, Mr Brock.' The commander nodded again and wandered off.

'Did you mean that, guv,' asked Dave, once the commander had gone, 'about reviewing the evidence?'

'What the hell else can we do, Dave?'

'Have another go at Danny Todd, who appears to be bleeding Rose dry, to say nothing of what else he may be up to.'

'Good thinking, Dave. I think it's time we spun his drum.'

Dave and I, together with four scenes-of-crime officers, hit Todd's luxurious penthouse flat at six o'clock on the Thursday morning.

Todd was furious, which came as no surprise to us.

171

'What the bloody hell's this all about?' he demanded, pulling his full-length brocaded-silk dressing gown more firmly around him.

'It's about the murder of a prostitute called Kim Light, known to you as Gloria,' I said, handing Todd his copy of the search warrant.

'I've told you I don't know nothing about any murders and I've never heard of this Gloria you keep banging on about. And right now I'm going to give my lawyer a bell.'

'Not till we've finished you're not,' I said.

'And what d'you think you'll find?' asked Todd with a sneer. 'The bleedin' crown jewels?'

'As far as I know they've not been reported missing,' said Dave mildly. Like me he knew that we wouldn't find any stolen property. Todd was too canny a villain to make that sort of mistake.

'Ha, ha, very funny.' But Todd was clearly disconcerted that Dave and I were making no apparent effort to search his flat. It was only the SOCOs who were at work.

It took about three hours, but at the end of it they had gathered quite a few sets of fingerprints that, with any luck, might prove to be identifiable.

'So? Satisfied?' demanded Todd.

'I'll let you know when we've done some checks, Danny,' I said.

'I'm going to make an official complaint against you for harassment,' shouted Todd as we left.

'Feel free,' I said, 'but I should warn you, there's a long queue.'

The speed with which fingerprints can be checked against the main index these days is breathtaking, thanks to computers. By four o'clock that afternoon, the results were in.

Linda Mitchell, the senior SOCO, was jubilant. 'We've got the set I think you've been looking for, Mr Brock,' she said. 'Kim Light's fingerprints were in Todd's bedroom, in his shower room, and in the jacuzzi.'

'Bloody marvellous,' I said. 'Frank, you may have the

172

privilege of going down to Docklands and nicking the bastard.'

If Todd had been furious when we executed our search warrant that morning, he was now incandescent with rage.

'This is diabolical,' he screamed when Dave and I confronted him at Limehouse police station. 'And I want my solicitor here. *Now!*'

'Already been sent for, sir,' said the custody sergeant, turning to me. 'He should be here in about ten minutes from now.'

'Good,' I said.

True to his promise, Todd's solicitor arrived on time. Wearing a sharp suit and rimless spectacles, he was about forty years of age, and his business card revealed that he had offices in Poplar, less than half a mile away.

'My client has a complete answer to the charge,' he announced. I assumed it was his standard opening.

'Your client hasn't *been* charged,' I said.

'In that case, what's he here for?'

'He's assisting police with their enquiries into a double murder,' I informed him.

'Ludicrous,' said the lawyer.

'Mr Todd,' I began, once we were all ensconced in the interview room, 'you have persistently claimed not to know a woman named Kim Light, also known as Gloria, whose dead body was found at twenty-seven Durbridge Gardens on the morning of Thursday the thirteenth of June. However, the fingerprints of the dead woman were discovered in your penthouse this morning.'

'My client knows nothing of this, Chief Inspector,' said Todd's lawyer.

'May I remind you,' I said to the solicitor, 'that your duty is to look after the interests of your client, not to answer questions for him. If you persist in so doing, I shall have you removed from this interview.'

'I hope you know what you're doing,' snapped the lawyer.

173

'Oh, I do,' I said. 'And I hope you do.'

The lawyer scribbled busily on his legal pad.

'I've had lots of toms down my place,' said Todd. 'I don't know the names of half of them, and I certainly didn't top any of them.'

'Can you account for your movements on the night of Tuesday and Wednesday, the eleventh and twelfth of June?'

'If I have to,' said Todd.

'Is there any reason why you shouldn't?'

'Tell him, Danny,' said the lawyer.

'Yeah, I was kipping with a tom, down my place at The Heights.'

'Name?'

'I told you, I don't know the names of half of them, but I do know I have a bird down there most nights.'

'Blimey!' said Dave enviously, but quietly enough for his comment not to be picked up by the tape recorder.

'In that case,' I said, 'I can see no reason why I shouldn't charge you with the murder of Kim Light and Duncan Ford.'

'Here, hold on,' said Todd, the first sign of alarm creeping into his protest. 'Who said anything about a Duncan Ford?'

'I did,' I said.

'Well, I don't know nothing about him. Or this Gloria you keep on about. But if you want to know who the girl was who was with me when they got topped, ask Rose. He supplies them.'

I never did believe that there was a code of honour among thieves, but it was nice to have its absence confirmed once in a while. However, I wasn't going to tell Todd that I'd already sunk his alibi, if for no better reason than I hadn't yet checked Penny Harper's story that she'd spent the night with a David Moore in Chiswick.

'There appears to be no reason for you to detain my client any further, Chief Inspector,' said the solicitor smoothly, 'and as he is only assisting police with their enquiries, we shall both leave now.'

He was right, of course. That Kim Light's fingerprints had been found in Todd's apartment was not proof that he'd murdered her at Durbridge Gardens. And as she was now known to have been an active call-girl, there was no reason either why she should not have been at The Heights. Or a hundred other places.

Eighteen

A t seven o'clock that evening we went to Chiswick and saw David Moore, who told us he was single and worked as a management consultant. At first he stalled when I asked him if he'd entertained a prostitute on the eleventh of June. But after I'd explained to him the reasons behind the question, he admitted that Penny Harper had spent the night with him. And he had paid Rose for the pleasure.

It was success of a kind, but it meant that Todd, as a suspect, was now firmly back in our sights.

But that wasn't all. When we got back to Curtis Green at nine o'clock, Frank Mead was waiting with the news that Todd had given the surveillance team the slip.

'I'm sure he didn't suss us out, Harry,' he said. 'I think he must have guessed that we'd put an obo on him and took the necessary precautions.'

'What did John Fielding at customs say about the warehouse?'

'He's interested, but he doesn't have the staff for a twenty-four-hour surveillance on the basis of purely speculative information.'

'Right, in that case we'll hit it ourselves. Early tomorrow morning. And I want a TSG unit there with us just in case it turns into a rough-house.'

'What time?' asked Frank.

'Five o'clock.'

We arrived at Wandsworth just before five, and the Territorial Support Group unit – an inspector, two sergeants and twenty constables – were already there in carriers discreetly tucked away in a side street.

While half the unit encircled the warehouse, one of the PCs made short work of the door and we were in.

'Blimey! Aladdin's Cave,' said Dave as he looked around. There were shelves stacked from floor to ceiling with cigarettes, rolling tobacco and alcohol.

On my instructions, the rest of the TSG fanned out and searched the entire warehouse. Of Todd there was no sign, but moments later, two PCs appeared from the back of the warehouse holding a weasel of a man between them.

'Found this guy doing a runner out of the back door, sir,' said one of them.

'And who are you, friend?' I asked.

'Ain't saying.' The prisoner was a small man, with the undernourished appearance of the habitual East End villain.

'Well right now this lot's down to you. Happy with that, are you?'

'I don't know nothing about it. I'm just the caretaker.'

'And you're caretaking about half a million quid's worth of bent gear,' I said.

'Look, guv'nor, I'm just paid to keep an eye on things.'

'So what's your name?'

'Fred Spicer.'

'Where's Danny Todd?'

'Never heard of him.'

Dave took a menacing step closer. 'I don't think you quite heard my governor,' he said quietly.

Spicer shifted nervously and began coughing uncontrollably.

'I hope you haven't been smoking the stock, Fred,' said Dave.

Eventually recovering, Spicer realized that the chips were down. 'I dunno, guv'nor,' he muttered. 'Mr Todd ain't been here for a few days.'

The caretaker's apparent ignorance of Todd's whereabouts was probably genuine. If Danny Todd was half as shrewd as I thought he was, there was no way he'd trust a loser like Fred Spicer.

'Put him in the van,' I said to the PCs. 'We'll deal with him later. And now,' I continued, turning to Dave, 'get on to Fielding's lot at customs and tell them to get down here a bit swift.'

Dave made the call. 'The duty watch will be here ASAP, guv,' he said, snapping shut the flap of his mobile.

Having previously arranged for Frank Mead and a couple of DCs to be parked up within spitting distance of Todd's penthouse in Docklands, I rang him, told him the outcome of the raid and asked him to see if Todd was there. Although our most-wanted had somehow evaded the surveillance team, he might just have managed to slip back into his flat.

'There's what looks like an office over in the corner, sir,' said one of the TSG sergeants, pointing towards the rear of the warehouse, 'but it's locked.'

The same PC who had let us in tackled the padlock with a pair of bolt cutters. The tiny room was little more than a cupboard containing a telephone and a fax machine.

Dave started by checking the numbers stored in the telephone's memory against the list in his pocketbook. 'Oh dear! How careless,' he said.

'What've you got, Dave?' I asked.

'Andrew Light's home number and the mobile numbers of Ford and Mark Light. Among quite a few others.'

'I think it's coming together, Dave.' It was more than I'd hoped for, but it still didn't provide any evidence of murder.

'Of course, customs might tell us that this stock is all kosher, guv,' said Dave.

'Yes,' I said, 'and I've just been appointed Commissioner.'

Twenty minutes after Dave's phone call to the customs investigators, three of their officers arrived.

'You must have burned rubber getting down here this quick,' I said.

'We broke a few speed limits,' said the senior officer, 'but don't tell the police.' He introduced himself as Les Wentworth. 'This all looks promising.' He glanced round the huge stock that the warehouse contained. 'How did you run across this lot then?'

I explained, as briefly as possible, our interest in Todd and how we'd come to search his warehouse. If it was his warehouse. For all we knew, he might just be part of a much bigger network.

Before very long the customs officers confirmed that the contents of the warehouse had all come from abroad. The chances of duty having been paid on it was remote, Wentworth observed drily.

So far so good, but Frank Mead's telephone call told me that Todd was not in his penthouse flat.

Half an hour later, John Fielding arrived, having been called out from home. 'Looks like you hit the jackpot, Harry,' he said, once he'd listened to Wentworth's report.

'Got good informants,' I said with a measure of triumph. 'What happens now?'

'I'll put a team in here and wait,' said Fielding. 'Some-one's got to turn up sooner or later.'

'I should make it a pretty strong team, John,' I said. 'If Todd's anything to go by, his little lot will be nasty bastards.'

'They all are, Harry, but I'd appreciate it if you could leave some of your guys here until my chaps arrive.'

'No problem, sir,' said the TSG inspector when I briefed him. I got the impression that his men and women would rather enjoy a punch-up.

'What's your next move, John?' I asked Fielding.

'From what you say, the Light brothers and Todd are in this up to their necks. If you can give me their addresses, I'll put an observation team on them.'

'OK, but Todd's my front-runner for the murder of Duncan Ford and Kim Light. If he shows up, perhaps you'll let me know. When I've done with him, I'll throw you the bones. If there are any left.'

'Thanks, Harry, you're a real pal,' said Fielding with a laugh.

'What happens now, guv?' asked Dave.

179

'We return to Curtis Green and regroup,' I said.

'Is that a euphemism for we don't know what to do next?' asked Dave with a grin.

But I knew exactly what we were going to do next: tackle the Light brothers. But that did not turn out to be as easy as I'd anticipated.

Melanie stared at me, a vacant expression on her face. 'If you're looking for Mark, he's not here,' she said.

'What time does he usually get in?'

'About nine, maybe half past. On the days he does come in, I mean.' The girl glanced at a clock on the wall next to a picture of the Eiffel Tower. Don't ask me why the Eiffel Tower. 'It's nearly two o'clock, too. He's not usually this late,' she added.

'I think you'd better tell me where he lives,' I said.

'I'm not allowed to give out his address.'

I sat down on the chair in front of the girl and, leaning forward, folded my arms on the computer table. 'I'm dealing with a very serious crime, Melanie,' I said gently, 'the murder of Mark's sister-in-law, and it's imperative that I speak to him urgently. Now, I wouldn't like to think that you're going to be difficult about this. It could have serious repercussions.'

'Oh!' She took a small dog-eared book from a drawer and flipped through the pages. 'It's flat seven, fifteen Captain's Walk, Chelsea,' she said, 'but don't tell him I told you. He'd be very cross with me.'

'Your secret's safe with me, Melanie,' I said in a pointless attempt at reassurance. Of course he'd know who'd told me. 'I won't tell him if you don't. I presume he lives there alone.'

'I don't know.'

'And you have no idea where he might be?'

'No, he never tells me anything.'

In my book, that made Mark Light an astute operator. Melanie did not strike me as being among the brightest, but she did exude sex – oodles of it – and I wondered why her

180

boss didn't take her with him wherever he went, especially when he went to bed. I'm pretty sure his brother would've done, given the chance. There certainly didn't seem much point in leaving her here to look after the business. This was the fourth time we'd visited Mark Light's run-down offices and although there was a row of wooden chairs along one wall, there'd never been a client waiting to be interviewed. But then I don't know much about theatrical agents and the way they work. Maybe it's all done on the phone.

'When he shows up, perhaps you'd ask him to ring me on this number,' I said, handing the girl one of my cards.

Melanie studied it closely before placing it between the pages of the address book and putting it in the drawer. 'Yeah, right,' she said.

I had no great hope that the message would ever reach him.

Captain's Walk lay between Kings Road, Chelsea, and the river. Number fifteen was a block of service flats. There was a security entry system and I pressed the bell for flat seven several times before having to accept that Mark Light was not at home.

'What about trying the resident porter?' asked Dave, pointing to another bell-push.

'He'll only tell Mark we're interested,' I said. 'I'd rather catch him unawares.'

'I reckon he's done a runner,' said Dave.

'Looks like it,' I said, being a suspicious sort of bastard, 'but why? I doubt if he knows that we spun the warehouse this morning.'

Dave shrugged. 'Got something else to hide,' he said, but didn't expand on that profound statement.

'I wonder if his brother knows where he is,' I mused.

'We could ask him,' said Dave.

We went back to Durbridge Gardens, but Andrew Light was no longer at home.

We were getting back into our car when Debbie Wilson

181

sashayed across the road. She tapped on the window. 'Are you looking for Andrew?' she asked.

'Yes. D'you know where he's gone?'

'Not exactly,' said Debbie, lowering her voice and leaning into the car so that her ash-blonde hair fell across her eyes. 'But he got into a taxi about an hour ago. He had some luggage with him.' By now she was almost whispering.

'Thank you,' I said. 'You've been a great help.' I fished out another of my cards. 'If he returns, perhaps you'd give me a ring. Er, without letting him know, eh?'

Debbie Wilson was obviously delighted to be involved in official police business. 'Of course.' Leaning even further forward, she gave me a coy smile and tucked the card into the top of her bra.

Nice try, love, but you're not my type.

'Looks like we're up the proverbial gum tree, guv,' said Dave as we drove away.

I spent the rest of the afternoon with Dave going through what we'd collected so far about the murders. It was a mess. Our likely suspects were Todd and Dent, in that order. Personally, I thought that Dent was too much of a tosser to be capable of committing the sort of sophisticated killings that had resulted in the deaths of Kim and Ford. And the Stows were out of the loop.

Todd had to be my number one suspect. The problem was going to be proving it. Admittedly he was a vicious criminal, but we still had no substantial evidence that would put him in the dock for murder. If I gave the Crown Prosecution Service what we'd got so far, they'd throw it straight back at me. But right now that was academic. Todd had disappeared and we hadn't a clue – literally – where he'd gone.

I looked glumly at the picture gallery in the incident room. The photographs of the living stared back at me, as if defying me to identify any one of them as the murderer.

The commander appeared, as usual at an inopportune moment, but then he always did appear at an inopportune moment.

'Any progress, Mr Brock?'

I outlined the state of the enquiry and the commander grunted.

Then he turned his attention to Dave. 'How are you settling down here, Sergeant Poole?' he enquired. This despite the fact that Dave had been with the group for over a year.

'Fine, thank you, sir,' said Dave, 'and it helps to have a good governor.'

'Of course.' The commander preened himself. He obviously thought that Dave meant him. 'Incidentally, I've always meant to ask where you come from, Sergeant Poole.'

Dave assumed an air of naïve perplexity. 'Er, Kennington, sir.' He knew what the question was aimed at: it was because he was black. But he also knew that in these days of enlightened racial tolerance, even the commander had to tread warily.

The commander laughed nervously. 'No, I meant before that.'

'Before that, sir?' asked Dave innocently.

'Yes, I mean where did you come from originally?'

'Bethnal Green, sir,' said Dave with a straight face.

'Really? And you're married?'

'Yes, sir.'

'And what is your wife? Is she, er . . . ?'

'She's a ballet dancer, sir.' Dave was really playing him along now.

'Ah!' said the commander.

'Oh, I see,' said Dave, who had seen all along. 'You meant is she black, sir. No, she's white.'

'Well, no, I, er . . .' The commander lapsed into silence, having been hit head-on, something he'd not expected from a sergeant.

But then Dave really fronted him. 'If you want to know where my ancestors come from, sir, it's no secret. My grandfather came across from Jamaica in the nineteen fifties – he was a doctor – and set up practice in Bethnal Green. And my old man's an accountant. But I disappointed them all.

After going to university I became a copper.' Dave chuckled. 'What you might call the black sheep of the family.'

'You went to university, then. Mmm, how interesting,' said the commander and retreated to his office.

While this exchange had been going on, I'd been working myself up for a row with the commander, but decided that Dave's neat demolition job of him made any intervention on my part quite unnecessary.

Dave picked up a banana and started to peel it. 'So what do we do now?' he asked.

'It's beginning to look very much like the death of Ford was connected to bootlegging,' I said, 'and the first thing is to track down Todd, and Andrew and Mark Light.'

'But won't John Fielding want them?' asked Dave.

'Yes, but we've come to an agreement. If Todd was the killer, I want first bite of the cherry. Murder still takes precedence over smuggling.'

'D'you reckon that Light's trip to Stockholm had anything to do with the smuggling, guv?'

'I don't know. What's so special about Sweden when it comes to smuggling?'

'Nothing that I can think of,' said Dave.

'To hell with it,' I said. 'The Lights and Todd have all disappeared, so there's nothing we can do this side of Monday at the earliest.'

'Unless Fielding's redbreasts spot them,' said Dave.

'Redbreasts?' I knew Dave was going to come up with a smart answer. And he did.

'Yeah, a guy called Fielding was the boss of the Bow Street Runners, guv, and they wore red waistcoats.'

I had given everyone, save a minimal staff, the weekend off in the hope that they would return refreshed and bursting with ideas.

On Monday morning, my thoughts returned to Mark Light, who had vanished from his office sometime since last Wednesday without telling his secretary where he was going.

'I suppose he could have gone to Paris again,' said Dave.

'Why Paris?'

'There's a picture of the Eiffel Tower on his office wall,' said Dave.

God preserve me! 'A lot of people have pictures of the Eiffel Tower, Dave,' I said patiently, 'or a little model of it on their mantelshelf. I've even seen it on T-shirts.'

'Well, he might have gone there, guv. He's been before. But one thing's certain, there's something a bit sussy going on here. Don't forget that both of them were away at the time of Kim's murder. They might have done it again.'

'Another smuggling run, I suppose,' I said gloomily. As Dave had said, it was certainly suspicious. Either that or one hell of a coincidence. But without good, hard evidence there was not a damned thing we could do about it. 'Let's go back over the conversation you had with the Swedish banker that Andrew Light went to see, Dave,' I said. 'What was his name?'

'Jan Johannsson, guv.'

'Yes, that's the guy. He confirmed that he'd been visited by Andrew Light, didn't he?' I asked. 'And he said that they'd spent most of Tuesday the eleventh together, discussing business, went sightseeing the following day and had dinner that evening. Light left for home the next morning, having been given a lift to Arlanda airport by Johannsson. Didn't you say something about Light having had dinner *with* Mr and Mrs Johannsson, Dave?'

'It was Light himself who told us that, guv,' said Dave, rapidly turning the pages of his pocketbook. 'And he stayed at a hotel called the Grand in Castelgaten, Stockholm, so he said.'

'There's something worrying me in all this, Dave,' I said. 'The only confirmation we've got is your conversation with Johannsson. The rest is hearsay. Light could be saying anything.'

'I don't think there's any reason to disbelieve Johannsson, guv,' said Dave.

'Perhaps not, but I think it's time we found out what else Light was doing over there,' I said, making one of my rare instant decisions. 'Colin, look up the times of flights to Stockholm and provisionally book two seats on the first one tomorrow morning. It's time we did our own leg-work. In the meantime, I'll see the commander and twist his arm to get authority.'

'Good as done, sir,' said Colin, and turned to his computer.

'Haven't you got a timetable, Colin?' I asked, slightly piqued that, unusually for him, Wilberforce hadn't leaped straight into action.

'Old hat, sir. It'll all be on a website.'

'A what?'

'Keep up, guv,' said Dave, 'it's computer technology.'

The commander was never one to make a decision if he could find someone else to make it for him and was known to the lads as the antithesis of Mr Micawber: always waiting for something to turn down.

He muttered a lot of mumbo-jumbo about budgets and overspend and finally, in a crisis of indecision, telephoned the deputy assistant commissioner.

And so we were eventually given permission to go, but not before the commander had added his usual caveat about not spending too much of the Commissioner's money.

Meanwhile, Colin Wilberforce had been busy on the phone to the Swedish police.

Nineteen

The following morning we were met at Arlanda airport by an English-speaking police officer complete with a car. The policeman introduced himself as *Kriminalinspektor* Lars Åsbrink of the Stockholm CID.

Our first call was to the Grand Hotel in Castelgaten and Åsbrink introduced us to the hotel manager, a man called Petersen. Åsbrink apparently knew him quite well.

I explained the reason for our visit and, after the obligatory coffee had been served, asked Petersen to confirm that Andrew Light had stayed at his hotel on the nights of Monday the tenth, Tuesday the eleventh and Wednesday the twelfth of June.

Petersen summoned his secretary and ordered a printout from the hotel computer. 'Yes, that is so,' he said, running his finger down the list. 'On those dates precisely.' He put the list aside and placed the tips of his fingers together. 'Ah, now, I remember something about him,' he continued thoughtfully. 'Yes, on the Wednesday night . . .' He leaned forward again, glancing briefly at the printout. '. . . yes, the twelfth, the fire alarm sounded. It was about two o'clock in the morning. It was a false alarm, but we didn't know that at the time. The staff had to go round all the bedrooms and rouse the guests. When the third floor waiter went into Mr Light's room he found that he was not alone.'

Dave laughed. 'I'll bet he was in bed with a gorgeous Swedish blonde with big boobs,' he said.

'No,' said Petersen, laughing also, 'not a woman. He was in bed with another man. But in Sweden no one worries about such things.'

*   *   *

187

'You seemed surprised by that, Harry,' said Lars Åsbrink as we ordered lunch at a rather splendid restaurant to which the Swedish policeman had taken us. 'Did you not know that your man was gay?'

'Yes, I was surprised, Lars,' I said. 'Our enquiries about Andrew Light suggest that he has an intense dislike of homosexuals.'

'That's very often a gay's attitude,' said Åsbrink. 'And then you find they're gay themselves.'

I told him what Gill Stow had said about Andrew Light's concern that Peter Stow might have been bisexual.

Åsbrink chuckled. 'Not all gays fancy all other gays,' he said, 'any more than all men fancy all women.'

'Well, we'll definitely have to talk to Johannsson now,' I said.

After lunch, all the more enjoyable because the Swedish police footed the bill, the three of us drove to the bank, a magnificent building in the heart of the commercial area of Stockholm.

Jan Johannsson's office was much grander than Klein's, and Johannsson more affable than his British counterpart. As Dave had said, he spoke perfect English.

'Gentlemen, welcome to Stockholm,' said Johannsson. He was tall and slim with snow-white hair, a flowing moustache and pale slender hands. 'Please sit down. Annika is preparing coffee. Nothing can start without coffee, eh?' he added with a twinkling eye.

I got straight to the point. 'I'm investigating a double murder in London, Mr Johannsson,' I began, as Annika dispensed coffee in chunky china cups.

'So I understand. I spoke to one of your officers on the telephone about it, what, three weeks ago?'

'That was me,' Dave put in.

'Well then, I told you what little there was to tell,' said Johannsson, addressing Dave. 'It was the wife of the man who came to see me, a Mr Light, who was murdered, was it not? So what else can I help you with?' He took a sip of his coffee, made a wry face and shouted something in his native tongue.

Annika reappeared, mumbled what I took to be an apology and placed a bowl of sugar on the table.

'She's trying to get me to give it up,' said Johannsson, spooning sugar into his coffee. 'She keeps telling me it's poison. But to get back to this Mr Light. He made what I thought was a strange request. He told me he was married and in the next breath said that he wanted to find the sex quarter that he'd heard so much about.'

'D'you think he was looking for, er . . . ?'

'A prostitute?' Johannsson gave a great bellow of a laugh. 'Why else would one want to go there? Unless he was a university anthropologist carrying out a study, well then, maybe.' He shrugged. 'But I don't think a banker would be doing that sort of survey, eh?'

I liked this man. He was much more relaxed than Klein, and had a wry sense of humour.

'And did you tell him where to find this area?'

'Yes, I did.' Johannsson laughed again. 'I think it's still in the same place,' he said, 'but I haven't been there since I was a student.'

'Did Mr Light talk much about his wife?' asked Dave.

I wasn't sure why Dave had posed that question but, as I've said before, he's a pretty shrewd detective.

'Hardly at all,' said Johannsson. 'Mind you, most of the day I was talking about London – I haven't been there for some time and he was asking about Stockholm.' He paused. 'We hardly mentioned business, once Klein's document was signed and out of the way, but Mr Light wasn't very interested in business anyway. In fact, I got the impression that he wasn't very knowledgeable about banking. But then he told me he was a lawyer. What do lawyers know about anything, eh? Some of them don't even know much about the law.'

'They know how to make money, though,' said Dave.

Johannsson gave a grave nod in Dave's direction. 'About that, young man,' he said, 'you are perfectly correct.'

'When did you first meet Andrew Light, Mr Johannsson?' I asked.

'When he came to Stockholm last month.'

'You'd not met him before?'

'No.'

'I'd like you to look at this photograph, then.' I handed Johannsson the print of Andrew Light that had been taken by one of Frank Mead's team. The Swede's reply proved that it hadn't been a waste of film.

'Who is this man?' Johannsson asked. 'I've never seen him before.'

'You're certain?'

'I'm positive.' Johannsson handed back the print.

'That,' I said, 'is Andrew Light.'

'I think you've made a mistake, Mr Brock.'

I passed over the best of the photographs that had been taken of Mark Light. 'And how about this one?'

'That's him. That's Andrew Light, the man who came to see me.'

'In fact, that's Andrew Light's brother Mark. He's a theatrical agent.'

'You are sure?'

'Absolutely.'

'Ha!' Johannsson drove a fist of one hand into the palm of his other. 'I knew that man didn't know the first thing about banking. Sex, that's all he was interested in. But why should Mr Klein send me a theatrical agent? Does he want me to make a film about banking?' It was sarcastic humour.

'Mr Klein obviously didn't know that Andrew Light hadn't come to Sweden, Mr Johannsson. If he'd known that Andrew had sent Mark Light in his place, he'd probably have sacked him.'

'He has sacked him,' said Johannsson, with some obvious degree of satisfaction.

'Oh, you know about that.'

'The world of international banking is a very closed one, Mr Brock. What's that lovely English expression: "You scratch my back and I'll scratch yours"? We couldn't work without that sort of mutual co-operation.'

190

'It works between police forces as well,' I said.

'We have to know about the sort of swindles that Light carried out with his bank's computer and the diamonds.' Suddenly Johannsson became very serious. 'You're the policeman, Mr Brock. Tell me, is this some sort of fraud that these Light men are trying on my bank?'

'I don't think so, Mr Johannsson, but at this stage I'm not absolutely sure.'

'Then perhaps I should ring Klein, eh?'

'I'd be grateful if you could leave that until I've had a chance to speak to him myself. Tomorrow, I hope.'

Now we had something to work on. Mark Light had impersonated his brother in Stockholm, and it followed therefore that Andrew Light had probably spent the same four days in Paris.

What I didn't know was why they should have done so. Maybe the switch in identity was connected with their smuggling ventures.

We would have to wait until Andrew Light returned from Paris. But I now had sufficient evidence to justify having a very serious talk with his brother Mark. Down at the nick. If we could find him.

'We have obtained conclusive proof that Andrew Light didn't go to Stockholm, Mr Klein,' I said, when we arrived at the banker's office early on Wednesday morning. 'He sent his brother Mark instead.'

'But that's ridiculous,' said Klein. 'I told you that he went there in order to have an agreement signed. Johannsson telephoned me and said that he'd been there, and I have the document.'

'We went to Stockholm yesterday for the express purpose of showing Mr Johannsson a photograph of Andrew Light,' I said patiently, 'and he told me that he'd never seen the man before. But when we showed him a photograph of Mark Light, he immediately identified him as his visitor.' I didn't mention the incident at the hotel.

'What the hell was he playing at?' For the first time,

191

the normally temperate Klein displayed anger. 'I tell you, Andrew Light brought that agreement back and gave it to me personally, the day after his wife was found murdered.' He paused, his fingers drumming on the edge of his desk. 'But why should you have gone to Stockholm? I mean, why did you find it necessary? Do you suspect him of something, other than the fraud which, I would remind you, we are not going to pursue?'

The questions tumbled out, but I declined to answer any of them, not yet anyway. And I had no intention of mentioning Light's association with Todd.

'Do you have that agreement handy, by any chance?' I asked.

By way of a reply, Klein pressed down the switch on his intercom and asked his secretary to find the document. 'I can't believe it,' he said, while we were waiting. 'But then I wouldn't have thought he was the sort of man who would have smuggled diamonds and defrauded the bank.' There was an air of resignation about him now. 'Just goes to show, doesn't it?'

Klein's secretary entered the room and, without a word, placed the agreement on his desk.

'Now, what am I looking for here?' Klein turned the pages of the document.

'Andrew Light's signature,' I said. 'Presumably it appears on there somewhere.'

'Yes, here it is.' Klein paused and adjusted his glasses as though he was not believing what he was seeing. 'This isn't his signature,' he said, outrage apparent in his voice. 'It's nothing like it.' He looked up, an expression of betrayal on his face. 'Why? What was the point of him sending his brother? Is it another sort of fraud?'

'No, I think it's much more serious than that, Mr Klein,' I said, although I had no intention of sharing my suspicions with him at this stage.

Klein appeared to be struggling with the concept that there could be something more serious than defrauding his bank. 'Are you going to arrest him?' he asked.

'I shall certainly want to question him when he returns home. If he returns.' I had a nasty feeling that Andrew Light was abroad somewhere, and that it was his intention to stay well clear of the English judicial system for the foreseeable future.

Dave had taken a statement from Klein in which the banker detailed the circumstances under which he had issued instructions to Andrew Light to go to Stockholm. He also included, at my behest, his firm belief that the signature of Andrew Light – on the document which had also been signed by Johannsson – was a forgery.

Thanks to the constraints of the Police and Criminal Evidence Act, we were not in a position to seize the document until we obtained a circuit judge's warrant, but Klein allowed us to take a photocopy.

'Are we going after Mark Light, guv?' asked Dave as he moved the gear lever into 'drive'.

'Too bloody true,' I said. 'We'll try his office first. Make for Fulham.'

Mark's secretary Melanie was her usual unhelpful self. 'He's not been in since you were here last,' she said, 'and I've three people waiting to see him.' She waved a limp hand towards a trio of hopefuls lined up on the chairs. It was the first time we'd seen any would-be actors in Light's office. 'I've tried ringing his home, but he's not there either.'

That was no more than I expected, and my hopes now rested with John Fielding's customs surveillance team.

'I've just telephoned your office, Harry,' said Fielding when I got through to him on my mobile. 'I'm sorry to say that by the time we put an observation on the Light brothers' home addresses, both had already gone. However, Mark Light turned up at his flat about an hour ago, stayed for ten minutes and then took off again. According to my chaps he's just joined the M20 at Swanley. I've a shrewd suspicion he's on his way to Dover. Is there a problem?'

'You could say that, John,' I said and explained briefly why it was imperative that Light wasn't allowed to leave the country.

'Nice one,' said Fielding with a chuckle. 'We were hoping to give him a free run outbound and catch him on the way in with contraband.' He paused. 'So what are you going to do?'

'I shall get the Special Branch people at Dover to nick him,' I said. 'What's he driving?'

'A Range Rover,' said Fielding, and gave me the index number.

'That can't be right, John. Are you sure? That number's the same as that on Duncan Ford's Range Rover which is still in police custody at Lambeth.' Well, I hoped it was.

'Absolutely,' said Fielding. 'It's an interesting twist though. More to do with my job than yours, I'd've thought.'

I gave Fielding my mobile number. 'Keep me posted, John, will you? If he changes direction, I'd like to know about it. And thanks for your help.'

'Take it as read,' said Fielding.

I next called Colin Wilberforce in the incident room and asked him to check that Duncan Ford's Range Rover was still at Lambeth. It was.

'Good. Get on to the National Ports Office at Heathrow, Colin. I want a priority all-ports warning issued for Mark Light. He's to be nicked.'

'What for, sir?' asked Colin. In the background I could hear him tapping away at his computer keyboard.

I paused only briefly. 'Suspicion of car ringing, but not to be questioned.' The fact that Light was driving a Range Rover with the same number plates as the one we'd got in our possession was good enough. For a start, anyway.

'As good as done, sir,' said Colin, 'and I'll get a digital likeness of him transmitted by computer.'

'If that makes you feel better, Colin, do it.' I hadn't a clue what he was talking about.

Although customs had suggested that Light was making for Dover, he had plenty of options, the Channel Tunnel at Folkestone for one. And if he'd spotted his 'tail', he might just try to shake them, change direction and make for the car ferry at Harwich, the port for the Hook of Holland. But there were also numerous small airports in the south-east from where he could fly abroad.

However, I was putting my faith in John Fielding's surveillance team to tell me if he changed course.

Twenty

While we were waiting to see what happened about Mark Light, I sent Frank Mead to Horseferry Road court to get search warrants for Andrew Light's house – not that I had much hope of finding anything incriminating there – and for Mark Light's flat and his office at Fulham.

'What do we hope to find at Durbridge Gardens that the SOCOs didn't find, guv?' asked Dave, lighting a cigarette. He pushed the packet across the desk in my direction.

'It's what might have been put there *after* the SOCOs did their search,' I said. 'The murder weapon's got to be somewhere.'

'Bottom of the Thames, I should think. And I reckon it was Todd who put it there.' That was the trouble with Dave, he was a realist.

An hour later, a detective inspector from the Kent police Special Branch unit at Dover telephoned. 'We've nicked this Mark Light guy, sir,' he said. 'He's currently being held at Dover nick. What d'you want us to do with him?'

'I'm sending an escort,' I said.

'They *will* be pleased,' said the DI. 'He's an arrogant little bastard.'

In the absence of Frank Mead, still trying to charm some warrants out of the district judge at Horseferry Road court, I sent for his deputy and told him to organize an escort to bring Mark Light back to London.

I glanced at my watch. 'Time for a quick bite of lunch, Dave.'

'About time, guv,' said Dave. 'I'm bloody starving.'

* * *

196

Frank Mead was waiting with a clutch of warrants when we got back to the office. It was now one thirty.

'What d'you want me to do with these, Harry?' he asked.

During lunch Dave and I had been mulling over which address we should do first. Sometimes it's advantageous to organize teams and hit all the targets at the same time. But that's necessary only when each address is occupied and there's a possibility of a quick phone call warning the others that the Old Bill are on their way. The one thought at the back of my mind was that Mark Light might have used his one statutory telephone call to tell Melanie he'd been arrested, not that I thought she was bright enough to do anything but sympathize.

'Dave and I will do his Fulham office first, Frank,' I said.

If Melanie was surprised to see us again, it didn't show. Perhaps she'd forgotten that we'd been there that morning. 'Hello,' she said, a vacant expression on her face. The would-be actors had gone, presumably having exited stage left.

We showed Melanie the warrant, but her only reaction was to ask if we wanted a cup of coffee. But I knew that it would be instant and declined the offer.

The inner office – the one occupied by Mark when, rarely it seemed, he was there – was as sparsely furnished as Melanie's: a desk and chair, and another chair for clients. And a six-foot-high locked metal cabinet.

'Who's got the key to this cupboard?' Dave asked.

'Mark usually keeps it,' said Melanie, 'but he sometimes leaves it under the desk.' She moved Light's chair and bent down, running her hand along a ledge in the knee-well. 'Oh good, it's here.' She handed me the key and looked quite pleased with herself, a pleasure that Mark would probably not have shared.

'How very careless of him,' I said, really meaning 'how very helpful of him' in that we wouldn't have to force it open.

Dave unlocked the cabinet. It was stuffed with papers, most of which would probably prove to be of no interest to us. There were a few box files, a small cash box that a kid could have opened, a badminton racket and a few disparate books lined up on the top shelf. 'This guy's got a weird idea of what's valuable,' commented Dave as he started to empty the contents on to the desk. 'This for example,' he said as he unearthed one very old volume of the *Encyclopaedia Britannica* and put it on the desk. 'I wonder where the other twenty-seven are.'

'How d'you know there are another twenty-seven, Dave?'

'I don't,' said Dave, 'I'm guessing.'

I opened the large book. The centre of the pages had been carefully cut out to leave a cavity. In the cavity, wrapped in clingfilm, rested a .38 Walther pistol. Beneath it was Duncan Ford's passport.

With Mark Light now in custody and soon to be on his way back to London, I was suddenly in one hell of a hurry. There was no way we could keep him locked up on a charge of driving a vehicle with false number plates, thanks to the liberal bleeding-heart brigade and the bent lawyers who thought that it was the divine right of every villain to be bailed, no matter how grave his crime.

We went from Fulham direct to Fingerprint Branch and pleaded with a senior FPO to do a quick examination. But it was in vain.

'There's not a single identifiable mark on this,' he said, returning the pistol to me. 'Either the user wore gloves, or it's been wiped clean. And expertly at that.'

Expertly, eh? I immediately thought of Todd. Again.

I was stymied. There was no point in seeking the help of the ballistics expert at Lambeth. No rounds had been left at the murder scene with which we could compare a test firing; the killer had been careful to extract them from the wall in the sitting room at Durbridge Gardens and from the wardrobe door in the master bedroom there.

But it might not be the murder weapon. Mark Light could

be keeping it for self-protection. Some characters in the bootlegging business can be very nasty. Like Danny Todd for example.

But I did have one advantage. I now knew that Mark Light had been in Stockholm at the time of the murders and might not have known that the killer had, in fact, removed those rounds.

By the time we reached Charing Cross police station, just off Trafalgar Square, Mark Light was already there. And so was his solicitor: fifty-ish, spotted bow tie and a purple-veined nose.

The solicitor went on the offensive immediately. 'Chief Inspector,' he began, 'I wish to know why my client has been arrested on a ridiculously trumped-up charge of possessing his own car.'

'It's not his car,' I said. 'But that apart, your client was in possession of a vehicle identical in every particular – including the index mark – to one currently held in police custody. The vehicle we have is registered to Duncan Ford of flat two, thirteen Sawbridge Street, Pimlico, as is the vehicle which was being driven by Mr Light when he was arrested at Dover this morning. In other words, both vehicles appear to be the same. However, I'm sure you'll appreciate that this interview must be put on a formal footing.'

I turned to Dave. 'Administer the caution, Sergeant.' I had to let Dave do it. I could never remember the new version, even though it was now quite a few years old, and I'd lost the little card that it was written on. I'll really have to get another one, just in case I'm ever in this sort of situation on my own. Mind you, most of the villains I've come across would be able to help me out.

'I'm advising my client to say nothing about this, Chief Inspector, and I demand he be released immediately. This is obviously some administrative error and certainly nothing that should concern the criminal law. I suggest you're taking a sledgehammer to crack a nut.'

I could have made a facetious remark about nuts at this

stage, but decided that the best course of action was to ignore Light's solicitor completely.

'Show Mr Light the exhibit, Sergeant,' I said.

Dave took the pistol from his briefcase and laid it on the table.

'This afternoon, I executed a search warrant at your business premises in Fulham, Mr Light,' I said, 'and this weapon was found.'

Mark Light sneered. 'Says you. I've never seen that in my life before. It's obviously a frame-up of some sort. Everyone knows about police planting evidence.'

'I really don't see what that has to do with the alleged offence for which my client was arrested.' The solicitor was noticeably less hostile now, having clearly been wrong-footed by this dramatic turn of events, but presumably felt that he had to say something to justify his presence.

'It has nothing whatever to do with it,' I said, taking a sheet of paper from Dave. 'And to answer your client's allegation that the weapon was planted on his premises – not that it really warrants rebuttal – I have here a photocopy of a statement made by Miss Melanie Talbot, Mr Light's secretary, in which she testifies to having seen this officer' – I waved a hand in Dave's direction – 'remove the weapon from inside a volume of the *Encyclopaedia Britannica* which was in a locked cupboard in Mr Light's office. Miss Talbot gave us the key to that cabinet. The defence will, of course, be entitled to a copy of that statement in due course.'

'Stupid bloody woman,' said Light angrily. 'I expect she put it there.'

'I don't think she's that stupid,' said Dave mildly.

I went out on a limb. 'This weapon has been test-fired at the forensic science laboratory and the ballistics officer has high hopes of making a positive comparison with the rounds and shell cases found at the scene of the murders of Kim Light and Duncan Ford.' I sat back and waited for a reaction. The solicitor had the depressed look of a man whose client hadn't told him everything.

'I was in Stockholm when that happened,' said Light.

'Really? But you told me on several previous occasions that you were in Paris.'

'I lied,' said Light.

'So how did you come into possession of this weapon?' I gestured at the Walther.

There was a long pause before Mark Light spoke again. 'Andrew asked me to take care of it for him,' he said.

'Do you have a firearms certificate for this weapon?' I asked. I knew damned well that he hadn't, but it had to be asked.

'Of course not,' said Light with a sneer.

'In that case you will be charged with its unlawful possession,' I said. That would do for a start. Whether it was the murder weapon, and whether Mark Light was subsequently arraigned as a principal in the commission of the murders, or as an accessory, was something I still had to prove, and the erudite brains of the Crown Prosecution Service would have to resolve. It all depended on an interview with Andrew Light, if we ever got hold of him.

'I wasn't in possession of it,' said Light sarcastically. 'You found it in my cupboard. So you said.'

'It's what is called constructive possession,' I replied.

Sitting beside Mark Light, his solicitor nodded wearily, probably wondering why he'd got involved in what, at first, seemed to be a fairly simple matter. Once Her Majesty's Customs and Excise put in their two-penn'orth, he'd probably do a runner.

At Horseferry Road court the next morning, Mark Light was remanded in custody despite a lukewarm plea for bail by his solicitor. I got the impression that the lawyer's heart wasn't really in it but, even so, he said that he would make an immediate bail application to a circuit judge. I wished him luck.

'Mark Light's making a bail application before a judge in Court Thirteen at the Bailey this afternoon, sir,' said Colin

201

Wilberforce. 'The Crown Prosecution Service are sending a mouthpiece to oppose.'

'Anyone we know?' I asked.

Colin ran his finger down the open page of his day book. 'No one I've ever heard of, sir,' he said, and read off a name. I'd never heard of him either.

And so we trooped up to the Central Criminal Court at half past two.

A young woman with a very white wig began an impassioned plea for her client's release, larded with the offer to surrender his passport and listing the names of potential sureties. Halfway through this eloquent appeal for Mark Light's freedom, the judge, a crusty-looking fellow who must have been nearing seventy, glanced up and said, 'There'll be no bail in this case.'

'Your Honour makes it very difficult for me to continue,' said the young lady barrister haltingly, clearly flustered by this judicial intervention.

'That was my intention,' growled the judge. He knew that possession of a firearm was usually a precursor to more serious charges, particularly when the possession charge was brought by a senior officer from the Serious Crime Group at New Scotland Yard.

Next morning, Dave and I journeyed to Brixton prison, where Mark Light was being held on remand, and interviewed him once again.

But it was going to be a tricky interrogation.

'I don't believe your statement that you went to Stockholm instead of your brother,' I began.

'Well I did.'

'D'you seriously expect me to believe that you, a theatrical agent, could delude an experienced banker into thinking you were in the same profession? It won't wash. What interests me is why you should be making up this story.'

'But I did go to Stockholm,' protested Mark.

I knew that of course, but I was trying to lure Mark into

202

telling me what really happened. 'And this story about your brother Andrew having given you the pistol for safe-keeping is all nonsense. You were having trouble with Danny Todd, and thought you might need the weapon for self-protection.'

'How the hell d'you know about him?' I had clearly stunned Mark with that comment. Just as I had shaken his brother when I mentioned Todd's name.

'We raided the warehouse at Wandsworth and there's now a warrant out for his arrest for smuggling tobacco and alcohol,' I said. 'What's more, he was careless enough to store your number in the memory of the telephone there, along with your brother's and Duncan Ford's. So there we have it, a conspiracy to smuggle. And you're in the middle of it.'

Mark listened to this in silence. Perhaps he thought my only interest was in the smuggling and not the murders.

But I quickly disillusioned him. 'But I'm not interested in that except to work out how it bears on the murders. What happened? Did you, Andrew and Todd have a bust-up with Ford? Was he cheating, or had he had enough and wanted out? Going to grass on the three of you to customs for a massive reward, and your only answer was to kill him? And Kim just happened to be there. Who was it, Mark? Who pulled the trigger? You or Todd or Andrew?'

It suddenly dawned on the oh-so-clever Mark that he wasn't so clever after all, and that we knew a lot more than he'd thought.

'It was Andrew,' he suddenly blurted out.

So much for brotherly love.

'Why?' I asked.

'I don't know,' said Mark. 'You'd better ask him.'

'Where is your brother now?'

'I haven't the faintest idea,' said Mark with a sneer. 'And don't ask me where Todd is because I don't know that either.'

Twenty-one

'Now that we know Mark Light went to Stockholm, Dave, it must follow that Andrew Light went to Paris. The question is why.'

'Perhaps there's some guy in Paris who's masterminding the whole smuggling operation, guv,' said Dave, 'and it was Andrew who had to go because Mark couldn't handle it.'

'Maybe, but we'll start where we should have started in the first place.' I was annoyed with myself that I hadn't made the basic enquiries that I should have done in the first place. It was then that I recalled one of my mother's favourite sayings. Try to cut corners, Harry, she would say, and you'll finish up going the long way round. I never knew what it meant. Until now.

We drove to the Eurostar terminal at Waterloo station and I told the manager responsible for bookings what I wanted.

'No problem,' he said. 'Should be able to give you an answer in seconds.' He turned to his computer terminal and began to tap the keys. 'Yes,' he said, speaking slowly as he read the details from the display on his screen. 'On the tenth of June an Andrew Light was booked on the 9014 Paris service leaving London at oh-nine-twenty-three. He returned from Paris on Tuesday, arriving London at twenty-oh-nine, and went back to Paris again the following morning, leaving here on the service at oh-five-fifteen.' He looked up. 'That's the first one out. And he came back to London again on Thursday the thirteenth by the 9013 service from Gare du Nord arriving Waterloo at ten forty-three hours.'

'Let me get this straight,' I said. 'He went out on Monday

morning, came back on Tuesday night, out again Wednesday morning and finally returned on the Thursday morning.'

'That's it,' said the manager.

'But did he actually travel?' Dave asked.

The manager smiled. 'Well, someone did,' he said. 'But I can't tell you whether it was the person in whose name the tickets were issued. He might have bought the tickets for someone else. Does that help?'

'Yes, I think it does,' I said, trying hard not to display my delight at this latest revelation. But, knowing my luck, there would be some logical explanation for this latest twist. 'D'you have an address for him?'

The manager turned to his screen again and then glanced back at me. 'Twenty-seven Durbridge Gardens, Notting Hill. Paid by credit card.'

'Could you let me have a printout of all that. It's possible that it's relevant to my enquiry.'

'No problem,' said the manager.

'I do believe we've cracked it, Dave,' I said when we were back at the office.

'There's only one problem, guv,' said Dave gloomily.

'Which is?'

'We don't know where the bastard's gone.'

But then we had what turned out to be a stroke of luck.

'Peter Stow reported his wife missing at eleven o'clock last night, sir,' said Colin Wilberforce. 'At Notting Hill nick.'

'How did you know that?'

'They pushed it straight through to us, sir.'

'But how did they know we were interested?' I was puzzled that the information had come through to my office. We dealt with murders, not missing persons. Not unless the missing person was found murdered.

'I put the Stows on the computer, guv,' said Dave. 'I thought they were sufficiently close to the Lights to warrant an interest.'

'Well done.' I always knew that Dave Poole was a good

detective and he kept proving it. 'In that case, I think we'll have a word with Mr Stow. Right now.'

'If you want to see my wife, she's gone missing,' said Stow as he opened the door. It was an unemotional statement that implied that he wasn't too distressed about her disappearance.

'So I understand,' I said, as we followed him into the sitting room.

'How did you know?' Stow stopped and turned.

'You filed a report at Notting Hill police station late last night, Mr Stow, and anyone who is even remotely connected with a murder enquiry is of interest to us.'

'*How* are we connected?' Stow forced an unconvincing laugh. 'You're not suspecting Gill or me of being involved in some way, are you?'

'Certainly not. If I remember correctly, you and your wife were enjoying yourselves at the Passion House in Amsterdam.'

Stow forced a smile. 'Indeed we were,' he said.

'So, when did your wife go missing, Mr Stow?' Dave asked.

'Yesterday.'

'But you made your report at eleven o'clock last night. How did you know that she wasn't going to arrive here after that?' I asked, pretending that the whole thing was a mystery to me.

'She's gone to Paris to meet up with Andrew Light.'

'How d'you know that?'

'I don't know, but I'm bloody sure that's where she is.'

'Any idea where in Paris?'

'Not the faintest. And I'll tell you this much, I don't bloody well care.'

'I take it this came as a surprise to you, Mr Stow.'

'Not really. She's been carrying on with Andrew ever since our holiday in the Algarve last year, as I was with Kim.' Stow was quite open about the dual affairs. 'But

206

when Kim died we thought we ought to call it off. Out of respect, really.'

I suppose I should have been surprised at such hypocrisy, but I wasn't. Gill had been cheerfully hopping in and out of Andrew's bed while Peter had been having fun with Kim, but suddenly the Stows had got all pious because one of their quartet had been murdered. Somehow I doubted that.

'What was the name of the hotel that Mark Light claimed to have stayed at in Paris, Dave?'

'The Hotel New York, guv. Somewhere near the British Embassy, so he said.'

'So, given that Mark was in Stockholm, it looks likely that Andrew stayed there during that period. In which case, he might be there again.'

Dave rang his French-speaking mate in Special Branch and a quarter of an hour later got a call back.

'He's there, guv,' he said, and chuckled, 'together with a woman calling herself *Mrs* Light. And they're booking out tomorrow.'

Dave's next call was to our friendly manager at the Eurostar terminal at Waterloo.

'Mr and Mrs Andrew Light –' Dave chuckled at that – 'are due in at Waterloo at seventeen-oh-nine tomorrow, guv, and it doesn't stop at Ashford, fortunately.'

We got to Waterloo by five o'clock on Saturday afternoon, which gave us just enough time to have a quick word with customs, and to make our number with the Special Branch officers stationed there and explain what we were about.

'Dave and I will stay near the controls,' I said to the SB sergeant, 'but out of sight. If this guy spots us, he's likely to do a runner.' The last thing I wanted was to finish up chasing Andrew Light across the tracks outside the station in a scene reminiscent of the pursuit of an escaping prisoner – played by John Mills in the wartime film *Waterloo Road*. 'Take this,' I added. 'It's a photograph of him, just in case, God forbid, we should miss him.'

The passengers started to drift through just after a quarter past five. I spotted Andrew Light almost immediately. A pace behind him was Gill Stow. Each of them was towing a wheeled suitcase.

We waited until he was in the act of waving his British passport at the immigration officer and then stepped up to him. I suppose tomorrow's newspapers will say that we'd 'swooped'.

'Andrew Light, I'm arresting you for the murder of Kim Light and Duncan Ford. Sergeant . . .'

Dave rattled off the caution and took hold of Light's arm in a physical indication of arrest.

Beside him, Gill Stow's mouth opened in shock and she let go of the handle of her wheeled case so that it clattered on the floor. '*Andrew!*' was all she managed to utter.

To say that Andrew Light was stunned would be a monumental understatement. His face went white with rage. 'What the bloody hell are you talking about?' he spluttered. 'This is harassment.'

He was shouting now, and little groups of passengers had stopped to stare at the cameo being played out at the passport desk.

'I shouldn't make a fuss, sir,' said Dave.

'Don't make a fuss!' roared Light. 'You arrest an innocent citizen and you have the damned audacity to tell me not to make a fuss.' He made a sudden lunge at me, pushing me violently to one side, and shaking off Dave's restraining hand at the same time, before running towards the customs area. The Special Branch sergeant dived at Light's fleeing legs in an attempt at a rugby tackle, missed, and finished up sprawling on the floor, muttering the sort of obscene oaths that a discipline board would doubtless construe as conduct likely to bring the police force into disrepute.

Recovering quickly, we gave chase, Dave leaping over the still-prostrate SB officer. We legged it through the red channel watched by a couple of bemused customs officers and up the ramp towards the door leading to the taxi rank. By now we were only two or three yards behind Light who, clearly, was fitter than we'd given him credit for. But instead of making for the exit, he turned back into the waiting area for departing passengers. Shouldering them roughly aside, he sprinted – two at a time – up the moving staircase towards the main concourse of Waterloo station.

Once at the top, he ran towards that end of the station that led ultimately to Waterloo Road, pushing passengers violently out of the way in his desperate attempt to escape.

Dave was nearer to him than I was, but then Dave – a mere twenty-eight years of age – is younger and fitter than me. With a supreme effort, he launched his fifteen stone the last few feet and landed, fair and square, on Light's back, bringing him crashing to the ground.

As we laid hands on him, Light began to struggle again, but between us, Dave and I were able to restrain him, Dave eventually managing to handcuff him. A few passengers stopped to stare at the unseemly scuffle.

A railway constable appeared. 'And what's going on here, then?' he demanded officiously.

I produced my warrant card and waved it at him. 'DCI Brock,' I gasped.

'Ah! Want any help, sir?' asked the constable without actually stirring himself too much.

'Yes,' I said, 'you can assist me to take this prisoner to the police office so that my sergeant here can arrange transport.' I hadn't visualized that Light would cut up rough, and we'd travelled to Waterloo in the car we normally used. But a fractious prisoner was going to have to be conveyed in a police van. Having got this far, I didn't want to lose him again. If I did, I knew it would be the last we'd see of him.

We lodged Andrew Light at Belgravia police station, sufficiently far away from Charing Cross, where his brother was being held. I didn't want him learning of Mark's arrest until I was ready to tell him myself.

Predictably, Light's first request was for a solicitor, and being in the trade, so to speak, he was not prepared to make do with a duty solicitor. Instead, he sent for a smart City lawyer who, he said, was a close friend of his. Recalling what Gill Stow had said about Andrew Light, I wondered if he'd ever made a pass at the lawyer's wife.

It was now half past six and the solicitor, who, fortunately for Andrew Light and me had just returned from a round of golf, had guaranteed his arrival within the hour.

And so, at half past seven, the four of us – Light, his solicitor, Dave and I – sat down in an interview room and I started to question our prisoner about the killing of his common-law wife, and one Duncan Ford.

'Yesterday afternoon, your brother Mark was arrested at Dover and brought to London.'

'Arrested? What for?' From the look on his face, it was evident that that piece of information had taken Andrew Light by surprise. He'd probably thought that we were going to talk about his own arrest.

'He was in possession of a vehicle with false number plates,' I said. In fact, we didn't yet know if Mark's vehicle was the bogus one or whether it was the one we were holding at Lambeth. Not that it mattered now; compared with the murders, that was a minor matter. 'We subsequently searched his office at Fulham, where we found a Walther .38 handgun. Mark told us that you had given it to him for safekeeping.'

I'd hoped that Andrew Light would say something incriminating at this stage, but he'd been a lawyer too long to make damaging admissions. He knew perfectly well that the prosecution had to prove its case. And right now, I was the prosecution. 'I don't know anything about it,' he said dismissively. 'Mark must have had some sort of aberration. I really don't know where he got that idea from.'

I glanced down at my list of prepared questions. 'According to my enquiries, you went to Paris on Monday the tenth of June and returned during the evening of the following day. I put it to you that you then murdered your wife and Duncan Ford before returning to Paris on the morning of Wednesday the twelfth of June, and stayed there until your final return to this country on Thursday the thirteenth.'

Let's see how you get out of that one, sport.

A slow smile spread over Light's face. 'My dear Chief Inspector,' he said, 'I was in Stockholm for the whole of that period. You can check with Johannsson, the man I went to see, and you can check with old man Klein at the bank I used to work for. It was my brother who went to Paris, a short break for which I paid. But I told you all that before.'

'Oh, so you did.' I looked down at my papers, turning over a page or two and putting on a show of being confused. 'My mistake. Yes, it was Mark who went to Paris and you who went to Stockholm.' I gave Light an apologetic glance.

But I happen to know that you're a lying bastard.

Light sat back and folded his arms, a smug expression on his face that implied he was dealing with a stupid bloody copper who was no match for his forensic mind.

'What did you think of the entrance hall of the bank you visited in Stockholm, Mr Light?' I asked, still shuffling my papers, and deliberately trying to convey that I was stalling while I worked out what to ask next.

Although momentarily puzzled by the question, Light was far from being put out by it 'Much like any other,' he said, waving a hand of dismissal. 'Very ordinary.'

I arranged my papers in order as I asked the next question. 'But that huge fountain was rather imposing, wasn't it?' I adopted a conversational tone and smiled.

'Yes, that was quite a striking feature, I thought.' Light was very relaxed now and probably imagined I'd run out of taxing questions.

How the hell hadn't he yet worked out that I'd been there? And there wasn't a fountain, just an atrium.

'Refresh my memory, Mr Light. Where did you stay in Stockholm?'

'I told you that, too. It was the Grand Hotel in Castelgaten.' Light still had the air of a man able to talk his way out of

Mark's allegation that he had given him the pistol, and probably thought I'd been satisfied with his answer.

'Ah yes, so you did.' I looked at my aide-mémoire again, not that I needed to. 'During the night of the twelfth–thirteenth of June, I believe there was a fire alarm in that hotel. At about two in the morning.'

'I don't remember anything about that.' For the first time since the interview had begun, Light looked a little disconcerted. Wary, would perhaps be a better word.

'The staff at the hotel recall having to rouse you to go down to the assembly point. The porter who came to your room states that he found you in bed with another person.'

Light laughed again. 'Oh yes, I do remember that now. She was a rather gorgeous Swedish blonde I'd met in the bar. And very energetic she was too.' He contrived a dreamy expression as he pretended to recall the incident.

'The porter was adamant that the other person was a man.'

For a moment or two there was utter silence in the austere room as the sudden realization dawned on Light that he'd been led into a trap, ironically a trap that had been set unwittingly by his own brother. 'The stupid little bastard,' he said bitterly.

'You were not in Stockholm at all, Mr Light,' I said. 'It was your brother. We interviewed Mr Johannsson and showed him a photograph of Mark, whom he positively identified as the person who went to see him.'

'I advise you not to answer any more questions, Andrew.' The solicitor, speaking for the first time since the start of the interview, interrupted sharply. He'd appreciated, even if Andrew Light hadn't, that his client was now on very dangerous ground.

'That may be your advice,' I said, 'but I shall continue to ask them.'

'It'll be to no avail,' said the solicitor hopefully.

But he knew as well as I did that when the case reached court – and there was no doubt in my mind now that it would reach court – my evidence of questions to which, *on each occasion*, the accused made no reply would be far more damning than testimony of a blanket refusal.

'The rounds taken from your house at Durbridge Gardens have been compared with the weapon found in your brother's possession—' I began, but got no further.

'There weren't any rounds left there,' said Light smugly, 'so you can't—'

I never thought it would work, but suddenly Light realized what he had said and lapsed into silence. From the expression on his face it was obvious that he wished to God he'd never said it. But it was too late. *It was on the tape.*

He knew and I knew that apart from the investigation team, the only other person who could have known that the rounds had been removed was the murderer himself. Light slumped in his chair, conscious that he'd just implicated himself, but for the moment I ignored his damning admission.

'You claimed never to have heard of Duncan Ford,' I went on, 'but the vehicle which was in your brother's possession when he was arrested was registered in Ford's name. I have to tell you also that Mark is being investigated by Her Majesty's Customs and Excise in respect of the illegal importation of alcohol and tobacco, together with Danny Todd, with whom he is suspected of conspiring.' I didn't mention to Andrew Light that he was also under customs investigation. The waters were muddy enough as it was.

'I don't see the relevance of that,' said the solicitor. I think he had sensed that his client had as good as admitted to the crime, but I suppose he felt he had to say something.

Not that I was surprised. He was not as conversant with the twists and turns of the plot as I was, and neither was his client.

'Your brother Mark claimed that the relationship between him and Duncan Ford was purely a professional one,' I said, ignoring the lawyer's observation. 'That Ford was an actor and Mark his theatrical agent. But I suggest that it went much further than that.' I took a gamble that the letter from 'Eve' that we'd found in Duncan Ford's flat had actually been written by Mark Light. Added to the Poison perfume found in Mark's flat, DC Appleby's enquiries had revealed that Mark's full name was Mark *Evelyn* Light. 'Mark was a practising homosexual, wasn't he, and Duncan Ford was his lover?'

Light nodded. 'Yes.'

'Andrew!' The solicitor laid a cautionary hand on his client's arm, and addressing me, said, 'I don't see what this has to do with Mr Light. Mr *Andrew* Light, that is.'

Then it came to me, what I'd been searching for all along: a motive. Even so, it was to be a wild sortie into the unknown.

'But one day Mark introduced Duncan Ford to you and Kim. Kim was a highly sexed woman and she saw Duncan Ford, a homosexual with a film star's good looks, as a challenge.'

I'd met women like Kim. Women who regarded the seduction of a homosexual man as the ultimate test of their own feminine allure. They would flirt outrageously, deploying every artifice at their disposal in their determination to overcome his innate carnal preferences. And not giving a damn about the consequences.

'Some women love a challenge like that,' I continued, 'and Kim set out to seduce Duncan Ford, and she triumphed so successfully that they started an affair that continued until Kim's death. He would spend time with her in your bed as often as he could.' *Come on, Light, get spiteful.*

'And your frequent absences on business presented them both with the ideal opportunity,' I went on. 'Kim couldn't get enough of him, could she? I'll bet it was the best sex she'd ever had.' I continued to press him into losing his temper. 'You didn't mind your wife having sex with other men – so long as they were straight and she was discreet – but then Steve Wilson confronted you with the information that she was nothing more than a tart, a common prostitute. You even managed to live with that for a while, but you took grave exception to her making love to a homosexual.

214

Perhaps you thought she might infect you with some nasty disease as a result.

'As for your brother Mark, he was beside himself at the prospect of losing his lover to a woman, wasn't he? In fact, I suggest that he became irrationally jealous. And so did you, because you'd lost control of her. It was all right when she was sleeping with Peter Stow next door, and you were having sex with Gill Stow. You knew you could put a stop to that any time you liked. But Kim's propensity for sleeping with anyone who paid her, and her obsession with Duncan Ford was a different ball game . . . to coin a phrase. Kim just wouldn't give up, would she? As a result, your insane, unreasoning jealousy – yours and Mark's – combined to blind the pair of you to the extent that the only solution you could come up with was to kill them. And that's exactly what you and your brother conspired to do.'

'Yes, damn you!' Andrew Light shouted the words at me and, white of face, slumped in his chair, defeated. There had been but a short pause before his answer came, and I can only assume that in a moment of inner torment he had suddenly tired of the lies, the deceit and the attempts to sustain the web he had woven.

From the Andrew Light I had first met on the day the bodies of his wife and Ford had been discovered, when he put on a compelling performance as the bereaved widower, through the jousting, the overweening confidence and his undisguised contempt for us mere dim policemen, he had now been reduced to a man whose arsenal had been emptied of all its weapons. In front of me sat a murderer who, like so many other killers, had tried to be too clever by half.

As for Light's friend and solicitor – now doodling aimlessly on his legal pad – he had the appearance of a man who realized that the case against his client was as good as over before it had even begun.

And when Andrew Light opted to make a full statement, his lawyer just shrugged.

215

Twenty-Two

Back we went to Brixton prison.

In view of the seriousness of what I was about to put to Mark Light, I was legally bound to ask him if he wanted a solicitor present. To my surprise he declined.

'Your brother has made a full statement, a copy of which you are entitled to have,' I said once the tape-recorder had been turned on.

Mark Light took some minutes to read the lengthy type-written document, and then he read it again. In it Andrew Light had made clear that Mark had been a willing party to the commission of the murders.

'It was Kim's fault,' Mark Light began. *Well, that was original.* 'Duncan was besotted by the damned woman. She didn't care who she destroyed so long as she got what she wanted. And she wanted Duncan. He and I had a long-term relationship, several years in fact. But then he met Kim, and that was my mistake. I introduced them and she set her cap at him. He was a committed gay and that made her all the more determined. Poor Duncan didn't really stand a chance. She was going to get him into bed with her if it was the last thing she did.' He smiled as he realized the aptness of that comment. 'And it was.' He paused. 'I pleaded with Duncan to give her up, but he wouldn't listen. In fact, he told me that he wanted nothing more to do with me.'

'And so you and Andrew decided to murder them both.'

'Yes. But we arranged it carefully. I went to Stockholm in Andy's place. He said there'd be nothing to it. I was only supposed to get some document signed.' The offhand way in which Mark was talking made it sound as though he was

216

proud of how clever he and his brother had been. 'I honestly didn't think we'd get away with it – it was a bit risky, after all – but Andy said that he'd not met Johannsson before and the Swede wouldn't be any the wiser. And if I didn't understand something that was raised, Andy said I could always blame it on the interpreter's translation. But then I discovered that the bloody man spoke perfect English. Nevertheless I muddled my way through.

'Andy, meanwhile, went to Paris, claiming to be me. But as he said in his statement' – he waved a hand casually at the pile of paper on the table – 'he came back on the Tuesday. You probably know that he and Kim had a very open relationship, and he pretended to her that he didn't mind her having an affair with Duncan. As a matter of fact, he encouraged it, and suggested that while he was away she should invite Duncan to Durbridge Gardens to sleep with her. But just to make certain that Duncan *was* there, he rang Kim on Monday as he was leaving Paris. Having established that, he came back. Like he said' – again Mark waved at the statement – 'he went in and out of the back door of his house. Apparently he's got a neighbour who lives opposite who sees everything.

'He shot each of them in the head with a single round,' Mark continued in matter-of-fact tones, 'and later gave me the pistol to get rid of. Like a fool I hung on to it. I should have chucked the bloody thing in the river.' He shook his head at his own idiocy.

'And the kitchen window?' I asked.

'Oh yes. Andy said that he'd removed that to make it look like a burglary.' Mark continued almost as if he had been an innocent observer of the shocking events he was recounting instead of a willing participant. 'Anyway, before going back to Paris, he went to Duncan's flat – I'd given him my key – and removed all his paperwork and his floppy disks, that sort of thing, so that there'd be no trace of our association.'

To say nothing of your bootlegging operation.

'Your brother missed this though, didn't he?' I produced the letter signed 'Eve' that, even now, still held

217

the faint aroma of Poison perfume. 'You did write this, didn't you?'

Mark gave a listless nod and smiled ruefully. 'Yes.' Then came a flash of candour. 'We honestly didn't think you'd make all the enquiries you did, and I realize now that it was bloody silly of me to pick up that boy in Stockholm and take him back to my room at the hotel.'

It was a finely tuned conspiracy that had been an attempt to confuse the investigation, and it might well have succeeded but for a gay Swedish boy and a fire alarm.

It was, however, one of the worst cases of cold-blooded execution that I'd come across, made more chilling by the unemotional way in which each brother had recounted his part in the plot.

Our first glimmer of success had come when we learned that Andrew Light had a brother, something that he had not mentioned and probably hoped we wouldn't discover.

The second break came when we found out that the 'Andrew Light' who had been staying in a Stockholm hotel had been found in bed *with a man*. That was sheer stupidity on Mark Light's part, particularly as the Stows' lurid accounts of their sexual encounters with Andrew and Kim Light had made plain how unlikely it was that Andrew was bisexual.

Furthermore, neither of the brothers had expected that the police would actually go to Sweden armed with photographs, or that we would check the finer details of their travel arrangements with Eurostar at Waterloo, the Hotel New York in Paris and the Grand Hotel in Stockholm.

This time television had been on my side. If a murder has to be solved in two hours, the producers of so-called authentic police drama don't have the time to include all the dull, painstaking, time-consuming nitty-gritty of solid detective work.

Andrew and Mark Light certainly didn't know much about it.

A few months later, the Light brothers were arraigned at the

Central Criminal Court, each facing an indictment for the murders of Duncan Ford and Kim Light.

We knew from our cursory search of the Wandsworth warehouse that the Light brothers, Duncan Ford and Danny Todd had been involved in smuggling, and customs had done a superb job in gathering evidence of a conspiracy that would hold up in court. During that time customs had also arrested several couriers, suppliers and purchasers.

And it was probably Duncan Ford's involvement in this bootlegging ring that had resulted in him being introduced to Andrew Light, and thus Kim, in the first place.

It had been a tortuous and at times misleading investigation. Had Jonathon Wheeler not broken the arm of a hunt saboteur, we might never have discovered that Kim Light was a call-girl. And that led us to Rose's club and, thus, to Danny Todd. Contrary to my gut feeling, however, Todd had had nothing to do with the deaths of Kim and Ford. But we did do customs a bloody good favour.

The trial didn't take long. As I'd predicted, the brothers each entered a plea of not guilty and although their counsel did their valiant but vain best, putting forward the usual tired old suggestions that the Lights' damning confessions had been made under duress, and that they had been disorientated at the time, it took the jury less than two hours to convict them both.

The judge had no alternative in law but to sentence them to life imprisonment. In view of the evidence he had heard, I doubt that he would have wanted to give them anything less anyway. As it was, he whacked on a tariff of twenty-five years minimum. But then that particular judge has always been a generous sort of fellow.

In a second trial a month later the Light brothers received eight-year sentences of imprisonment for illegal trafficking in alcohol and tobacco, to run concurrent with their life terms, but it didn't seem to worry them too much. Danny Todd, however, had still not been found.

As for John Rose and his bouncer, Tony Lambert, enquiries are continuing into their living on immoral earnings and other associated matters. But as the Uniform Branch deal with such offences, it could be some time before the case comes to court.

Incidentally, Trixie was never sure whether Robert Dent had spent the night with her, even after Dave showed her a photograph of him. What was undeniable is that not long after we'd interviewed him, the local police were called to what in the job is called a 'domestic': one hell of a row between Dent and his wife Holly so violent that the neighbours feared for *his* safety. The upshot was a divorce. Oh well, tell me about it.

It must have been six weeks after the trial that I got a telephone call from a detective superintendent in the Thames Valley Police.

'Mr Brock, I understand that the name Danny Todd came up in the course of a murder you investigated recently.'

'Yes, sir, it did. But we've not found him yet. Customs want him for bootlegging.'

'Well, I've got good news for them,' said the superintendent. 'I've found him.'

'Oh, they will be pleased. Where?'

'Floating in the Thames at Runnymede. He'd been weighted down, but apparently his body broke free.'

'I always knew he was a clever bastard,' I said.

That the two rounds taken from Todd's body were subsequently matched to the Walther .38 pistol used to slay Kim Light and Duncan Ford was of no more than academic interest to me. I don't deal with murders in the Thames Valley area.